Books also By Robert Jack
Well Tended

SLAVES
IN A
LAND OF PLENTY

ROBERT JACK

WESTBOW
PRESS®
A DIVISION OF THOMAS NELSON
& ZONDERVAN

WestBow Press books may be ordered through booksellers or by contacting:

WestBow Press
A Division of Thomas Nelson & Zondervan
1663 Liberty Drive
Bloomington, IN 47403
www.westbowpress.com
844-714-3454

Because of the dynamic nature of the Internet, any web addresses or
links contained in this book may have changed since publication and
may no longer be valid. The views expressed in this work are solely those
of the author and do not necessarily reflect the views of the publisher,
and the publisher hereby disclaims any responsibility for them.

Any people depicted in stock imagery provided by Getty Images are
models, and such images are being used for illustrative purposes only.
Certain stock imagery © Getty Images.

ISBN: 979-8-3850-1854-3 (sc)
ISBN: 979-8-3850-1855-0 (e)

Library of Congress Control Number: 2024902574

Print information available on the last page.

WestBow Press rev. date: 03/20/2024

Dedicated in Love
Connie Travis DeLoach

If you are planting for one year, plant rice. If you are planting for ten years, plant trees. If you are planting for one hundred years, plant people.
Chinese Proverb

PART I

There is no growth without change, there is no change without loss; there is no loss without grief; and no grief without pain.
Rick Warren

PART 1

CHAPTER 1

The most challenging thing I have ever had
to do is follow the advice I prayed for.
Albert Schweitzer

It was a late September morning. The tinge of fall was crisp, and the windy, overcast skies blew summer to an end.

In the distance, a lone trumpeter played Taps. The tones drifted deliberately through the silent cemetery, like a fog creeping along the forest floor. A muted fluttering noise caused Nicki Boaz to flip her head back to view a large flock of sparrows darting back and forth. They would fork at a forty-five-degree angle and reengage to a solid formation. The flock was so large that they appeared like a gray naval ship as they moved forward. It looked like a choreographed routine, all in perfect timing, separating at a lightning tempo and then joining together. It was teamwork and hard work that made the sparrows productive. To Nicki's left, two large hawks appeared to be the instigators of this high-speed dance. Predators were herding them like sheep, forcing the sparrows to coward down in the branches of the low trees. Circling above the sparrows, the two predators held the huge flock captive. Nicki knew the feeling.

Hope had died for Nicki Boaz. The gold had lost its luster as the light rain drizzled on the mahogany casket. The beaded water

1

created a mirrored sheen that caused a grotesque reflection of Nicki's face. She accepted that ugly likeness as an image of her soul.

Nicki leaned her head on the right shoulder of her father, Bobby. Her left hand clasped firmly to her brother Robert, who held five-year-old Tracey. On her dad's left, Aunt Marjorie Israel. Behind Nicki is her fiancée, Thomas White. Standing at the foot of the coffin was Jon Marie, Nicki's square-shouldered and impressive grandfather.

The words were spoken, hearts broken, and the casket lowered as five bodyguards patrolled the perimeter of the gravesite. Nicki took Tracey out of Robert's arms and hugged her as if she would never see her again.

Judge Howard Job hugged Bobby Boaz. "Bob, she was born to be a great one. She had no peers, no fear of evil or its supporters."

Bobby Boaz hung his usually noble head, grunting toward the ground, "The promise is broken." With no facial expression, he crushed his sunglasses in his right hand.

The family stood silent in the rain, umbrellas opened, and they returned to the black town cars for the return trip to the family home.

The large TV in the living area was broadcasting breaking news from Washington. Prelate Malum, the Secretary of Religion, spoke live to the country. He was explaining the new organizational procedures for the Churches. Because of the recession and the lack of contributions to the Churches, the State would step in and pay each church's Pastors, Preachers, and staff. With variations in his voice, he explained that there would have to be a consolidation of thousands of individual congregations. The Prelate smirked a savior's smile to convey the State's concern for the people and their religious practices. "Everything will remain the same, except the state will provide the funds to keep the Churches operating. The President and Congress want to convey their love and commitment."

Nicki, red-faced, shouted at the TV, "Prelate, you're a lying powermonger, trying to take over the Churches. It is a setup; you killed my mom."

⤳

Stepping away from the TV cameras and into the dark of the evening, the Prelate and his assistant, Bishop Toyer, walked out of the Eisenhower office building into a black SUV. A driver and bodyguard in the extra-large car drove several miles along Massachusetts Ave. They turned left into a driveway that once belonged to the Vice President. On the pillars on either side of the electric gate, gold-plated placards boasted the words Drakon Trading and included a medusa design.

Stepping up to the massive entry doors, the Prelate waited as the mahogany doors opened. He was shown into the marble foyer and a large living area. The home belonged to Francis Vile, the heiress to Drakon Trading, the world's largest Privately held company. He knew that politicians, captains of business, and foreign dignitaries frequented this home. Standing at attention in the room, he clicked his thumb and middle finger fingernails. Usually, someone would bring him an envelope with instructions. He waited nervously, looking around the room covered with floor-to-ceiling black velvet curtains.

The curtains on his right repositioned like a puff of wind had set them in motion. Jumping back, he could see an outline, a separate set of black cloth against the curtains. Like an illusion, the shape moved again, and he saw two cream-colored patches. The hands and face of a lady appeared. He shuffled even further back and placed his arms across his chest. Walking out of the background of the curtains, he could see how her jet-black hair and dress coordinated with the drapes. His first look at her took away his breath. The Prelate twisted his head to look out, and he clicked his fingernails frantically. The thin, curve-hugging dress revealed a flawless body. He felt small. His male excitement exceeded his fear. He had heard of her beauty and knew it was true. Her shoulders supplied confidence to her approach. She understood the power of her exquisiteness. Authority covered her perfection as she pressed forward toward him. Her smirk was intoxicating. The Prelate couldn't control all he felt, and he sweated. Her beauty was stimulating yet terrifying at the exact moment. He wished he had not come. Francis Vile's face was like an angel, skin like cream, every angle perfect, eyes, lips, and cheeks hypnotizing. He got a chill as she approached. He tried to move away but could not. His thoughts were out of control.

He bowed at the waist.

She said in a smooth tenor voice and a slow, sassy sway of her hips, "Prelate."

"Yes," he said, two octaves higher than usual. He stuttered because the strong taste of Francis Vile's perfume landed on his tongue.

"I need you to take care of this," handing him a gray envelope. Moving within six inches of his face, her strikingly bright green eyes pierced his soul.

"Open it," she said.

She backed away, aware her closeness was overpowering him. His shaking hands opened the clasp and slipped out a picture and a typed page. He read it, and his head shook back and forth.

"Any questions, Prelate?"

He kept his head down, not wanting to make eye contact. "No, Miss Vile."

"Thank you," she said, walking back toward the curtain and turning her back to the Prelate. Her rehearsed sensual walk hijacked his lingering strength.

The Prelate staggered out of the house and back into the car. He sighed a huge breath of relief. His cowardice slowly left; his confidence returned. He thought to himself, Embarrassed for the second-highest-ranking *man in the country*. He made a phone call while the car sat still. His voice was bold as he told someone to meet him in thirty minutes. The car slowly drove the length of the quarter-mile driveway and turned left on Massachusetts Ave.

"Is everything all right, Prelate?" Bishop Toyer said.

"I saw her," he paused, "and what they say about her is true."

The night grew darker as the car turned left and cruised several miles north, turning right and right again into the side entrance of The Washington National Cathedral. The bodyguards opened the car door, and the men entered the building through the administrative offices. They moved quickly, purposely down the stairs into the crypt.

Two men in business suits entered the room from the opposite stairs. The Prelate sat powerfully in a sizeable ornate chair in his Tom Ford black suit and double-banded clergy collate. As the Prelate clicked his fingernails, the bishop laid his hand on the Prelate's arm, resting the unconscious habit. The chair in the room for his private use sat just outside the labyrinth carved on the floor. The barrel-vaulted roof seemed to push the room toward the center. The bodyguards with the Prelate positioned themselves in the corners of the room. Bulges under their jackets were meant to show power. A few feet back, the businesspeople, with their lumps under their coats, took their turn, kissing the ring hand of the Prelate, and backed off several feet.

The Prelate had no power or authority over the National Cathedral. Still, he felt powerful and vital having his clandestine meetings in the National Church. His office at the Eisenhower Office building was humiliatingly small. The Very Reverend Randolph Parshall, the Dean of the Cathedral, carried enough weight in Washington to keep him out of the Church Management. Still, he allowed indulgences to protect all the Churches from an all-out takeover from the Prelate.

The meeting was brief.

∽

The grieving group silently moved around the house at Nicki's parent's home in Plentywood, Montana. Nicki's face, wet with tears, walked humped over like a person with pneumonia. Nicki's Dad held her right arm, and her grandfather had her left. They moved into the kitchen of the beautiful house built by Nicki's Mom. Nicki's Dad put his forehead on Nicki's, and they cried together.

"Dad, why?" the three letters of the word extended into an increasingly loud and long shriek.

"Nicki, God is sovereign; he knows everything from the beginning to the end."

Nicki pushed her dad back with her strong arms, and the tears glowed with fire in her eyes. "Don't give me that, Dad; Mom was sold out to God. Do you think he let her be killed? Really, Dad?" He should have saved her. Isn't that what he does, saves people?" Nicki lifted her head, and her eyes begged her dad to agree.

Bobby Boaz pulled his daughter back into his embrace, "I love you, Nicki, and your mother adored you. Let's say goodbye to your aunt and grandfather before they leave."

The Boaz family hugged and cried together. They formed a circle with their hands around each other's waists and prayed with deep moaning—some distant rumbling noise, like a clap of thunder, added to the harmony of the moans. Then, raising their heads from what seemed like a consecrated moment, they looked intently at each other, silently transmitting some hallowed communication. Thomas White, standing outside the circle, could see they connected. He felt uncomfortable; he always felt uncomfortable with Nicki's family.

Aunt Marjorie and Jon Marie grabbed their bags, leaving for Jacksonville, FL, to prepare for next week's public memorial service. Thomas White would head for New York, and Nicki would go to The Capital to clean out her Mother's Washington office. Bobby and Robert would stay in Plentywood to take care of the business.

Nicki's Mother's home office was a sizeable room with custom-built bookshelves and comfortable chairs. The focal point was a prominent white secretary. The fold-down leaf of the desk had room for spacious writing materials and files. In front of the desk was a Herman Miller chair. Nicki glanced into the room and then walked across to the chair. She placed her hands on the chair's arms and lowered herself, exhaling as she eased down. Her mid-length black dress rose, revealing her muscular legs. Well-cut biceps flexed as the sleeveless dress showed off the extent of her well-maintained body. She could sense her mom's presence in the room. Leaning her head back, she could recognize her mother's voice echoing in her mind.

As Nicki sat erect at her mother's desk, her five-foot-six frame fit as if it belonged in the chair. She was a professional, intelligent, and beautifully appropriate woman. In a slow-motion glance to the four-foot round mirror to her right, Nicki's striking face reflected as a replica of her mother. Her mom's blue eyes and ash blonde hair overlayed a younger and brasher woman. Nicki leaned forward to look at the papers on the desk. The documents were neatly stacked and rested in a worn manila folder. In her mom's cursive writing was a title in black ink, *"We are slaves in a land of plenty."* At the bottom of the page was a description of the contents: *Ted Talk Speech* and a date. The date was a year and a month before the next election. Her mother had mastered delivering her powerful messages in eighteen-minute TED talks to the country.

She lifted the papers in the open file and tilted them in both hands. Unexpectedly, she added three tears to the bright white paper. A typed paragraph centered on the page was the only printed words on a sheet of handwritten notes, numbered lines, penciled thoughts, and little scribbled diagrams. The tears rolled down the inkjet paragraph and across the handwritten words, leaving smudges and blurred comments.

She read the words out loud:

Slaves in a Land of Plenty

36. "So now today we are slaves here in the land of plenty that you gave our ancestors! We are enslaved people among all this abundance! 37. The lush produces of this land pile up in the hands of the

government you set over us because of our sins. They have power over us and our property. We serve them at their pleasure and are in great misery."

Nehemiah 9:36 *The Message Eugene Peterson Nava Press*

Nicki thought, *a Bible verse?* It had an attribution, chapter, and verse. State publishers did away with chapters and verses decades ago. How did Mom get this version? Nicki savored the words. Her mother was a freedom fighter who spoke against the evil that engulfed the land. The Government had set itself up as the authority and god. Their words were the final judgment.

Nicki's mother had refused to bow to the government idol.

Nicki glanced at the pages of handwritten notes. Some diagonals, some vertical, and several lists of numbers. It was as if her mom was asking questions. There were Bible chapters and verses with tag lines and short, incomplete sentences directed to her as if she were responsible for the answers.

Nicki held the file folder between her forefinger and thumbs. She could not understand the outline's intent or make meaning out of the scribble. Her pain was so intense that she physically hurt every part of her body. She couldn't create a complete thought. It was like being frozen under two feet of snow.

Her Dad leaned into the doorway and said, "Nicki, it is time."

Nicki closed the folder and ran her hand firmly over the front cover. She repeated the words, "The Crisis we are in," everyone knew we had a crisis. Still, the state would not allow any recognition of a disaster, only acceptance of their power. Nicki's mother had planned to speak out, stand up, and defy the state. Is this why she is dead?

Aunt Maggie called Nicki into the kitchen and gave her a bear hug. "I love you, girl. Hold out your hand." Looking into Marjorie Israel's eyes, Nicki put out her right hand, and Maggie slowly lowered a chain into her hand. Like sand trickling out of a tight fist, it formed a little pile, like an hourglass. On top of the chain arrived a small rectangular piece of metal, translucent grey, so shiny it almost disappeared.

Nicki recognized it, "From my mom's bracelet?"

"Yes. Nicki, the bracelet I gave her when she started her journey years ago. The other charms are buried with her."

"My Mom treated her bracelet like it had some special power."

I made it into a necklace. I will tell you more when I see you at the memorial service next week.

Nicki placed her mother's charm around her neck. It was warm as if it had energy.

CHAPTER 2

Misfortunes subdue little minds; great minds rise above them.
Washington Irving

"Nicki's Dad drove her to the Plentywood airport for a commuter flight to Dallas, then direct to Washington. She intended to clean out her mom's office and then return to New York until the memorial service.

"Dad, how is Robert holding up."

"Better than I expected. He has come a long way. Your Mom and I were so proud of his recovery. Little Tracey had become the light of our lives. "Tell me, Nicki, how is your heart?"

"I don't know, Dad, I am angry," biting her finger and shaking her head like a spoiled child. Explaining in a high tone, "I cannot understand one thing about Mom's death. Where was her God?"

Bobby calmly said, "I understand, sweetie. Maybe we can spend some time talking after the Memorial Service. Aunt Maggie, your grandfather, and I have some things we need to share with you."

"Like what, Dad?"

"Your Mother's story and how it is related to you."

Bobby Boaz pulled in front of the small, flat-roofed building. Opening Nicki's door, he hugged her and handed her the key to her mom's office. "You are looking for a five-inch thick, three-ring binder. It contains all your mom's research for her big speech next year. Love you, please be careful and don't take that snotty bore Thomas White with you?"

"I might, Dad. I will marry him, and you better get used to it. She smiled her faint first smile in ten days."

On the two-and-a-half-hour flight to Regan Airport, Nicki played a game in her head. It was a game like chess, not with pieces but with words. Nicki learned the game in the woods the summer she was to graduate high school.

Shaking herself out of the mental game, she opened the folder with her mother's unruly notes. Turning the pages sideways, she tried to decipher her mom's thoughts. A list of numbers one through five is in the top left-hand part of the page.

1. _____
2. Lincoln
3. Henry
4. Roosevelt
5. King

She pondered the names. At first glance, she thought, all Presidents, but no. The top spot is blank, and which Roosevelt? Directly below the list on the left in her mom's cursive, "The power of the truth is gone," then the word gone is crossed through and rewritten as *taken*. The scribbling next to the sentence had doubled underlining; *I will find it*. On the top right was written, "like lambs to the slaughter." The colors and textures of the pencils and pens look like they were all written at different times. Below is a stanza: "We are weak, self-consumed, lazy of soul; we rely on our wisdom." At the bottom of the page, in black ink, it says, "It is all about feeling good about self. No sin, no rebukes, no human responsibilities." Under the typewritten words was a pencil-written sentence about the government tightening its grip on the Church and education and loosening its authority on morality. There were twenty words like freedom, wisdom, fear, and power. There were unexplained capital initials, like DUTO. At the bottom of the page, where the footer belonged, were the words: <u>WHO WILL GO WITH ME?</u>

Nicki could not put her mother's thoughts into a coherent story because her pain distracted her. Still, she was familiar with her mother's formulaic speech-writing techniques. Nicki thought *I would figure it out*. Her headache pounding, she closed the folder and looked out the window at the beautiful Washington landscape.

Closing her eyes and leaning back on the headrest, she whispered, "I will go, Mom. I will go with you."

Landing at Regan Airport, Nicki took a cab to 10th Street N.W. to the largest Law firm in the city. Her Mother had friends in the firm, and they provided her with a small office in exchange for work in her area of expertise. Nicki introduced herself to the receptionist and cleared security. The security officer escorted her to the basement office. Nicki unlocked the office to find the destruction. The drawers were pulled out and strewn about the room, and chairs were sliced open. The officer stepped in with her and cautioned her about touching anything. Nicki didn't listen. She tried to locate the five-inch three-ring binder. She spent over an hour looking. Nicki found two family pictures, removed them from the broken frames, and placed them into her briefcase. She gave her contact information to the guard. Before leaving the building, she called her dad to find out if her mother had a close associate in the tower. Her Dad told her Nancy Durden was a close friend of her mom's; they went to Law School together in North Dakota. Her Dad cautioned her to get out of the building and DC. Nicki checked with the receptionist to see if Ms. Durden was in the office. She called her assistant, who said Ms. Durden was not in then. Hoping she might see her at the Memorial Service, Nicki left her card and exited the building. Nicki turned back to see the receptionist looking at her, holding her card, and talking on the phone.

Standing on the sidewalk, Nicki looked back again and felt like she was in danger.

Nicki originally planned to fly to New York and spend several days with Thomas White. Then, she would go to Jacksonville, FL, for her mom's public memorial service. Nicki opened her Uber app, looked at the moving cars, and then hailed a cab, fearing her destination could be monitored. Arriving at the Airport, she bought a ticket on a direct American Airlines flight to Jacksonville. She would stay with her grandfather until the service.

Nicki's grandfather had always lived close, even in college and grad school; wherever she lived, he lived too. She called and informed her grandfather of her arrival time, and he agreed to pick her up. She texted Thomas while on the runway, explaining she would see him in Jacksonville in a few days.

Jon Marie was waiting with a big smile at the end of the terminal exit. Nicki gave him a big hug. She always felt safe with her granddad. She said, "I told you to pick me up outside. You don't always have to come inside. I am not a baby."

Jon smiled.

Her grandfather said, "Tell me what's frightened you?"

I wasn't frightened. I was concerned."

"Why," her Granddad replied.

"I can't tell you because I don't know. Maybe old memories."

"Ok, I was staying downtown, but I have moved us to the Ponte Vedra Club for the next few days."

"Thanks for understanding, granddad."

He always understood, part sage, part bodyguard, and part frontman. Since her senior year in high school, he had always been within a few hundred feet.

After settling in, Nicki went for a long walk on the beach, one hundred yards behind, and her granddad followed. She grieved deeply over her mom; Nicki knew her death was no accident. Her mother had been a hard charger for good and the right, and she didn't pander to anyone or give up. But to die for her beliefs was beyond comprehension, Nicki thought; *this was America, the land of the free, or it used to be.* Her wandering mind thought every strange thought a grieving heart could conjure up. A breakdown was at hand, but Nicki knew how to handle it. She walked back to her grandfather, and they strolled along the white hard-packed sand.

"Where is Aunt Maggie? She was going to tell me about this charm?"

"She had to return home. You will see her tomorrow."

Jon rousted Nicki for a beach breakfast at Ellen's Kitchen the following day. She ordered a surfer #7. Heading south, Jon took Nicki to the tiny house where her mother grew up—a two-bedroom block house with a carport five short blocks from the beach.

John pulled into the driveway, and they sat looking at the house. Your Mom would sit on those steps with her friend Linda and plan summer fun. Your Grandmother made an exceptional home for them both. This house is where they lived when your grandmother died. Your Mom was beginning high school. Later, Aunt Maggie arrived to take care of your mom.

"Where were you, granddad?"

"Nicki, he paused, "I made some terrible mistakes. In my youth, I bought the lies of fortune and power. The short story, I sold my soul to the devil. It is a sad story. God did rescue me, but the cost was high and hurtful. I will tell you about it someday. Let's drive to the little Church, your grandmother and Mom attended." The little single-story beige Church sat as it always had at the corner of 4th Street and 4th Avenue North. The parking lot was grass. Nicki looked through the front door but could only see the foyer, which looked newly decorated. Standing back and looking east toward the ocean, Nicki could visualize her mom running around like a 12-year-old child. Effortlessly, she could feel the comfort of the small beach town where her mother grew up. Still, she could not understand what had happened to her grandfather and why he wasn't a part of her mom's childhood. He told her that when Aunt Maggie arrived, they went to the Mega Church downtown, which your mother loved passionately.

"Nicki, are you interested in going downtown?"

"No, Granddad."

"OK, kiddo, let's go back to the hotel. I want to sit and talk for a few minutes. If things don't go perfectly tomorrow, we need a plan."

"What do you mean?"

"I want to be prepared. It is always good to have a plan B. I have heard that the state is not very happy with you."

"I haven't done anything except fire off a few in-your-face emails and tweets. They are big men; they should be able to take it."

Jon Marie schooled his granddaughter in persistence, patience, and planning as they sat on the veranda overlooking the ocean. She didn't understand the purpose of his lesson. Still, she paid attention to her grandfather because he was wise and stern and knew his way around dangerous situations.

"I don't understand what this is all about."

"Nicki, since the bridge incident, I have been able to live close to you. I have been a grandfather and a guardian with the intent to love and protect you. I was a lousy Father to your mom, but what a privilege it has been to be your grandfather. You have been a great student of all I have taught you, and I love you.

"Protect me from what."

"Nicki, I have some things to take care of. Enjoy the afternoon, and I will see you at the hotel at 9:00 AM."

"Love you, Grandad," Nicki studied her grandfather, walking away. She didn't understand what he was talking about but realized he was always around, and she could trust him.

At 9:00 AM, Jon Marie drove to the hotel's front in a black town car. Dressed in a Brooks Brothers Black suit, looking like a Senator, he opened the door for his granddaughter. He introduced her to Rick, the driver. Her grandfather told her of his friendship with Rick and his wife when your grandmother and I first moved to Jacksonville. They drove west into town, thirty miles away. Arriving early at the Church, Rick parked on the side street west of the Church. Nicki's grandfather walked around and opened the door. He had a sad look in his eyes. Nicki started to say something, but he shook his head and waved his hand, then hugged her, and they walked to the front door of the massive Church.

⌒

The late afternoon sun shone level into Todd Miller's face, forcing him to walk with his head downward. He observed his boots kicking the light-colored dust as he hiked to the Sea Camp dock. On each of his shoulders rested a coil of yellow braided rope. In his hand, a hollow glass ball covered by a thin rope meshwork, afloat, used by fishermen to mark their nets. A hundred-year-old glass globe painted yellow, orange, and blue swirls looked like the Earth from outer space. Todd's white tee shirt was wet with late autumn coastal sweat that stuck to his chest—traversing the hurricane-damaged dock, jumping from one board to the other. Vaulting onto the boat, he found a seat on the back rail of the old thirty-two-foot trawler. Removing the ropes from his shoulders, he circled his hat in the air and gave the let's go wave, and the boat pulled out into the Intercoastal and headed north. The government supply boat made monthly trips to Dungeness Dock and Sea Camp. Today, the trawler will travel nine miles to Plum Orchard Dock to drop off a box of instruments the college interns use on their projects.

Todd relished the afternoon sunlight and the breeze of the water. He tied carabiners to the ends of his two ropes.

The easterly turn into Plum Orchard dock was tricky. The island and the mainland were close, marsh to marsh thirty yards apart. The sawgrass thickets on the mainland made a beautiful dark green and yellow brilliance against the fast-moving dark water.

Coasting into the dock still idling, the captain handed the box to a young lady and turned the boat, chugging and jerking, diesel fumes floating north. Todd leaned over the back of the ship, his right foot catching the railing to keep him in the boat. Hooking one end of the rope around the dock pole and then through the carabiner, the line and the steel clip disappeared into the salty water.

As the boat tugged out into the middle of the channel, Todd let his yellow rope slide leisurely under the surface. Todd attached his globe to the final carabiner, massaging it as if it had some unusual power. He kissed his ball and flung it toward the sand, landing between the grassy reeds. Todd Miller stuck his hand in the water, which was cold for a warm day. His blue eyes glimmered, he took his hat off, and the wind blew his hair. He smiled a Clark Gable smile.

⌒

A large crowd of diverse people was expected, and at 9:45, they started filling the Church's lower levels. Nicki's Mom had mentored hundreds of girls, politicians, friends, and foes. They filled the seats, wearing blue suits, white shirts, and red ties. There was excitement that a homeless man named Chester would show up. He was rumored to be Nicki's mother's formable guardian angel. Gossip also circled that several of the *Faithfull Forty* Congressmen would pay their respects. With their help, Nicki's Mom had fought hard for significant changes in helping the country's people. Most of their good works had disappeared as the nation's love for God and each other had grown cold. Disrespect and insults replace law and religion. Everyone demanded their way, claiming Democracy gave them the right to do what they wanted.

Once the largest in the modern era, the Church was built for music and speech. The podium of this Church was once the podium for the Nation. As the crowds proceeded, a violin, piano, and classical guitar backed by a two-hundred-person choir performed the song Amazing Grace. The music was captivatingly sweet, the words wondrously floating to the church's top. The crowd's noise lowered to an extreme silence as they played the song's moving 4th stanza. A quartet of erect, barrel-chested tenors in tuxedoes harmonized the words in pure tones. The goosebumps were communal.

Bobby Boaz and Jon Marie sat in the first row alongside Marjorie Isreal. They were impressive figures looking larger than life in front of the church. Nicki, Robert, and Tracey joined them in the front row. Thomas White sat to the left of Nicki's grandfather, and Nicki sat with her dad. A large black man in a starched and pressed Khaki shirt and pants sat beside Nicki's grandfather. His arms were as large as jackhammers, and his smile was as pleasing as heaven's light. The crowd was awed as Bobby Boaz hugged him and wept.

Judge Howard Job ascended to the massive platform. He was straight and tall, secure, and robust. He called the crowd to prayer. It was not the state's scripted prayer but a humble servant's supplication. He boldly asked for forgiveness for the sins of the country. He begged for restoration and deliverance from the slavery the citizens had brought on themselves. He asked God to receive his helper, Carrie Marie Israel Boaz. While everyone's head was bowed, Nicki's Dad leaned over and kissed his daughter on the cheek. He tapped her granddad on the shoulder and pointed toward the exit. He handed her a small plastic bag. Jon Marie led his granddaughter through the exit door, down one flight of stairs, a dimly lit hallway, and up one flight to a metal door opening on the street. Thomas White stood up, but Nicki's Dad pushed him back down.

On the sidewalk, Nicki said, "No, Granddad, I want to stay."

"No, Nicki."

She lifted her eyes to meet her granddad's earnest gaze, a commanding presence not to be rebuffed.

He led her to the black town car parked on the street.

Jon Marie told the driver outside the car, "Rick, it is time, and I want to thank you."

"No, Jon, we thank you and Nicki's family."

"Rick, here are the instructions, and the car loudly idled.

Nicki's grandfather said," Niki, give me your phone."

"She looked at him, shocked. She pulled back, finally obeyed, and placed her phone in his hand."

"We will know where you are; you will be safe, I promise. There are instructions in the plastic bag. Follow them exactly."

"Rick, Go quickly."

Jon Marie reentered the Church. As the Judge closed his prayer, and in response, a loud amen echoed in the 8,000-seat venue.

The Judge started his preamble, "Carrie Marie Boaz, the bravest soul of our times, without her, we could have lost it all?"

Six wooden double doors into the sanctuary banged open, and sunlight beamed in the auditorium at his next word. Twenty men in black suits raced like ants down the aisles and onto the stage.

An articulate, well-dressed, and tall man gently pulled the Judge back from the podium, leaned into the microphone, and said with a sincere smile, "This is an illegal assembly. The speaker is not state-approved, and there is no permit for this religious assemblage. The Prelate has gracefully allowed you to leave without penalty. Please rise and leave at this time."

He looked at the first row and saw the empty seat between Nicki's Father and Grandfather. His sincere smile turned into an angry red face.

The crowd rose with no fight or push-back. Positioned at the exit doors were members of the swat team, examining in detail the departing funeral guest. The tall man waited for Nicki's Dad, grabbed him by the arm, and whispered something in his ear. Bobby Boaz, being the more muscular man, pulled away.

CHAPTER 3

"I learned a long time ago the food we eat on the
mountaintop was grown in the valley!"
Fred Smith

In the back seat, Nicki leaned forward and asked, "Where are we going?"

Rick said, "To Fernandina."

"I remember Fernandina; it was a quaint, shrimping town."

"Well, it is still small, but the government used most of the town to support the Navy Base just a few miles north into Georgia."

"What will I do there?"

"Nicki, relaxing is hard, but you can trust us. My wife Treasa and our friends cared for your mother many years ago. We all went to church together."

"That little Church at the beach?"

"Yes"

"We have about fifteen minutes before we arrive. I want to cover the details your grandfather gave me. I will park and go to the boathouse office; you will stay in the car. After I finish with the arrangements, I will come to get you. While you wait, get your travel bag out of the trunk and put on some flat shoes."

"Ok"

Rick drove a mile west on Centere Street into the waterfront parking lot of Brett's Water Way Café. Jumping out of the car, he negotiated a series of floating docks. Nicki could see him enter a small twelve-foot by twelve-foot wooden office with signs plastered all over the building *Amelia River Cruises*. Nicki was impressed with the confidence Rick showed in this covert operation.

In ten minutes, Rick was sitting back in the car, "Nicki, are you ready?" Inside the tiny wooden shack, Rick introduced her to Jim Rowell, the owner of the boat fleet.

"Hi, I'm Jim," he said my wife was friends with your grandmother."

"Does everyone know my grandmother?"

Rick said to Nicki, "Jim is trustworthy. Do as he says. We will all know where you are and that you will be safe. Make sure you have your plastic bag." He bowed his head like he was praying. He lifted his head, smiled, and hugged her. He waited in the car until she and Jim left the building and walked down the dock.

Nicki was comforted by Jim's peaceful demeanor. Fidgeting, she focused on all the radio equipment behind the counter. It looked like a radio station. She was going to ask about it, but Jim spoke first.

Jim talked slowly and deliberately, "Nicki, I own a fleet of tourist boats. The only ship I have today is the Shrimping Eco-tour boat that drops an Otter Trawl Shrimp net. The vessel will be crowded, but we will work around it. The state monitors my sailings because of the Naval base, but we will safely get you to your exit point. I will skipper this tour, and Captain Buster will be our mate. We will follow our standard route through the Tiger Basin, and then Buster and I will prepare you. It would be best if you relaxed in the cabin.

"Yes, Mr. Rowell."

They reached the double hull 45-foot-long Miss Kaylynn at the end of the dock. There were several people already aboard. Nicki followed Jim to the back and went to the small cabin next to the bathroom.

Another 15 people boarded, then ten more. Jim and Captain

Buster cast off and headed North. Nicki could hear the children's excitement about dropping a shrimp net and hauling in the catch.

The small cabin was behind the captain's seat. Nicki sat in a stupor as if none of this was happening. Fifteen minutes later, Jim came in and sat down and, with a warming smile, said, "Nicki, this is the plan; in forty-five minutes, we will pass the Plum Orchard Dock. The visitors will be in the front of the boat, excited over the catch in our shrimp net. You will spring off the back of the ship and grab a yellow and blue painted glass ball floating to the boat's right. The float will be on the edge of the current line, and as soon as you get in the water, you must grasp the rope and ball, or the current will race off with you.

He sheepishly handed her a black wet suit and told her she could change in the ladies' room but quickly return to the cabin.

Nicki's eyes got big, but she did not move. She had not understood a single word.

Mr. Rowell, "I did not understand."

Jim said kindly," I cannot stop the boat. The Coast Guard boat would be on us in five minutes; I must stick to the regular route."

Nicki remained still.

Jim reached out, took her hand, and rubbed it between his hands. "This will work, Nicki; Rick and your grandfather know what they are doing." He went over the plan again.

"What's next," Nicki's expression of fear and uncertainty mixed with despondency caused Jim to sigh deeply.

Nicki stood apprehensively. Jim opened the door for her and said, "I will be back in twenty minutes. Put your stuff in the waterproof backpack."

Nicki squeezed into the undersized wetsuit. She thought it was probably for a teenage surfer boy. Nicki could not breathe; it was so tight. She returned to the cabin and put her belongings into the neoprene backpack. She then sat quietly and gazed hypnotically at the bay and the Islands. She was one deep breath away from a breakdown.

Jim returned, "Do you have your black plastic bag?"

"Yes"

"Make sure it is in the backpack."

"It is time, Nicki." Walk between the cabin and the bathroom to the back of the boat. There is a small platform through the railing gate. Sit down on the platform and slide to the left. I will sound the horn in ten minutes. Look to your left, and you will see the dock. Get ready to slide off as soon as you see the glass ball. It will be about ten feet off the boat, push off the platform, swim to the float, and hold on for dear life."

"What do I do next, she said.

Jim said slowly, "I don't know what, but I know the people who sent you here are trustworthy. They are worthy of your faith. Bobby Boaz is not going to let anything happen to his daughter."

"You will be ok," He gave her a Father's pat on the head as she made her way to the lower platform.

"Hold the rope," he said over his shoulder.

She sat crouched with her spine against the back of the boat. The engine bubbled and rumbled and vibrated. In intense fear, she thought, *Dear Jesus, please, my mom just died.*

The horn blew.

Nicki trembled.

The dock passed on her left. Nicki slowly slid off the back of the boat into the salty water. She could see the floating glass ball as she pushed off. It was only a few feet away.

Nicki had both arms in front like a baby reaching out to be held. The yellow rope wrapped on her arm, gripping it tightly with her right hand, and the glass ball slid under her left armpit as a safety stop. The swift-moving tide carried Nicki into the middle of the river. Using her feet as a rudder, she pulled the rope tight to gain speed to launch toward the shore. The current flowed faster closer to the shore, and erosion had left a deep drop off inches from the beach. The water started to surge into her face, and twice, she gulped in a big mouth of water. Coughing violently, she turned over on her back to gain a breath. Nicki started spinning; her grip slipped, and her arm ached. She wanted to give up and let go and take a chance swimming. She reached out with her left hand, and the glass ball floated from under her arm. Nicki thought *That was a mistake.* She couldn't escape the turbulence keeping her inches off the shoreline. The force was like two magnets of opposite poles repelling, pushing her away from safety.

Coughing out water and closing her eyes, she turned on her side, using both legs to do a dolphin kick and power her body to the land. Lifting her chest with all her energy, she felt a sharp, stabbing, burning pain in her right side, like jellyfish tentacles wrapping around her stomach.

Water filled her mouth and nose. In her struggle, her eyes and mind went dark.

Coughing up water, the white sand beach beneath her came into an unfocused view.

Something was holding her head off the sand. A hand pushed firmly on her back and rolled her over.

She gagged a clean gulp of air, gasping; the next breath started pumping her back to life. A strong arm lifted her into the sitting position. The light from the afternoon sun reflected on her savior's face, and he smiled with his lips and blue eyes.

Nicki's right arm lay hanging loose on the sand; she lifted it, balled her hand into a fist, and swung at his face in a mighty move.

He ducked, then grinned.

He dropped Nicki back to the sand and said," That is no way to treat the man, that risks his life to save you."

Sitting with her arms behind her, palms on the sand, she said, "Todd Miller, I told you. If I ever saw you again, it would be the end of you."

"Nicki," It is good to see you again."

"You are a lying sack of garbage, Todd, you slimebag."

"Nicki, I had to go."

"You didn't have to go. You ran, you coward, you used car

salesman. You pretended to care for me. You're a deceitful insect. You went with your friends on one of your boy's adventures."

He picked her up in both arms.

"What - are you doing?"

"I fished you out, and I can release you back. Nicki, you're a pain."

Nicki reached up to Todd's head and rubbed the hair on the back of his neck, and he purred like a kitten, "Put me down, Toddy."

He lowered her to the sand, "I see you have been working on your negotiation skills." He turned and walked away.

As Nicki took her first two steps, she bent over and put her hands on her knees. Water poured out of her nose, mouth, and ears. Her head hung low as she wobbled. Woozily standing, she packed her glass ball in her waterproof bag and followed Todd.

Turning back, he said, "You look pretty good in that wet suit, Nicki." She kicked sand on his back, smiled, and frowned simultaneously.

"Really, Todd, you're a nasty boy."

Todd followed the path to a dirt road; turning left, they walked in the wheel ruts. Nicki increased her pace to get shoulder-to-shoulder with Todd. She tilted her head to the right, looking up at Todd.

"Where are we going?"

"Plum Orchard," Todd said brashly.

"Is it a farm?"

"No, never had a Plum grown on that land, but it is special."

"Todd, what are you doing here, and where is here? How did you find me in the river? Where have you been? I can't believe that you saved me. It is wild." Nicki's voice transitioned to a whisper, why did you ...?"

"Relax, Nicki, don't try to make a miracle out of this. I brought Dr. Bernie Maker from California to the Island. He is a political prisoner. He is having his hands slapped for being uncooperative in his teachings. This Island is a compound for people who make the State uncomfortable.

Nicki acted puzzled, "A prison?"

"A no security prison. Guarded by the world's most advanced Nuclear Naval Base on the other side of the river, nobody makes a move without them knowing. I was repairing the dock so the supply boat could safely arrive. It is just that simple. I travel on special assignments; it is a coincidence you washed onto the shore."

"I heard about your mom's death. I am sorry. She was an amazing lady. How are your dad and that lunatic brother of yours?" Todd stood to her side and asked in a low, slow voice, "Nicki, how is your heart?"

"Mom's death was a shock; thank you for asking. Dad is doing well, and Robert is ok. It is emotional turmoil. If that is not enough, I mouthed off to The Secretary of Religious Activities and several Senators. A week after Mom died, I wrote a scathing op-ed in The Journal and torched them for their evil ways. They're hunting for me. They say for a conversation, I say for retribution. You know the government and their no opposition policy." I believe they had something to do with Mom's death.

Lifting her chin with his forefinger and looking into Nicki's eyes tenderly, he said, "Sounds like a lot."

Nicki thought, *that's my sweet Todd*, and said, "I am doing ok, Todd. I believe depression is holding me back, but it is also helping me move forward. All I want to do is lash out at God and the government. I might even be angry at you.'

He put his hands on her shoulders and leaned his forehead against hers --"I understand."

They walked east; their shoulders would touch as they bounced over the ruts. They looked like a couple. The way was dry and dusty but easy to see in the late light of orange and gray. Todd stepped off the road and followed a small path into thick woods. Nicki stopped and watched. He disappeared; Nicki called his name three times, "Todd, Todd, Todd," louder and faster.

He returned from the thicket and said, "Come on, Nicki, it is a shortcut."

Nicki, wearing her unzipped wetsuit, started sweating. Acid poured into her stomach. "No, Todd, I am staying on the road."

"Nicki, it will take 10 minutes off our walk. There is nothing in here but hogs," he grinned.

"No, Todd." She held both hands out in the stop position, "I will stay on the road." Her face turned pale, and she looked sick.

Todd returned to the road to catch up with her, "Nicki, what is the matter? Joe says, 'The enchantment of this Island is the forest, clear water, and blue sky."

"I don't care what Joe says. I am not going in the woods." She tightened her lips and walked deliberately. "Who's Joe anyway?"

The road forked in twenty minutes, and they turned to the right. In the distance, in brilliant white, the Plum Orchard Mansion stood colossal and out of place in such a secluded location.

Nicki took two steps back to appreciate the majestic oaks gracing the property. The heavy, low-hanging moss blew ever so slowly in the breeze, looking like a scary movie in the soft gray light. The white mansion anchored the panorama, standing silently as the sunset bathed it in afternoon pastels. The sprawling marsh and winding river framed what could be a world-class painting through the trees. Her tight, deep muscles were unwound, her breath released, and her tranquility blended Nicki Boaz into the picture. She went willingly.

They marched up the quarter of a mile-long driveway, and Todd started to give Nicki the lay of the land.

Nicki, eleven people live permanently on this Island. Cumberland Island belongs to the Federal Government and is a National Park. Not too long ago, it was a beautiful attraction for nature lovers. Horses run wild on the Island and have for over a hundred years. In the 1800's it was a Cotton Plantation, but the Civil War ended slavery, and the plantations went out of business. On your trip to Sea Camp, you will see some of the cotton fields. For a brief time, the Island was a refuge for the well-off and celebrated. Thomas Carnegie and his wife Lucy raised their family on the island, and Mrs. Lucy built several mansions. The island to the north of Jekyll

Island was home to many wealthy Industrialists, whose homes still stand. Across the river and due west is a Nuclear Submarine Base.

Today, Cumberland Island is an island the government uses to keep leaders who will not conform to the state's wishes. It is not a prison with guards and bars but water and the U.S. Navy. Access is restricted to the government supply boat, Alcatraz, ultra-light.

His grin grew, his thoughts showing before his words, "You are the first volunteer prisoner and the only one who swam to the Island."

The sun faded onto their back as they walked to the large plantation porch with 30-foot columns. Todd banged on the screen door.

"Todd, it is good to see you; come in." Mrs. Frank stood motionless as Nicki came from behind Todd. Mrs. Frank's eyes fixated on Nicki. Her expression seemed to be asking a question and answering it all simultaneously.

"Please come in, young lady," Mrs. Frank roared.

"This is Nicki," Todd said as he pushed her out in front of him, within Mrs. Frank's reach.

"Welcome, Nicki. I am Evonne. She paused for what seemed to be five minutes—twisting her head back and forth as if she were looking for something inside Nicki. My husband Joe and I are the temporary caretakers of this incredible mansion. Come right in." Reaching out, she took Nicki's hand, and her eyes focused on her face.

"Nicki,' Todd said, "I must go to the other end of the Island. Stay with the Franks. They will treat you with kindness and keep you safe."

"Mrs. Frank, may I take the 4-wheeler back to Sea Camp?"

He reached out to hug Nicki. She pulled him in and put her head on his chest; she inhaled his white V-neck tee shirt deeply. He touched her shoulders and gently pushed her back, "It will be fine, Nicki."

"Come," Nicki, and get out of that wet suit," Mrs. Frank said.

They were proceeding to the central staircase, located in the grand hall. The stairs split right and left. The owners had built a fireplace under the stairs with two built-in benches. Arriving on the second floor, they walked to the backside of the landing wall to a small door. Mrs. Frank turned on the pale yellow lights and proceeded up several flights on the narrow, windowless staircase. At the top appeared another large room, like a family room, with chairs, tables, and table lamps. Mrs. Frank pointed out a private exit at this landing: "It is next to the bookcase. The stairs lead down to the side yard by the Kitchen Porch."

Mrs. Frank advanced toward a large wooden bookcase, walked to the right side, and slid it across the wall like a barn door. In the opening was a double-wide staircase; at the top was gleaming sunlight. Cresting the top of the stairs, Nicki could see the grand marshes and river behind the mansion from the dormer window.

Mrs. Frank said, "The attic has been remodeled to create three apartments. Built 25 years ago by the Park Service to keep the main portion of the house original, it made it possible for caretakers to enjoy modern comfort. You are number two; to your left, we are number 1. The key is in the door. Take your time, and when you are ready, come to sit on the porch and talk."

Inside apartment #2, Nicki saw a sizeable one-bedroom efficiency apartment. The living area was large and separated from the kitchen, with a modern island with a stone countertop. The walls and flooring were all new, neat, and contemporary. The furniture could have been a hundred years old. Off the living area is a door leading to a 12 X12 bedroom and an extra-large bathroom with a separate shower, tub, and large vanity. Nicki thought, except for all the stairs, this is nice. She showered and dressed into one of the three outfits she had stuffed in her waterproof bag.

She slid into her black lycra pants and a matching turtleneck and left her bright room. She walked to the large window at the top of the staircase. Taking in the fantastic property surrounded on three sides by rivers or creeks, the green grass contrasting the blue water calmed her.

Nicki descended the staircase with the fireplace and built-in seats. The double doors were open, and she walked out on the large porch under the supporting columns. Mrs. Frank sat in a rocker; smiling, she waved for Nicki to sit in the early evening shade.

"How are you feeling, Nicki?"

"Full of the river. Every time I bend over, it flows out," Nicki said with a slight smile.

"Mrs. Frank's eyes riveted on Nicki, looking into her meaningfully.

"What is it, Mrs. Frank?"

"Call me Evonne," she said.

"I will; thanks for the rope and the glass ball. It was a grand and dangerous entrance."

Mrs. Frank smiled, looking past Nicki to a tall, lean man walking straight and robust across the 100-foot-long porch.

"Hi, Mom," he said to Mrs. Frank, but focusing on Nicki, he stared hard and long, turning to his wife to ask critical questions. She gave him the back-and-forth shake of her head. He shrugged back and said, "Who do we have here?"

"Nicki," she said as she stood to shake his hand, but the water ran out of her nose, and she had to put both hands on her face to contain the flood. Mr. Frank handed her his handkerchief.

"Well, hello Nicki, it is nice to meet you. Are you ok? I have never seen a girl spill out so much water."

"Todd Miller brought her. He said he fished her out of the river. She is the guest he told us would arrive," looking at Nicki, she continued, "but we thought you would be a political prisoner."

"I am not a prisoner yet." But in reflection, she said, "Maybe I am a prisoner of sorts."

Joe's bright blue eyes, silver hair, and smooth, deep voice made him attractive. The Franks were older, but they looked like movie stars with the kindness of farm folks. They seemed moved and excited by Nicki's presence.

Joe said, "Where are you from, Nicki?"

Originally from Montana. In the last few years, I have been at college in Florida, law school in Philadelphia, and recently from Los Angeles. And this morning from my Mom's Memorial Service in Jacksonville.

Mrs. Frank said, "Nicki, we are so sorry. What is going on that you are fished out of the river the same day as your mother's funeral?"

I have made a few enemies. I worked for my mom and dad after law school. My Dad owns a business, and my mom was a lawyer fighting for freedom for the people. She was a fantastic woman, highly respected and influential, and perhaps the most persuasive platform speaker of her time.

Nicki said, "You seem like nice people; how did you get here, and how do you know Todd?"

"We work for the state as caretakers of this historic property. We came from Atlanta but raised our children south of here and would bring them to Cumberland Island for magical getaways. We couldn't stand the pace of life in Atlanta, so we took this job for peace. "Todd works for the state and brings people to the island."

"Todd works for the state," Nicki said, horrified. "Never could trust him anyway, the dirtbag." Just hearing that Todd worked for the state took the energy out of Nicki.

Joe said, "Nicki, you can trust us, and you can trust Todd."

Mr. Frank said, "Nicki, life looks complicated for you today. A prisoner of your choice, but you will find it may not be as bad as it seems."

Nicki hung her head low, "At the funeral, my grandfather handed me this small plastic bag with a strange-looking device and specific directions on using it."

Mrs. Frank could see Nicki's exhaustion and said, "We would understand if you wanted to go to your apartment. I will meet you in the morning at nine. A small summer kitchen is off the back porch to get fresh coffee. Knock on our door if you need anything."

Nicki said," Thank you, I will. I am exhausted."

Joe said, "Nicki before you turn on the lights, close the curtains and fasten them to the Velcro on the wall. We prefer that no one know someone is in the mansion."

"Yes, sir."

Nicki pulled herself up the staircase, shoulders slumped and lonely. The day had been beyond exhausting. The Memorial Service for her mom disrupted a boat escape and a near-drowning event, finalized by seeing Todd Miller. It was a lot.

"Good night," Joe said, and in his next breath, looking at Mrs. Frank, he said, "How could it be?

Mrs. Frank said, "Joe, like the first time, a divine act?' Should we say anything?

Joe paused and, after deliberation, said, "Let's wait."

CHAPTER 4

"A change of place plus a change of pace
equals a change of perspective."
Mark Batterson

Good morning, Mrs. Frank.

"Good morning, Nicki."

"What time will Todd come by?"

"He is not coming by; he left this morning."

"Oh, did he say anything? Do you know when he will be back?"

"No, he didn't say anything, and I don't know when he will be back. Sit, and let's talk. Maybe you could tell me your story, how did you arrive on our Island?

"I was working for my dad's company in Los Angeles. My main job was research and presentations for Congress members to protect larger businesses. I would also help my mom, who is focused on restoring the country to its full potential. My Mom was an incredible lady, powerful in fighting for the good and right and helping those in need. The government was jealous of the influence she had on the people. My Mother often asked the citizens of the United States to do something – millions of them acted. She was a Godly leader fighting evil with good. Loved by the multitudes, hated by the crooks and most in the government."

"One of those who hated her murdered her on the steps of the

Capital. Some enemy killed her and ten others. She was gunned down trying to help the wounded. They never located the shooter. The government reported that she was an innocent bystander. I say—not. I say killed by the corrupt and those who don't want opposition or oversight to their powerful way of life."

"To let them know how I believe. I pushed and shoved for answers, for justice, for the truth. They didn't like the pushing; they pushed back to get even. They were looking for me at my mom's service in Jacksonville. The government forcefully stopped the service, claiming it was an unlawful assembly."

What was your mother's name?

"Carrie Boaz"

"What was her maiden name?

"Marie, Carrie Israel Marie."

"Joe and I have heard of her. We listened to her speak. Some said she was a great one, gifted, touched by God."

"Some said that."

"I am so sorry for you, Nicki. I know your heart hurts."

"How is your dad?"

"It is hard to know; my mom and he had the love affair of the century. His business grew to hundreds of millions of dollars, and he didn't change. They were drop-dead poor before that. He is rare and God-confident inside and out, making him an impressive man. He has not said a word; I know he is deeply hurt, but he is working on a plan. He is a tactician.

"How long do you think you will be staying with us?"

"I don't have a clue. I don't know how I got here. I have no insights; I feel lost. But I feel compelled to complete my mom's work. But I am unlike my mom with kneeling prayers and a wait-on-the-Lord philosophy. She looked at her enemies with love and tried to conquer evil by doing good, seeing what got her—killed. I have laid back and been uninterested in our government. Still, now I need to be about action, moving toward the problem," her voice raised three octaves in response to her feelings. She whispered back to herself, *change the world, Nicki, you, and everyone else.* "I need to get in touch with my dad or brother."

Nicki, we are void of communication on the Island. Charlie and Beth Tender have a monitored government phone; the only computer connected is at the ranger station. We receive mail monthly, but it gets inspected before delivery. It is a prison, a beautiful one, however.

"My Dad gave me a small square plastic device, like a communicator. It had a note with longitude and latitude and a date and time. But I am unclear what to do with it."

"Let Joe help you; he is technology handy."

Since you put yourself on the Island, I don't think anyone will be coming for you, but we need a plan. Until you have a revelation, let's put you to work.

"First, we must add your needs to our supply list. We need to get you some Island clothes and shoes, but we can't alert anyone to a new resident. You know Nicki, the people on the other side of this river aren't prisoners; they are enslaved but don't understand it."

Nicki stood silent. Mrs. Frank stood, determined.

Nicki broke the silence, "Me too."

"I have someone who can help with the clothes. Todd returned the 4-wheeler, and we can take it to Dungeness to meet Connie. Later, Joe can drive you to meet the others on the Island.

Nicki returned in thirty minutes with the list of her needs. Mrs. Frank looked it over, and they walked to the back of the mansion and climbed into the green 4-wheeler. They drove to the end of the entrance of the Plum Orchard Mansion. Mrs. Frank put the paper in a mailbox at the end of the long driveway and raised the flag.

"You have a mailman?"

"Kind of," Mrs. Frank smiled. "Taylor Samms resides at the settlement at the Island's North end. In addition to being an economist and publisher, he is a motorcycle enthusiast. The government allowed him to transport ten of his bikes to the Island. He rides from North to South daily and moves notes from one place to another—the nicety of 11 people working together.

35

The drive was noisy and dirty; the dry white sand put off a thin layer of dust, like smoke. Mrs. Frank called out the landmarks of the famous old Island. Heading south, she pointed out the remnants of a golf course and an overgrown tree-lined road. The remaining forty acres of cotton fields looked like a pasture with horses grazing in the distance. On the right, they passed the Stafford house, once the home of the plantation owner. Bernie Maker, a Professor from California, lives in this small mansion overlooking the fields. They continued as Mrs. Frank taught the most fantastic history lesson of Island life, Cumberland style.

Stopping, Mrs. Frank said, "Nicki, the next turn is into the ruins of Dungeness Mansion. I was hoping you could close your eyes and listen to the music and the sounds of happiness that encircled this home. Even in ruins, it has a life of its own. The rivers and marshes bring energy to the expansive lawns. The back of the mansion is the first place you will see the wild horses; they seem to like being close to the house. It is remarkable."

Mrs. Frank slowed to reduce the noise. A colossal sunbeam lighted the mansion on its ruins. It was easy to envision parties, lighted lawns, and high-fashion ladies adding to the joy of life at Dungeness, even in its dilapidated sophistication. They coasted the quarter of a mile to the house entrance to Lucy Carnegie's beloved Dungeness.

Mrs. Frank drove around the massive house. At the river, old docks and boat slips are rusted to ruin. To the South, greenhouses remain in working order. A slight turn takes you to a small white cottage used for the accountants and a half-mile-long stone garden gazebo. Several herds of horses grazed the lush grass, some raising their heads to look; others could care less.

Nicki could imagine the children's life playing by the grand fountain full of shooting water and the grass, a magic carpet for Lucy's nine children.

Mrs. Frank completed the circle and headed North, on the left of the laundry house, further out; the stables were still in proper order.

On her immediate right was a concrete building, the equipment barn. Caddy Corner sat a two-story white house. It appeared to be in excellent condition. Mrs. Frank pulled close to the front door and parked. The four-wheeler slid sideways because of the soft sand surrounding the house. "I don't know why they had to build this house in all this sand," Mrs. Frank said.

Nicki was surprised at how it looked. It was like a house, in her hometown. "The Doctor's house," Mrs. Frank said, "We use the bottom floor for our community center." Going through the door, an older lady said, "Evonne, great to see you. Who do you have with you."

"Connie, this is Nicki," she said.

"Someone new on the Island, what a surprise. Usually, I am the first to hear of a new prisoner," she said with a big grin. She called for Evelyn in the back room.

Evonne said, "She brought herself and swam at Plum Orchard dock. Todd Miller fished her out of the channel."

"What! Nobody swims over. It has never been done before," said Evelyn.

Nicki and Mrs. Frank walked to a large round table with Four Kings in a Corner and Mexican Train games. "Do you want to play? "Evelyn said.

"No," Mrs. Frank said, "Nicki needs some clothes. She arrived with a limited wardrobe, and I don't want to order any for her from the mainland. Can you make her daytime clothes? She needs Island shoes?"

Connie pulled a rolled measuring tape out of the table drawer, and the three ladies quickly measured her, including her feet. "No problem," Connie said, "Come back in two days and be ready to play," they all smiled like carnival barkers in the mid-way.

"Great," Evonne said, "Remember mum the word."

They all hugged goodbye. Nicki and Mrs. Frank stepped out the front door. Mrs. Frank pointed to her left. Six tiny houses were tightly squeezed under the oak trees in the distance, all with a continuous white picket fence. Connie and Evelyn live in the first two, and the college interns live in the others. Screen porches adorned the narrow white houses, southern row houses on a cream-colored dirt road.

On the four-wheeler, Mrs. Frank drove between the horse barn and the equipment barn on the road to the beach. Mrs. Lucy's children had to stop between the two buildings and wait for an adult employee to walk them to the beach. Mrs. Lucy's oldest child had an incident with a shark. After that episode, nobody went swimming by themselves.

Captivated by the Island, Nicki felt she should be in deep mourning. Her anger kept her from accepting that her mother was dead and her father was alone 2,000 miles away. Nicki's brother was a recovering alcoholic, struggling each day. Her fiancé Thomas was lost to her whereabouts. She had much to mourn and much to fuel her anger.

A mile past the street sign heading north, the high-pitched sound of a motorcycle came from behind and passed around them on the left. The driver popped a wheelie and waved.

"What was that," Nicki said.

"Taylor Samms, that is what."

"Wow," said Nicki. This place is like a circus."

"You haven't seen anything yet," Evelyn smiled and turned to the right on a small path; palm fronds slapped them in the face. Silently driving under the canopy of trees, the four-wheeler stopped by two buildings up on poles.

"What is this," Nicki said.

"Let's get out. The building on the left is a bathroom, and the building on the right is showers. "Expensive conveniences for the campers that used the primitive campsites," said Mrs. Frank, "In excellent condition to this day." Nicki thought this place was like a deserted Jurassic Park; it was not about the strange dinosaurs but the eccentric people.

They continued out of the trees into a bright open space of blue skies and dunes, over the top, and to the beach. Mrs. Frank drove halfway to the water and stopped. The beach was a quarter of a mile wide and the whitest of whites. As far as they could see, no people, buildings, or condos were sighted, a virgin beach and a soft easterly breeze.

"Amazing," Nicki said, "I would like to have it as all mine. She let all her air out." She wanted to say something else but pushed out the fresh air in exchange for heavy air. Her head dropped to her chin.

Mrs. Frank drove on the hard-packed beach, passing sand dollars and conch shells. She slowed as they came upon a wall of trees, bleached white, dead trees scattered over the beach, some standing attached to their roots, some lying on their sides fifty-foot long.

"Driftwood beach," Mrs. Frank said, "amazing, isn't it?" Before the hurricanes, these trees were on the land; they moved from the forest to the sea, and then the sea backed out.

As she stood in the four-wheeler, Nicki shouted, "Can we stop?"

She ran over to a tree lying sideways; a towering pine once had become petrified sideways, limbs and trunk in tack. She was like an 8-year-old, running, climbing, and swinging from the limbs. Fifteen minutes had passed, and she returned with wet, matted hair and a smile.

"I shouldn't be having fun; I should be sad."

They drove back to Plum Orchard at an even pace. Halfway between Plum Orchard and Dungeness is the Stafford House, standing watch over unkept cotton fields. Still, a few plants can produce high-quality Sea Island Cotton.

"I thought I would let Joe introduce you to Bernie Maker, but since we are here, let's stop and say Hi."

Mrs. Frank knocked on the screen door on the porch and called out, "Dr. Maker, it's Evonne Frank."

From behind them, Dr. Maker called back, "Good day, Mrs. Frank. Are you and Joe well?"

"Yes, thank you, Dr. Maker. Please say hello to Niki Boaz."

"Hello, Miss Boaz, Boaz as in the Bible?"

"Yes, no—it was my dad's family name. I know the story, but we are not related."

"What an unfortunate incident. Boaz was a prodigious man, and his wife Ruth, a heroine."

"Nicki, Dr. Baker is a leading theology professor. Most of the Preachers who lead big Churches have been in Dr. Maker's classes; he is the one who makes Doctors out of Pastors. Dr. Maker is in exile because he will not conform to the state's program for teaching Pastors. He is too famous for killing and influential to be housed in a real prison. He is out of the way, and his wife is in California with their children, under watchful eyes."

"I am sorry, Dr. Maker; I am estranged from my family too."

"He gave her a half-smile, a confirmation of compassion. Please return soon, Nicki. I have alienated most of the people on the Island, and you might as well get your chance.

Mrs. Frank said, "Dr. Maker is doing his best to make a joke."

"Sure, Bernie, I will be back."

Driving away, Nicki said to Mrs. Frank with a smile, "Dr. Nerd, for sure."

"True, Nicki, but you are one of the smartest nerds in our country. You will do good to get some free high-priced schooling," Mrs. Frank said with no smile.

They drove to the Plum Orchard entrance and parked on the right side of the house. Mr. Frank sat at a picnic table under the mossy oaks; he waved them over, "lunch is ready," he said. Joe had set the table with a plate of sausage biscuits and a bowl of scrambled eggs.

Mrs. Frank said, "Joe, I see you are eating your heart-healthy diet again."

"Relax, Evonne, eat. Nicki and I will run and meet Charlie and Beth and try to get to the Settlement to meet Taylor Samms if we have time."

Nicki smiled, watching a gust of fresh Georgia air blow the tablecloth. She gazed off at the white clouds hovering over the river that wandered through the marsh. The scene relaxed her to the point of numbness.

After they headed out, Joe filled Nicki in on all the Plantation Homes after the meal. Mrs. Lucy wanted her adult children to stay on the Island, so she built mansions. Some children stayed, some didn't, but the Greyfield stayed in her family. Charlie and Beth are the owners. Charlie is related to Lucy; he spent his youth on this Island, went to school in the Northeast, and brought Beth back to the Island, and she loved it. They married at the same place a President's son got married, at the settlement. They enjoy special privileges because Charlie's family runs in political circles and has power and influence. They spend time in Washington and remain active in the robust lifestyle. They own this land and the building, not the state.

Joe turned right onto the hard-packed shell driveway. He stopped at the bottom of the mansions, 30-foot-wide steps leading to the second-level porch. Joe and Nicki reached the top step and heard a voice from the yard, "Joe, how are you doing?"

They looked toward the river behind them; Charlie and Beth were transporting a six-foot-long duffle bag into a golf cart. Smiling and sweating profusely, they drove to the steps and carried the bag to the top, then to the side of the large porch. Nicki and Joe followed. Laying the load on the wooden floor tenderly, Beth unzipped the entire bag's length, and a dark-haired young woman sprang out.

Nicki jerked back and got behind Joe.

Charlie said, "The sawgrass islands block the base cameras, but they fly drones along the shore, so we bag them," Charlie laughed. Beth showed the girl inside, and Joe introduced Nicki to Charlie.

"Hi, Nicki. What brings you to our beautiful Island."

"Visiting," Nicki said, careful not to reveal herself.

"How long will you be with us?"

"Not sure."

Beth came out the front door, rolling up her sleeve, and with a big smile, she held her hand toward Nicki, "I am Beth. How are you? It can be a little scary to see people carrying a girl in a bag."

Nicki squinted and grimaced, "Yes."

"Well," Beth said, "To make things worse, Charlie and I are smugglers. We smuggle people."

Nicki pulled back.

"You can relax; it is all good work. I will tell you the next time you come by."

Charlie said with a smile, "I call it the Lord's work."

Joe said, "We better be going. I wanted to introduce Nicki so you wouldn't bag her if you saw her." He thought it was funny; Nicki didn't. Confused, she did not know what to believe, thinking, *Beautiful Island, strange people.*

"We will have to wait to go to the settlement. If you think that was strange, wait until you meet Taylor Samms; he is one of a kind."

Arriving back at Plum Orchard, Joe locked the main doors shut. "Come to dinner; we are eating fresh Georgia shrimp."

Apartment number one looked like a house out of Coastal Living Magazine, a spacious two-bedroom apartment tastefully decorated in Plum Orchard style. Contemporary accessories adorned the home. It all fit Mrs. Frank flawlessly.

Mrs. Frank said, "Hi to you both; how were Beth and Charlie?"

"Hauling girls in bags is how they were."

Joe laughed, "She is right; one of their underground properties is passing through."

Nicki drifted around the room as they talked, looking at Joe, Evonne, and their family pictures. Sitting on the desk was an 8X10 picture of the Franks with three young girls. The image was old because the Franks were young.

Nicki said, "Your girls?" and held the picture so Mrs. Frank could see.

"The one on the right is Gina, and on the left is Lisa, our girls."

"Nicki said, holding the picture, "You know the girl in the

middle looks like me. She held it closer, "Really, it looks like me. We could be twins."

Mrs. Frank walked from the kitchen, stood before Nicki, stared into her eyes, and said, "Not you—your mother."

Nicki laughed because she didn't understand; her eyes drifted back to Mrs. Frank's eyes.

Mrs. Frank nodded her head to say— yes.

CHAPTER 5

"Life shrinks or expands in proportion to one's courage."
Jane Austen

"Nicki, Joe, and I knew your grandmother and your mother. Although from Atlanta, we spent our early years in Jacksonville Beach and attended a small church a few blocks from the ocean. Joe was a Deacon and was part of the events that brought your grandmother to our protection and church.

Your Mom and our girls were best friends and even came to this Island with us for a day trip. Carrie Marie, your mom, was born for something unique.

Your Mom left town after she graduated college. She was on a mission to find herself. She ended up in Plentywood, Montana. We all loved your mom and followed her life. We prayed for her as she became one of the country's most influential women lawyers and public speakers.

We only saw her one more time during the incident under the bridge. We didn't meet you there; we only stood by your mother's side.

When we saw you at the door with Todd, Joe and I recognized you immediately. You look exactly like your mom, only more beautiful, more formidable."

Nicki said, "This is an unbelievable story. How can this be? "Why would my mom and Grandmother need protection?"

Nicki looked at Joe, stunned. Joe looked back with a deep sense of kind-heartedness. Mrs. Frank was happy Nicki was here and hoped for an extended stay.

"What now?" said Nicki.

"A fresh Georgia shrimp dinner, that's what." beamed Mrs. Frank

Broiled and fried, Nicki devoured the large shrimp caught fresh off the island.

Nicki casually asked about her mother as a child. Mrs. Frank could fill in most details, except details about her arrival at the little church and the incident. Nicki could smell the avoidance and the fresh corn on her plate.

Nicki showed Joe the small device and the note that went with it. He smiled. We have a few days, according to the date and time in your message. I will show you tomorrow.

Nicki went with Joe to the front porch and sat in the green rockers. The gentle breeze blew the moss like a gray ghost flying in the early darkness. Joe smoked a cigar with the biggest of smiles as the smoke floated smoothly across the porch. Nicki's brain sorted twenty thoughts simultaneously in the peace of the moment. She bit her lip and rocked quickly, thinking, *How long will I be stuck here?*

"When is Todd coming back?"

Joe said, "We never know. He shows up. He is guarded about his visits, usually spending time with Beth, Charlie, and Taylor Samms. Then he is gone. He treats us so well. He is a great friend. Joe grinned with the cigar still in his mouth, "Nicki, it seems he is more than a friend to you."

She paused, looking out onto the large front yard, "Oh no, just a college friend."

Joe laughed," Who are you kidding?"

"There could have been something once, but we could never light the flame again. There was always so much going on. Todd could never sit still, and I was not very trusting."

Joe shrugged and said, "Tomorrow, we will stop by your

coordinates, and then we will travel north to the settlement and meet Taylor Samms. The Island's north end is isolated but full of history and surprises.

"There is no TV or internet here; there are books on the second-floor landing. The chairs are comfortable, and the view is beautiful. He said, "If you feel adventurous, take the 4-wheeler to Dungeness and play cards with the old biddies."

Evonne said, "You mean those sweet ladies?"

Joe said," They made me dizzy with all they're carrying on. They think they are the owners of this Island."

"That is a great idea. I think I will read it tonight and try it tomorrow."

At 7:00 the following day, Mrs. Frank knocked on Nicki's door and left a tray with eggs, bacon, and biscuits. Nicki struggled to the door, brought the food in, and sat at her table gazing out the back of her apartment. The view was extraordinary. She could see the water moving through the tidal marsh; the winding trails led back to the Intercoastal and eventually to the Atlantic Ocean. The early sun cast a bright yellow haze against the heavenly blue skies. This place felt very comfortable.

At eight o'clock precisely, she showed up on the front porch, and Joe rocked back and forth, drinking a mug of coffee.

"Good morning, Mr. Frank."

"Joe, please."

"You ready?" Walking down the steps, they climbed into the four-wheeler. Heading north at a leisurely pace, Joe gave her the history tour. The Main Road was the only road North and South. The settlement was six miles straight ahead and then a quick turn east.

Joe expertly told Nicki stories of the Island's 16th and 17th centuries history. It was a Spanish settlement. In 1684, the missionaries and the natives abandoned the Island. They retreated to St Augustine because the pirate Thomas Jingle attacked the Island.

He spoke proudly about James Oglethorpe arriving in 1736 and how Cumberland Island was given its name. A young Yamacraw Indian named Toonahowi had returned with Oglethorpe to England. They called it for the Duke of Cumberland, son of King George II.

Oglethorpe built a hunting lodge called Dungeness in the southern part of the Island.

Small farmers and Innkeepers initially used the north end because of the shipping activity at St Andrew's Sound. During the Civil War, the Union occupied the Island. The war ended; most people left, leaving the enslaved people, now called freedmen, to the settlement home.

In the late 19th and 20th centuries, tourism came back with large luxury hotels. The settlement became home to those who worked and supported the thriving tourist businesses.

The dirt road came to an intersection. Nicki looked down the crossroad, and it looked like it had been a subdivision at one time. On the corner stood a house in good condition. Joe told her about the women who lived there who helped educate the settlement people. The house had been restored as part of a tour, and modern bathrooms were built inside. Driving past the home, Joe pulled into a wide-open lot. A rectangular wooden building in the middle of the lot is a wooden box, undoubtedly a Church. The First African Baptist Church, established in 1893, had a stone plaque with the founder's names attached to the building. They pushed the door open; Nicki was shocked it was not locked. Joe replied to her shocked look, "Who would break in?"

They sat in the thirty by the twenty-foot church; all but one pew was original. Nicki felt at home for some reason. What a fantastic old place. The silence was holy, and the building was as plain as the lot.

Joe's history lesson continued, with the son of an American president and his beautiful bride married in this little Church as it is today. It was very secretive; only forty family members attended. After the wedding, this place became like a national monument, but it faded quickly because of its remoteness.

Exiting the Church, Joe led Nicki to his right across the lot and a house. They walked up to the fence while the central air conditioning kicked on. Nicki thought, what a contrast in time travel.

Joe yelled, "Taylor, are you home? Taylor Samms, it is Joe Frank, and I have someone you would like to meet."

A voice from two buildings away said, "Joe, my friend, how are you?" A five-foot-five smiling man was walking toward the fence, wearing an orange Home Depot apron covered in grease and a Russian mink cap with dog ears in the down position.

Nicki was somewhat frightened at the sight. Come in, Joe, come in, and he pulled back a gate not opened in years. Taylor, this is Nicki Boaz.

"Howdy," he said as he walked them to his new, oversized garage. They entered through the ten-foot sliding barn doors and into a room like a showroom at a new car dealer. Every modern piece of equipment hung on the walls or a moveable tool chest, many of them as tall as Taylor. In the back of the garage, lined up like transformers, were fifteen motorcycles standing at attention on the sparking grease-free floor.

Nicki, wide-eyed, gazed at the modernist in an old remote location like it was a movie. "How did all of this get here, Mr. Samms?"

"When they exiled me to this Island, it was conditional. I would need my tools and my bikes." Tilting his head to the right and staring at Nicki, he said, "You look a little too pretentious to ride bikes. Are you a rich girl?"

Joe smiled and looked at Taylor but spoke to Nicki, "What do you think, Nicki?"

Her brow wrinkled, "Maybe I should punch him in the nose."

Taylor chuckled and asked, "Would you like a coffee and chocolate chip cookies fresh from the oven?"

Joe laughed, "I thought you only used your oven to clean the grease off your motorcycle parts."

A huge smile gave him away, "You're right, fresh out of the microwave oven."

Nicki, "How long will you be on our beautiful Island?"

"Only a few days. I am staying at Plumb Orchard with the Franks."

"If I can be of any help to you, let me know. Come on up if you have a hankering."

"Taylor, it was good to see you. Please stop by the house and have coffee and real cookies with Evonne and me. I wanted you to meet Nicki; she is a friend of Todd Miller."

"Oh, a friend of Todd's? I insist that you come back now."

"I will, Mr. Samms."

Joe and Nicki walked back through the fence and closed the gate. Joe smiled a big smile, "So what did you think?"

"This island is the most beautiful and intriguing place I have visited. I don't know what to say about Taylor Samms."

"Nicki, Taylor is a brilliant man. Don't let his country act fool you. He is an economist and a newspaper publisher, a powerful man in his own right. That is what earned him a trip to prison on this Island."

As they walked away, Joe continued his history lesson, "The Naval Station on the other side of the channel is more than a Nuclear Submarine base. They watch Taylor's every move, knowing when he breathes in and out. Nicki, your coordinates are directly across from the base itself. They are directly opposite the giant satellite dish that captures every electronic signal for a hundred miles. Let's go, and I will show you."

"Mr. Frank, more history, please."

"Nicki, things get spicy when the Carnegies arrive. Lucy Carnegie loved this Island and rebuilt Dungeness. She brings high society to bug-infested Cumberland Island: golf courses, gymnasiums, gardens, and lawns. Many of Lucy's relatives live north on the next Island, Jekyll Island, where all the millionaires had huge homes and a club built to keep people out. There were grand parties and extraordinary times on Cumberland Island.

"I will drive you to the coordinates on your note. The exact point is south of Plum Orchard and Stafford, about ½ mile south of Greyfield Inn."

The main road drive was just as enjoyable heading back. Joe showed her the overgrown tree-lined roads famous in the Gilded Era. He pointed out the location of the old Golf Course. On the left, just as they came upon the Stafford House located on a 30-acre cotton field, occasionally producing famous sea island cotton. To her left, Nicki saw what she thought was a diagonal road through the square area. Because of the height of the cotton plants, it seemed hidden.

"Stop, what is that in the cotton field? Nicki said as she lifted off her seat.

Joe stopped, backed up, and pulled to the side of the field. They got out and walked through the plants until they stood in the middle of a smooth dirt road. It was fifty feet wide and had tire marks much more expansive than the cart tire. They stood in the middle and looked southeast as far as they could see. At the end, in the distance, ever so slightly to the right, was a big green metal building.

Joe said," Welcome, Nicki, to Cumberland's private airport. This road is the runway. Hidden in the middle of this cotton field for secrecy. In the hanger in the distance is a small 4-seater private plane used by the owners of the only other private residence on this Island."

"Really, this Island with eleven people has an airport?"

"It is not an airport, more like a landing strip."

"This is so strange, Joe; what goes on here?"

"It is no big deal, Nicki; let's get going."

Just past Greyfield Inn, Joe turned to the right down a minor road that led to the river. Joe walked to the edge of the road and toward the river. The lush green grass curved around a giant oak tree onto a sand path. Two palm trees flanked their right, and tall scrub bushes rose ten feet high. They turned right, disappearing into a patch of heavy brush, and stepped onto a hard-packed sandy shore. There was a small wooden platform over the water. Joe said, "Nicki "X" marks the spot."

Nicki looked around; there was nothing much to see. The area was well-worn. The platform was tiny, like a place to hang your legs off while fishing. An island was about fifty yards out in front of the platform. It looked like any other intercoastal Island. It was above water sometimes but covered most of the time. Short pine trees along the Island ran north and south for about a ½ mile. "I don't see anything special about this spot, do you, Joe?"

The Island is called Drum Point Island, and it is a good fishing spot, but it is off-limits because on the other side of the Island is the Nuclear Submarine Base. Occasionally, people with small boats try to sneak up the channel to fish but are run off by the Navy guards.

"What is that big grey thing over the top of the trees?"

That is one of the satellite dishes that guard the area. It is ultra-sensitive, and it is the one that keeps us from using our electronic devices. It picks up everything.

"Why is this place so well worn? It looks like people are there all the time. There can't be that many people that come here to fish."

"What do I do?" Nicki asked, looking at her electronic device.

"Just show up when your note says and bring your little pod."

"Then I must be back here at 1:46 PM today."

They piled back into the cart and headed back to Plum Orchard.

"You are on your own the rest of the day, Nicki. I have some things I must do.

"May I borrow the four-wheeler?" Nicki said.

Mrs. Frank was downstairs in the small summer kitchen. She cheerfully baked pecan pies, Joe's favorite.

"Hello, Nicki, how did you like meeting Taylor Samms."

"It was a treat; he has an amazing garage for living on a deserted island. And the little Church had a strong attraction to me. I don't know why it is only one room on an empty lot."

"It is a famous place, for sure."

"May I borrow the 4-wheeler for the afternoon? Joe is busy, and I thought I would ride back to Dungeness and meet the ladies again."

"Sure, Nicki, but stay on the main road until Joe shows you

the lay of the land. We have a lot of wildlife on this Island, wild Hoggs especially. The Island used to be a Hogg hunting paradise. Still, we only get one or two groups a year. They are government cronies interested in drinking and telling stories. Watch the weather; powerful thunderstorms bring wind, lightning, and heavy rain, and they pop up quickly.

After lunch, Nicki pulled up to the two-story white house. Nicki politely knocked, and Connie walked to the door, "Hi, Nicki, welcome, come on in. Do you want something to drink?"

Nicki said, "Do you have sweet tea?"

"We have the sweetest tea you have ever tasted," she smiled big and giggled. "There is a thunderstorm brewing. Have a seat, Nicki, and tell me your story."

Nicki thought, *I never drink tea, much less sweet tea; what is with me? I am now Southern.* "It would have to be the short story, Connie. I have to get the cart back to Mrs. Frank."

"My family lived in Plentywood, Montana. My Mom, Dad, brother Robert, and I enjoyed the small-town life. In our early life, we were poor. My dad and brother invested their paychecks in a start-up business, and my mom traveled the country giving speeches. My mom became famous and influential, and she used her fame to help many people. She was in a war against evil, and evil was after her and our family. My Mom had a spiritual awakening and was charging hard for God. The country was on a downward spiral. My Dad and Uncle Tim grew their start-up into a billion-dollar business, and life became easier. But there were always strange things happening. As a teenager, I was kidnapped; it was terrible. I graduated college, went to law school, worked for my dad and Uncle, and occasionally helped my mom. I preferred being out of the limelight. My Mom was accidentally shot helping an innocent person at a protest in Washington. I came here hours after her memorial service, which the authorities stopped. That is my short story."

"That was short. Why did you come to our Island?"

"I don't have a clue. I want to talk with you about this beautiful Island, but I have a place I need to be.

"You have a place you need to be on our uninhabited island?"

"Yes, I will come back soon."

Nicki had left herself more than enough time to ride from Dungeness back to the small dock at Drum Island. She was slowly getting familiar with the Main Rd. She circled Dungeness and headed north, passing the Icehouse and Sea Camp. It had stormed while Nicki visited with Connie, and the dirt road was wet and puddled.

Nicki came upon a pine tree across the Main Road five minutes past the Sea Camp dock. The tree was over forty feet long, and it blocked the road. Lightning had hit the tree, blowing parts of the tree fifty feet in all directions. It was too heavy for Nicki to move. The lower branches made it impossible to climb over the fallen tree. She looked at her watch. It was only twenty-one minutes to drive to the platform. To her right, she saw a path that went to the west. She thought maybe it went to the river and she could follow the shore. But after fifty feet, it turned north into the thick woods. Nicki stopped and backed up, sweating as she investigated the dark thicket. She made her way back to Main Rd. Relieved, she discovered she had only used ten minutes of her time. Nicki paced and looked at the problem again. She walked to the tree, laid down on her stomach, and dug under the tree. One of the large branches had held the tree off the ground about six inches. She dug enough to get her head under and shoulders, though barely.

Mud in her mouth, she jumped up and started running. She had once been a six-minute mile runner, but she needed to go faster today.

She made the left turn, heading toward the river. Nicki stepped onto the platform and looked at her watch. It was 1:50 and 30 seconds. She switched on the small pod, a small light turned green, and she heard her name through the small device. Hello, she said. The light turned red. Nicki tried turning it on again, but the red light went off, and she had nothing. Soaking wet, she sat on the ground. Was this her one chance? The voice sounded like her dad. She repeatedly tried to contact someone who could help her. She kicked and waved her wrathful arms and pitched a red-faced fit, crying and screaming at her failure.

No green or red light flashed, only the dripping rain and an opportunity misused.

Nicki walked back to Plum Orchard in the light rain. Looking down the long road at the giant white plantation house, she had no feelings. In the distance, she could see Joe on the front porch smoking his cigar. Soaking wet and muddy, she sat beside him and said nothing, rocking in unison as she thought of someone or something to blame.

"I was too late to contact my dad. The light turned green for one second, then red, then nothing."

Joe smiled as he did when his wisdom could solve a problem. "Do you know why the grass was so worn at the dock?"

"That is the one spot on this Island where you can safely communicate with the outside world for ten minutes. The time you had on your note was Spring Tide. That is when the high tide is higher. The satellite dish on the other side of Drum Island must tilt several degrees upward to avoid the saltwater. It tilts up the dish and leaves an unmonitored area for five minutes before the Spring Tide and five minutes after. Your device could tell when the signal was present."

"How often does this spring tide occur?"

"Every two weeks."

Nicki bent her pointer finger, stuck it in her mouth, and bit down hard, "You mean I must be on this Island for another two weeks? I cannot do it. I must get off this Island."

"Well, Nicki, you can go right back and try again. A Coast Guard boat will arrive within five minutes and take you off the Island and into a real jail."

"What am I going to do for two weeks? I need to get off this Island. I have things I have to do."

"You will make yourself useful. Everyone works here."

Niki didn't cry.

Chin sticking out, Nicki murmured, "I will need a saw to cut a tree tomorrow to get the 4-wheeler back to Plum Orchard."

Conquered and exhausted, she slowly and wobbly stood up like an aged woman heading to her apartment. She didn't have to fall asleep to have nightmares; she lived them. A disheartened sleep might bring her relief.

PART II

"That Life will never come again is what makes it so sweet."
Emily Dickinson

CHAPTER 6

You are never a failure until you quit, and
it is always too soon to quit.
Rick Warren

The marsh breeze blew the curtains close to Nicki's face. After sleeping twenty hours, she sat in bed, pulling her knees to her chin. Trapped for two more weeks, she whimpered. *I must get off this Island.*

Every minute of the day, she experienced personal pain. It started when her mom died. She missed her dad, Robert, and little Tracey. Her fiancé, Thomas White, was occasionally on her mind. Nothing came close to distracting and comforting her hurt.

She needed to get home, get safe, and get going to carry out her mom's mission. She wanted retribution for her mom's death, but her project today was to bring the 4- 4-wheeler back to Plum Orchard. Projects made her purposeful.

Meandering downstairs, Nicki found Mrs. Frank in the kitchen on the back porch.

"Good morning," Nicki said quietly. "Where is Mr. Frank?"

"Morning, Nicki; he is off to work."

"Off to work? On a deserted island."

"It is just a term I use. He is just not here right now. He left a chainsaw and instructions by the rocking chair. How about some breakfast?"

Nicki liked talking to Mrs. Frank. After breakfast, she walked to the front porch and saw the small chainsaw in a gray plastic case with the blade sticking out.

Nicki thought, *I do not know how to use a chainsaw, and I have never even touched one. How am I going to get this done without a YouTube video?*

She carried the chainsaw as she walked south on the hard-packed road. She chuckled as she walked and thought, *The Main Road is the only road.* She liked the simplicity of Cumberland Island. Her real life was full of complexity. After walking for thirty minutes, she arrived at the pine tree. She read Mr. Frank's note, saying to wear these goggles and follow the instructions. He underlined that you follow the instructions.

Really Joe, a little smart aleck, she thought.

Nicki opened the case, glanced over the instructions, then walked to the tree and created a plan. She would have to cut the tree in two places and then cut the middle piece into smaller pieces so she could roll them off the road. Pondering how extensive each section should be, she wanted the most minor cuts. It was more like a business plan than a lumberjack decision.

Nicki followed the instructions, adding a few choice words appropriate for the fifty unfruitful pulls of the engine cord. Finally, it started. Nicki struggled to control the wild, noisy cutting machine. Cutting on the left and right, the saw sliced quickly and efficiently. Nicki was happy with the results. Finishing the cut on the right side of the tree, it fell into the path with a colossal thud and then rolled a few feet forward.

Feeling like a victorious soldier, she stopped the saw, took off her goggles, and admired her work. Looking down at the log, she noticed a pair of well-worn brown boots. She followed them up to see a young man in dark green khaki pants and a light brown shirt with a matching hat. It was an official uniform with badges, medals, and pins.

Nicki froze. She wanted to run.

"Hi," she said apprehensively.

"Hi yourself," in an authoritative voice. "Who are you?"

"I am a guest of the Franks."

"We don't have guests on this Island."

"I am a guest. My mother was a close friend of Mr. and Mrs. Frank's, and they have been helping me for a few weeks. My name is Nicki."

"My name is Craig, and I am the park ranger. Cumberland Island is a National Park, and I oversee the Island. Let me help you clear the road, and I will go with you to Plum Orchard to meet with Mr. Frank.

Nicki and Ranger Craig rolled the pieces off the road. Craig never said a word or made any facial expression that would clue Nicki into her fate. Drenched in the hard-working sweat of the last days of September, Craig told Nicki that when trees fall, they stay natural except when they interfere with roads. The Ranger proudly announced that roads were essential to the Ranger's job. Nicki bolstered his pride with an "I never knew that," including a girlish smile. Ranger Craig did not respond, and Nicki could not read his intentions. Pulling into Plum Orchard, Mrs. Frank was sitting on the porch reading.

She stood as the 4-wheeler rolled up into the circle.

"Morning, Craig."

"Good morning, Mrs. Frank. May I have a word with you?" Craig tipped his hat to Nicki as she walked into the house.

Nicki, nervous, went to the kitchen and made a cup of coffee. She tried to eavesdrop but could not hear a word.

Ranger Craig left after a few minutes.

Nicki burst onto the porch, "What did he say? Am I going to jail? How long do I have?"

Mrs. Frank said, "Calm down. Joe will handle it."

"Ranger Craig did say that you did a good job cutting the tree. I am impressed. I didn't picture you as an outdoors person." Mrs. Frank said with a big smile.

I have not been outdoors much in the last few years. I grew up in the great outdoors. My dad, brother, and Uncle were always off on some skiing adventure in the mountains and deep woods of the Northwest. I had an incident before college that kept me out of the woods.

"Do I have anything to worry about? Will Ranger Craig call the people looking for me?"

"Joe will handle it."

Joe says I have another chance to reach my dad in two weeks. I will study my mom's file folder to prepare for leaving. I do not want to waste time keeping my promise to help her. If you need me to do anything, I am willing.

"May I use the cart?"

"Yes, Joe is using the Bronco today."

Still worried that Ranger Craig's incident would end in her arrest, she grabbed the file folder out of the dry bag and set out for a place to interpret her mom's writings.

Nicki drove south on the Main Road, passing the secret communication point near Drum Island. Nearing the Sea Camp Ranger Station, she turned east and took the trail to the Ocean. There was a large white and black striped pole to mark the entrance to the trail. At the beach, she sat momentarily, looking for a location that matched her mood. Nicki couldn't find her peaceful spot and headed back to the trail. The trail running back split, and Niki chose the route to the left. The brush was thin and low, and the path led down into a small ravine. It was the most unusual thing she had ever seen. Ten wooden benches made of pine boards laid across sawed-off tree trunks. There was an aisle down the middle. At the front was a log-built podium. It looked like a Church or a schoolroom. Canopied with scrub oak, it was like a room. The easterly breeze causes the branches to grow west, creating an eerie look like witches' fingers. The floor of the natural room was oak leaves, several inches thick.

Nicki, completely enchanted with the peacefulness of the forest church, opened her backpack and reviewed her mother's notes. The notes must have been the research topics for the missing notebook. There was no single paragraph, just scribbles, lists, and thoughts with no conclusions. Nicki reached inside herself for her mom's words that could lead her to clues or answers. There was no revelation from the notes, but the location was otherworldly.

Nicki headed back north toward Plum Orchard. On her right, approaching the Stafford House, was the forty acres of Sea Island Cotton. She slowed to appreciate the cotton plants. Horses grazed in and around the cotton. It was like a picture out of Southern Living Magazine.

In the distance, she could see Dr. Maker in the front yard of his home. She drove to the house, pulled the cart to the left, and said, "Good Morning, Dr. Maker, "How are you today?

"Fine, Nicki, I am fine. Has your short stay on the Island been productive?

"I am restless. My brain tells me I have much to do, but my body cannot grasp it. I will lose my mind if I cannot find something useful to accomplish. I have tried working on understanding my mother's notes, but I am naïve. Maybe you could help. She has a lot of Bible verses and religious thoughts."

"Are you aware of the purpose of your mother's notes?"

"Yes, she was preparing a speech to change things in our country. My Mom was a powerful and convincing speaker."

"I am familiar with your mother's influence; she spoke at my college, and the people were moved to action. As time presents itself, I would be privileged to assist you."

"Thanks, Doc."

Dr. Maker looked at Nicki with disdain, "Please stop by soon, Miss Nicki."

Nicki thought something good had happened, a relationship that could help her. She grinned at her pretentious rhetoric, calling him Doc.

Nicki was not comfortable about feeling good. The reality was that her mom had died, and she was a hostage on an isolated island with a few other people. Nicki needed help figuring out what to do. She had ten days until the high tide and talking to her dad. She was sure he would have a plan. He always had an idea, most of them successful.

Returning to the Mansion, Nicki decided to help Mrs. Frank until she had further details. Mr. and Mrs. Frank were not picture-perfect caretakers for this old house. It seemed to her that they came from a different genre. They were well dressed, intelligent, moved, spoke, and acted with greater confidence. They were kind and wise. They also had a past with her mom and Grandmother. When she saw her grandfather again, she would get the low-down on this couple.

"Hi, Mrs. Frank," Nicki said with a bounce in her step.

"What is making you feel so good?" Mrs. Frank said.

"I don't know. How may I help you today?"

"It would help me if you could take this plate of cookies to Connie and Evelyn."

"No problem. Anything else I can do while I am at that end of the Island?"

"No, I cannot think of anything else but wait. I think it would serve you well to become familiar with the estate. Walk around Dungeness, including the greenhouse and the covered arches. I will make your lunch, and there is no better place to eat than under the pergola and trellis. Walk out of the entrance and look back at the grandness of the place."

"Why, I will be leaving soon. I will probably never come back."

"My Dear Nicki, I can assure you that neither you nor I know what tomorrow will bring."

"Yes, Mrs. Frank." Nicki knew she had been rude.

Nicki did not have a clue as to why Mrs. Frank wanted her to walk the entire ruined estate of Mrs. Lucy Carnegie.

Nicki pulled into the white house, knocked on the screen door, and called in. "It's Nicki."

"Nicki, come in. It is great to see you. What brings you this far south?"

"Cookies from Mrs. Frank."

"Cookies, get yourself in here, and we will get a fresh glass of lemonade and have a party."

Nicki passed the cookies to Evelyn and sat with Connie at the card table.

"How are you doing?"

"Fine."

Connie said, "I understand what fine means. Do you want to tell me about it?"

"I am stuck here. I missed my connection with my dad and didn't know what to do. It is frustrating."

"Are you safe, Nicki?"

"I guess, except I fear Ranger Craig might turn me in."

"Are you fed?"

"Yes, I am. I am well-fed."

"Do you have friends?"

"Yes."

"Couldn't you just be grateful for being safe, nourished, and loved for a few days?"

With deep embarrassment for her bad attitude and a reflective pause, Nicki said, "Yes, I could,"

"Here are the cookies and lemonade. Do you want to play a game of Mexican Train?"

"I would like to, but I am under orders to wander around Mrs. Lucy's ruins for some mysterious reason."

"Good for you," Connie said." The beauty of Lucy's place will never leave you."

Nicki left the 4-wheeler at the house and walked south toward a ruined Dungeness. She followed the well-worn path to the back, crossing the massive backyard on the marsh. A giant fountain adorned the center of the lawn. Like in a movie, this wide-open green space must have been fanciful for parties and Lucy's nine children.

She stepped down to the boat docks as wild horses sauntered by. The salty, muddy smell enhanced the slight easterly breeze as she headed toward the greenhouse. It must have matched the Arboretum at the Biltmore in its heyday. Although it was almost October, the grass was summer green. Wildflowers sprang up for a dessert for the Cumberland Horses. Nicki walked to the manager's house, now called the Tabby house. To the left was an impressive pergola a quarter of a mile long that looked like a colorful train tunnel. Nicki walked the pergola until she found a seat under a wild vine, creating soothing shade. Eating her lunch, she leaned back on the tabby column and breathed out. With the air went her stress. On the second exhalation, she went limp, and on the third exhale, she closed her eyes. She fell into a deep, hard sleep that only happens at total exhaustion.

Nicki's slumber turned into a dream. The dream was triple time and covered months in a few seconds. To see Nicki's face in her sleep, you would have seen expressions of pain, suffering, and joy. Although sitting in the shade, she was sweating when she woke up. Groggy, she tried to stand but wobbled. She attempted to remember all that happened in her dream, but just walking was the immediate issue. Feeling heavy, she walked out of the pergola toward the front of the Mansion. Standing at the head of the drive, she could comprehend the greatness of the estate, the location, and the sheer magnificence. It was as if Lucy's charm had touched her.

Shaking her head, *this is weird,* she thought. *I must be more tired than I realized. Now I have visions.* But Nicki Boaz knew she liked Cumberland Island.

Walking back to the 4-wheeler, Nicki wiped the sleep out of her eyes with her sleeve. She waved to Connie at the front door.

Nicki drove slowly back to Plum Orchard, trying to retrieve her dream. Parking in the back, she saw Mrs. Frank in the kitchen. Offering a weak wave, Nicki walked through the house to the living room. She sat in a giant Queen Anne chair and stared through the darkroom.

Mrs. Frank followed Nicki and asked, "Are you ok?

"Yes."

"How were Connie and your excursion around Mrs. Lucy's house?"

"Connie was good. The tour of the property was ok."

"I have to get off this Island," Mrs. Frank, when will Joe return?"

"At dinner."

"I am going to go to my room and rest. I will see you at dinner."

Nicki could not rest tossing and turning, trying to solve the puzzle of all she had to do. She didn't know how to do anything but corporate law, just paperwork. Adding to her uneasiness was the mystery of why me. Her thoughts created a torrent of emotions. It was everything she could do to remain in her skin.

Nicki raised her hand to knock on the Frank's door as she casually gazed out the window overlooking the back of the house. A man walking briskly across the back lawn looked like Todd Miller. Nicki turned away from the door and banged on the window three stories above the man. The man couldn't hear her pounding. Joe opened the door, and before he could say hello, she pointed to the man driving off in the four-wheeler. "Is that Todd?"

"Yes, Nicki, it is."

"Is he coming back?"

"No, not now, Nicki. He had to go."

She threw her arms up and said, "He always has to go, Mr. Frank, always."

"Come in, Nicki. We must calculate the time for your new high tide. While Mrs. Frank finished the meal, he taught Nicki about the tide changing every six hours and adding roughly 54 minutes to the change every day. The tide would be eleven hours and 15 minutes later, at 1:15 AM.

"Do you think my dad will know?"

"I am certain he does."

"You will have to walk it in the dark, and you need to practice walking to the location, and you cannot take any light. It would be a dead giveaway. We will check the moon phase to see if you will have any moonlight."

Nicki did several dry runs over the next two days, getting down to the river and the tiny platform. She wanted to avoid making a mistake again. It was easy, a clear, wide path with only two big trees. The steps were easy to count and remember. She was excited to talk to her Dad and hear his plan to get her off this Island.

The day came with a twinge of freshness, a different smell, and a slight crispness to excite Nicki. Waiting was going to be complicated. It was a long time between now and 1:15 AM.

Nicki thought of returning home to Plentywood and meeting Thomas in San Francisco. She felt free and light as her thoughts turned to Todd Miller. She blushed like a 16-year-old girl just asked to the Cotillion. After completing her last practice run at Drum Island, a sinking spell fell over Nicki. *I am not going to be free,* she thought. Dad will get me off this Island, but then what? I cannot go home or see Thomas. Her excitement now waned as she counted off her last few steps. *Maybe I can live with Granddad. Nobody messes with him. Dad will know what to do.*

After dinner, Nicki lay in bed reading a book she found on the shelf, *The Greatest Salesman in the World.* It was a dingy old paperback, once white, now turned yellow. Her Mom once told her a fantastic story about it. It was a small book easy for her to read. Nicki could relate to the short story in every way and repeat the mantras with strength and conviction. "I will not be led like a lamb to the slaughter. I will succeed. Never before or after will there be another person like me." The words pulsated out of the book. They gave her goosebumps.

At 12:30, she left the Plum Orchard Mansion, allowing her 45 minutes for a ten-minute walk. She could not wait to go. Two long weeks marooned on this irrational Island had depressed her. She had made some great friends but was sure Ranger Craig would turn her in.

Her practice getting to the location paid off well. Reaching the platform, she sat and hung her legs off the tiny dock. Watching the lights from the Naval Base kept her in heightened focus as she watched the communication device.

Red light, Nicki jumped up to her feet. Holding it close to her face, she took a deep breath, and the green light happened.

"Dad, Dad," she said. She waited.

"Dad, can you hear me?"

"Nicki, sweetie, how are you?"

"Good Dad, what is the plan to get me off the Island."

There was a pause.

"Nicki, you are going to have to stay there a while. Things are not good here. They have ramped up their search for you. The government is putting more pressure on companies to nationalize. The Prelate and his cronies are slowly taking over the Churches. I am sure they will try to suspend the election before November, claiming it is temporary, to get through the crisis. They will say it is for the people's good with eager faces and evil intentions. It is a mess, Nicki. Our plan for you is to stay."

"How long, dad? What about Thomas and Robert and Tracey?"

"Maybe a year, Nicki; I am not sure."

"A year," Nicki threw her arms in the air, waving madly. She screeched, "Not going t to happen, Dad. I cannot do it."

Do not give up; good people are doing good things, and there is hope. Thomas is sucking up to the government, recommending that we agree to their terms. I am sending Robert to take your place in San Francisco to watch him. What do you see in Thomas? Aunt Maggie has agreed to come to Plentywood and take care of Tracey. Your Grandfather is doing the Lord's Work somewhere."

"Dad, I cannot stay here a year."

"Nicki, you must trust me on this. There is nothing you can do."

"I will call you every two weeks on the high tide. Do not do anything to draw attention to yourself."

"Who is leading this cause, Dad?"

"Nicki, I think I know what your mom would say to you, "Waiting on God is time that is never wasted.""

"Dad, really, I don't want to do it this way."

"I know, sweetie. I will talk to you in two weeks. Love you."

The light changed from green to red, and the conversation ended.

"Love you too, Dad."

Nicki slumped down on the dock, leaning back on the weathered wood and looking at the sky. "Really, God, I can't do this!"

CHAPTER 7

One of the largest tributaries on the River of
Greatness is the Stream of Adversity.
Cavett Robert

Francis Vile summoned the Prelate to a meeting at the National
Cathedral. He hated the thought of taking her to the Church.
Reverend Randall Parshall would never let her in. But she insisted,
and she wanted to enter through the front doors. The Prelate was
in a panic. Bishop Toyer tried to calm him, but he, too, knew that
letting her in the Church would be like Antiochus killing pigs in
the Jerusalem Temple.

Bishop Toyer and The Prelate arrived first and stood by their
town car. The Prelate clicked his fingernails. The bishop reached
over and grabbed his hands. The highest-ranking man in the country
was wet from sweat.

The Black SUV swung into the driveway. Francis Vile stepped
out with power and grace. Her beauty was enough to cause the
most confident man to step back. The Prelate bowed and took her
hand.

"Take me to your private meeting hall, Prelate. We have much
to discuss."

Followed by two bodyguards, they walked fifteen steps toward
the front doors of the Cathedral. Out of the center glass door stepped

The Right Reverend Randall Parshall. Standing tall and confident, he stopped at the curb.

"Good morning, Randy," Francis Vile said.

The Prelate grimaced.

"Good morning, Francis," The Reverend replied. "What are you doing here."

The Prelate replied, "We have a meeting."

"Francis, you know I cannot let you in."

She moved toward him with an exotic walk, ending within six inches of his face, "Sure you can, Randy." Her breath landed gently on his face.

The Reverend put his hands on her shoulders to push her back. Her two bodyguards stepped forward, then out of the five glass doors behind the Reverend poured twenty-five priests and four swat-looking men with rifles. The whole strength of the Cathedral's workforce stood next to the Reverend's shoulders, like the wings of an archangel.

"Got your own little army, I see, Randy."

"Temple guards, you might call them."

The Prelate stepped forward and asked in a low tone, "Can you please let her in."

"She knows she cannot come in, and she knows which side of this curb the power resides."

"The Prelate walked her back to the car. She said, "Prelate, you have not concluded the business I ask you to perform. Bring the girl to me or else."

Sheepishly, the Prelate answered, "I am sorry, Miss. Vile, she has disappeared, and we cannot find her. But we will."

"You had better." Then she turned, looked back at the Reverend over her shoulder, and gave him a wicked smile."

He put his hands together in the prayer position and returned the smile.

The following day, the Right Reverend Randall Parshall was found dead, lying face-up on the altar in the main sanctuary.

Bishop Toyer rushed into the prelate office in the Eisenhower Office building to report the news.

"Who do you think killed him."

The Prelate dropped his head on the desk. "I am next unless I can find Nicki Boaz."

"Oh, no, Prelate, you will be the next President."

Please prepare the country's highest honors for the Reverend. Spare no expense and ensure the media is hot on the trail of the terrorist who killed him."

"What terrorist, Prelate?"

"You heard me, a terrorist killed the Reverend."

"Yes, sir."

The President of the United States, Bill Smith, spoke at the Reverend's service held at the Cathedral, the giant hall filled with people who would never grace the inside of a Church. But it was politically correct and fashionable to be upright and seen on National TV. The Prelate spoke of a great loving relationship and God's grace. He extolled that Reverend Parshall would ask forgiveness for the terrorist. The Cathedral Reverends, Bishops, and lay leaders scowled at the public lies.

Bishop Toyer held the Prelates' arm as they exited at the head of the procession, preceding even the Reverend's immediate family.

The President's car led the procession, followed by the Prelates car, which left the caravan and turned right into the gates of Drakon Trading.

⌒

Nicki lay on the dock facing the stars for thirty minutes, thinking and forcing creative thoughts that would give her the plan to leave the island. Not one idea came to her. Her Dad's call was devastating.

Heading back to Plum Orchard, she inhaled delicious fresh air.

It was fulfilling, like comfort food with a crisp, sweet smell. She felt calm, thinking she should feel depressed.

Joe and Evonne were drinking coffee and welcoming the sunrise over the marsh. Joe asked, "Well, Nicki, did you get your dad?"

"I did."

"I might be here a year."

Mrs. Frank smiled and jumped.

Joe said, "Sounds severe, Nicki. What is going on?

"Dad said the country is digressing every day. The government is nationalizing businesses and now pays pastors in Churches. Dad's concern is that they will try to suspend the election in November. He says they are ramping up their search for me."

"You will be safe here, Nicki."

"What about your Thomas?" Mrs. Frank said.

"I miss him. We have been together for a while, but dad has never liked or trusted him. You would think Thomas would be moving heaven and earth to find me."

"What would I do here for a year?" Nicki said with a considerable emphasis on the word year.

Mrs. Frank said," This charming island offers much for one who is looking."

Nicki smiled a half-crooked smile, thinking there was nothing she was looking for on this Island.

Joe changed the subject, "Ranger Craig said a category three hurricane could be heading our way. The National Hurricane Center sent alerts and warnings to all Federal Employees."

Nicki said, "I have never been in a Hurricane."

"Let us hope you don't get a chance. You can help me with getting our plan ready."

"What do we do first, Mr. Frank?

"Get into the cart, and we will see everyone on the Island. We will start with Taylor Samms. We aim to get everyone to the Plum Orchard Mansion, the safest building on the Island. Taylor will not want to leave. Next, we will see Dr. Maker and then Evelyn and

Connie. Ranger Craig will take the students off the Island. Beth and Charlie have a government-issued cell phone, and we should be able to follow the storm if they are at The Greyfield.

After giving Dr. Maker and Taylor Samms the news, they hurried down Main Rd. to Dungeness and the white house. He stayed on the shell road instead of trying to navigate the soft sand. Connie and Evelyn were making an uproar over a game of Mexican Train. Joe did not knock. He walked in. "Morning ladies, a hurricane is out in the Atlantic, and we are under warnings. I need you to be prepared to move to the Mansion."

"Joe, these hurricanes never hit our little bend on the coast. We will be fine here."

"Ranger Craig is taking the college students off the Island tomorrow, and I am not sure he will be back. We will be on our own."

"Don't worry, Joe, we have been through this before."

"You know this old house sits on soft white sand, and if the water comes over the back of Dungeness, you will be a goner."

"It will be ok, Joe."

"Let's go, Nicki, those two give me a headache."

At top speed, Joe and Nicki headed to Greyfield Inn. They walked around the house, and down at the dock, they saw Charlie loading the boat.

"Charlie, I guess you heard about the storm?"

"Yes, Joe, I have been following it on the phone. I must make a delivery before the weather gets bad. The reports are difficult to read with the storm so far off the coast. I hate to do this, but I must have the phone to get through checkpoints. I will try to get back before the storm."

Joe gave Charlie a shake, and Nicki hugged Charlie.

"I will see you soon, Nicki. I understand you will be here for a while.

"Bad news travels fast," Nicki said.

"It might not be so bad. Beth and I will enjoy your stay."

"Thanks," she said with a smile and big eyes.

"Nicki, let's get back to the Mansion. We have things to do."

Arriving back at Plum Orchard, Joe took Nicki to the basement. It was like a treasure hold. Fine antiques on wooden shelves, an old ice machine, paintings, and a handmade toilet from France are scattered around the large room. We must move things off the floor and onto the shelves.

Nicki said, "Mr. Frank, what is with all the brick and stone down here."

"See the sizeable horizontal opening on the back wall?"

"Those are to let floodwaters into the basement. See the opening across the room? Those are for the floodwaters to run out. A brick floor on top of the rock base. How smart is that, Nicki."

"Does it work?

"House is still here."

Mrs. Frank called, "Joe, Ranger Craig is here to see you."

Let's go, Nicki."

"I think I will stay."

Ranger Craig reported that the steering currents had pushed the storm further into the Ocean. The storm's eye will hit north near the Outer Banks unless something abnormal happens. Maybe we would get some rain but nothing much else."

"Joe and Mrs. Frank sighed. Ranger Craig could have been happy, but you could not tell.

The incredible excitement had left Nicki in a mild depression. Her remedy is to walk the beaches in solitude. After three days, she sat at the pergola pondering the remnants of the Dungeness House. It must have taken some extraordinary patience to build these mansions on this remote Island. She wandered over to the white house and knocked on the door. Connie called across the room. "Nicki, come in, how are you?"

"Not so good, Connie. I am stuck here for a year. I must finish my mom's mission. But first, I must find out exactly what she would do. My dad needs me. He believes that if things don't change, it will be the end of the elections and our hope for a return to freedom and democracy. I do not know what I am supposed to do, and I am afraid to do anything."

"Saving the country sounds like a heavy load for one so young," Connie said with a slight smile.

Nicki said, "Sounds a little self-important, doesn't it?"

"Well, young lady, we can achieve great things one step at a time. Sit down, and let's start with a game of Mexican Train."

"Might as well, nothing to do or nowhere to go."

Connie laid the pieces out and explained the rules. She was a cunning and competitive game player, always playing to win.

After several minutes, Nicki was having a difficult time. She needed clarification about the randomness of the play and the overabundance of pieces in the game. She had in front of her 12 dominos and no game board.

Connie explained, "It may seem random, and circumstances are in control, but there is a strategy and a tactic for every circumstance."

"Really, it seems that everything about this game is random," Nicki said, puzzled.

"Evelyn stepped in and showed her a simple trick of playing on other trains, taking advantage of others' positions before their next move.

The game lasted forty-five minutes, and Nicki lost in a disarray of domino pieces.

Evelyn went to the kitchen, and Connie leaned over the table and said, "Your circumstances are not unlike this game. Many pieces with no apparent order. It all starts with one step. Nicki, you are on an Island with several of our country's most intelligent, powerful, and influential men. Why do you think they are here? To keep them from teaching others. You should take advantage of them and learn all you can from them. They are here, and you are here. It could be random or not. What do you have to lose?"

"Nicki said, "I don't think they have anything to teach me. One is a Preacher, the other a lunatic economist and publisher, and I am a corporate lawyer."

"Nicki, let me ask you a question. Do you want to win?"

Nicki stared at Connie, silently studying her face, believing she knew what win meant. "Yes, I want to win."

Thinking stubbornly, leaning over the game table, Connie said, "Then change your attitude, quit whining, and get on the train."

Nicki stood up and exhaled loudly. Crossing her arms, she walked out. It was all too much for her. *Connie was not very compassionate to me. If only she knew all my troubles*, she thought.

Nicki kicked the sand up into a pile of smoke as she walked to the four-wheeler. She turned and headed north. Nicki passed the Stafford house at full speed. Abruptly, she put both feet on the brakes and slid to a stop. She did a short radius U-turn and pulled into the driveway. Nicki knocked on the screen door and called Dr. Maker. Are you home?"

Dr. Maker walked to the porch with a big smile and a monotone voice, "Nicki, nice to see you."

Nicki angrily attacked him, "Why didn't God save my mom?"

Dr. Maker stood still and looked into Nicki's eyes with kindness. He had heard those questions thousands of times. He did not have the answer she wanted.

Nicki was crying and mad. Dr. Maker asked her to sit on the step.

That is a profound question, Nicki. Tell me how your heart feels.

"Dr. Maker, I am so angry at God. My Mom was completely sold out to his work. She lost her life following him. He should have saved her; she was one of his. Why do bad things happen to good people?"

Dr. Maker's voice delivered a well-measured. "God is sovereign."

"My dad says that; what does that mean?"

"He has the final say on everything, Heaven and Earth."

"What about the Devil? Doesn't he do bad things to hurt people?"

"Stay here; Dr. Maker went inside and returned with a well-worn paperback book about trusting God. Sitting down beside her, he handed the book to Nicki. This book may help you. It is a required read in my doctorate classes. Read it and come back, and we will talk about it."

They remained sitting for a while. Nicki told him of her conversation with her dad and that she was a prisoner, too. As her red face turned back to the cream color, she said, "Even if I were not angry, I do not know what to do, and I would be afraid to do it.

He said in his slow, nerdy tone, "When I got here, I felt the same way. After a time, I was able to change my thinking. I came to believe my being here was good, and this could be my place of preparation. Think of Moses exiled from the palace to the desert. A place provided for him to focus, learn, and prepare for something new. These circumstances are not a curse but a blessing. God knows I am here. Those who exiled me did me a huge favor. Don't get me wrong, I miss my family and work back home, but a new purpose now fills my soul.

"You're a sick man, Doc," She smiled through the lingering tears. After learning how to become the most excellent salesman in the world, I will read your book."

Looking puzzled, he said, "Come back soon, Nicki."

Walking back to the four-wheeler, Nicki thought to herself. He never answered my question.

⏎

The two cars left simultaneously. The President's car turned right, and the Prelate's car turned left. To the public, the President was the country's leader. Still, everyone knew the Prelate was in charge, and his power had been an anointing by Francis Vile.

The Prelate's car turned into the National Cathedral, and he went unopposed to his hidden office in the crypt. He liked the Reverend and stopped by to pay his condolences. He was the 267th person to be laid to rest in the Cathedral. The Prelate met with the two thugs tasked with capturing Nicki Boaz. He yelled until his face was blood red and used words that Priest should not know. "Kill her if you must. I am tired of fooling with you two." One of the thugs reached inside his jacket, and the other put his hand on his chest. "Do not worry, Prelate. We will not let you down."

The Prelates' final word to them in the most fearful voice was, "I die, you die."

"In the car, he said to Bishop Toyer, "Mark, things are a mess, and time is running out. I am going to die one way or another. If Francis Vile doesn't kill me, God will."

The Prelate ordered the car to Wade's Gun shop. The driver ran in, returned with a large gun case, and put it in the trunk. Arriving at the Eisenhower Office Building, the Prelate stayed in the car, and Bishop Toyer went to his office. The Prelate and his driver headed to the Bible Museum.

The Prelate had commissioned an elegant seven-foot-high cross made from brass. Hand-made by one of the most creative and well-known artists, it was timeless in its beauty. It was delivered to the Museum's warehouse for storage until it could have a place on the roof of the East Building of the National Gallery of Art. It would take its place next to the stations of the cross exhibit and the fifteen-foot-high Blue Rooster that looks over Pennsylvania Ave. The Cross would sit in the outdoor sculpture garden.

The driver opened the trunk, handed the Prelate the case, and waited while he entered the warehouse's backdoor. The Prelate came out empty-handed, saying he loaned his gun to the Manager of the Museum.

⌐

Nicki completed her book, *Greatest Salesman in the World*. Full of memorized mantras, she felt eager about her future.

Nicki saw Dr. Maker's book about trusting God on her kitchen counter, shaking her head in dismay. She thought *I promised him I would read it.*

She was not past chapter one when she banged her fist on the kitchen counter. "What is wrong with Bernie Maker giving me this book? The sovereignty of God is not like the God my mother taught me. This book says God permits everything, good or bad." Niki kicked the Queen Anne chair hard enough to push it over, ran out the door down the back stairs, jumped in the four-wheeler, and sped off to the Stafford House. Sliding to a stop in front of the house, she ran around to the front porch, screaming Dr. Maker's name with hate-laced tones, "Dr. Bernie Maker, Dr. Maker, come out here."

"He appeared behind her, coming from the backyard, wiping his horned-rimmed glasses with his handkerchief, "Nicki, what is wrong."

"Why did you give me this book? What is wrong with you? It says God killed my mother. It says he gave the ok for her to die. What is wrong with you? The next thing it will say is that God killed Jesus. Don't ever speak to me again. You're no, Pastor."

"Nicki, you did not..."

Nicki threw the book as hard as she could at Dr. Maker, hitting him in the shin.

He looked at Nicki's back as she ran away from him. Her pain was enormous.

Nicki's mind did NASCAR laps repeatedly. Who would ever want Dr. Maker's God for his God?"

"Nicki drove to the community house to vent on Connie and Evelyn.

Connie said, "Sit, my angry child."

"How did you know I was angry?"

"Connie pointed to the mirror over the credenza. Look at yourself."

Nicki turned to see somebody she did not recognize, a wild person with red eyes and ears and a fierce frown—a face like a balled-up fist.

"Wow," Nicki said, "I didn't realize that emotions can control your physical appearance."

"What's going on."

"That Preacher Bernie Maker and his God, that is what."

Connie said, "He is an intelligent guy."

Evelyn said, "People wait in line to get a seat in his class."

"He is not for me," Nicki bit down on her lips hard.

"What did he say that made you mad? Connie said.

"God killed my mother."

Evelyn said, "I am positive he didn't say that."

"Close, he said God is sovereign in everything, I mean everything, requires his permission."

"I am sure that is what sovereign means," Connie said smoothly.

"Then why didn't he use his sovereignty and save my mother."

"You ask a question Dr. Maker cannot answer. Only God knows."

"Really, you too."

"I am not as educated as Pastor Maker, but I have much experience with God. She went to a drawer and pulled out a calling card. Above her name was a sentence in quotations. "All power in heaven and on earth belongs to God; nothing can rise above him, and he is good."

"You can trust me on this, Nicki. I don't know what happens on the road to life, but God is good and the ultimate power. I cannot think of anything better. Today, you may know the what, but you will know the why in five years. Keep the card in your wallet. Let me see your necklace. It is gorgeous," she said. She held it and closed her eyes like some power was charging her. There are those of us who have heard of this charm."

"It was my mom's. She wore it as a bracelet with two other charms. My Aunt Maggie was going to tell me about it, but things went bizarre."

Connie smiled and said, "It means Faith. The metal is translucent; you can only see it if you hold it at an angle. Nothing is on it, no writing, saying, or marks, because Faith is invisible. Faith believes at the highest level. Accepting God's promises and living every day as though they will come true, no matter how bad things look. Although Faith is invisible, it reveals the most dominant characteristic of a man. Nicki, I would love to stay and feel sorry for you, but I have things to do, and I think you do too. Don't fight the education that lies at your feet; be the student so you can be the teacher one day. Your Faith, followed by your positive attitude, will allow you to think, act wisely, and lead with power.

Nicki said under her breath, "Love you too, Connie. I don't know why I came here.".

Nicki headed back to Main Rd., half of her anger displaced by Connie and Evelyn's wise but uncompassionate care. Nicki was annoyed that Connie had given her a lesson on her mother's charm; what did she know? She began planning her subsequent conversation with her dad. Nicki could not stay on this Island. Her dad had to help. Heading north, she wanted to take the road east to the beach and drive around Dr. Maker's house, but it was a long way out. In the distance, Nicki could see the home, and on the left, standing at the fence, was the Preacher Man himself. Nicki decided she would slowly pass and wave but not stop and certainly not smile. The road came within twenty feet of the fence as she passed. Dr. Maker smiled, motioned with his left hand, and tossed the book into the four-wheeler in a gentle softball lob. "I hate him," Nicki punched the cart's accelerator and sped up on the sandy road.

Parking in the rear of the Mansion, Nicki dragged herself up the steps and into the summer kitchen. Mrs. Frank sang and made chocolate cookies to spread around the Island.

"Nicki, how are you?"

"I am angry, Mrs. Frank. It seems the people on this island don't like me much."

"What do you mean?"

"Dr. Maker, Connie, and Evelyn don't have much compassion for all that has happened to me."

"Nicki, I know them to be wise people. What is it you want from them?

"Comfort, Mrs. Frank, comfort. I want them to know how I feel."

"So that?"

"What do you mean, so that."

"There has to be a *connection* to your desire that they know how you feel."

"Mrs. Frank, you are one of them, too."

"Nicki, we love you."

"Where is Joe?"

"Gone to work."

"Really, you always say that. Where do you go to work on an Island of eleven people? I think I am going to lose my mind. All of this must be a bad dream."

CHAPTER 8

Blessed are the flexible, for they will never be bent out of shape.
Robert Ludlum

The Prelate and Bishop Toyer arrived in Atlanta to meet with the Southern Baptist Convention Trustees. The Trustees took a hard stand against the government, paying the Pastors and Priests. Along with the Catholics, they could feel the government slowly sucking the lifeblood from their congregations.

Arriving in Air Force One, they met in a banquet room at an airport hotel. The tables were set up in a square, enough to seat thirty people. The Prelate and the Bishop sat in the middle on the right side. Bishop Toyer was the moderator. Calling the meeting to order, he turned the floor over to the Prelate, who went around the table and called each man by name with a loving smile. Alternatively, he would ask about their family or congregation. Everyone in the room was astonished by his knowledge and intimacy. The battle was over without even one harsh word. The Baptist and Catholic leaders never even knew they had been to war.

He used the story about Joseph in Egypt to promote his position. He extolled Joseph and how he saved his family and the country. He did it by centralizing the resources during the great famine. He wanted to make them comfortable with how the government made it through the hard times by giving Joseph complete control over the land. He also encouraged them by telling them that Joseph's family went to Egypt as seventy-five people and flourished under the hand of the great Pharaoh. He was excited about the leaders that they, too, could succeed. His speech was inspiring but not the real story.

At the end of the meeting, the Trustees shook the Prelate's hand and hugged him. He certainly would take care of them and their people.

The Prelate was working diligently on the November election. Once elected, it would be the last election for the country. Francis Vile had convinced him that the citizens could not have a say in running the government. Only the chosen could lead. Only the predestined could understand the complexities. Only the selected were intelligent and worthy of elevated positions. Only the invited could sit at the king's table.

The Prelate's faithful past life could never digest the fact that Francis Vile was doing the choosing. He, as well as the rest of the world, would have to kneel at her table.

⁓

Nicki scouted Dr. Maker's book from the 4-wheeler and carried it inside. It was a hated object, a thorn in her side, and a view of God she did not believe in. Nicki placed the book in the window seat to avoid it. But it seemed every move she made in her apartment caused her to turn her head toward the book, like a horrible car accident you didn't want to look at but couldn't turn away. Nicki Boaz, spellbound by the book, was compelled to finish it.

Mrs. Frank continued the Island history lesson over eggs and bacon at breakfast. Today was about Mr. Stafford and his progressive management of the plantation and its slaves. Mrs. Frank told Nicki about life on the plantation under the rule of the Stafford Family in detail. She suggested that Nicki stop by the Stafford family cemetery behind the house.

Nicki replied, "I did not know there was a cemetery on the Island."

"Several, actually," Mrs. Frank said, "At the Island's south end is the Carnegie Family Cemetery."

"I have never seen it."

"It is not surprising; it is hidden, but if you keep a close eye, it is on your right, just south of Sea Camp. You will only be able to see a portion of the locked gate. The perimeter is fenced, and the bushes have grown up around it. Gardeners come every two months to maintain it. Mrs. Lucy made all the arrangements before she died. Smiling, she said, "You know how much she wanted to keep all her family on this Island."

Nicki sensed why Mrs. Lucy Carnegie loved this Island and wanted her family to stay together there. It was paradise.

Against her will, Nicki finished reading Dr. Maker's Book. She threw it across the room several times. Hating the book more than Dr. Maker himself, Nicki was sorry she learned about the topic. She didn't like that evil existed, people's souls hurt to the core, and tragedies encircled those who believed and didn't believe. She thought God should fix all of them instantly. Nicki could not grasp that a good God would allow those things to happen. But the books said God did allow it. The book's last few chapters took a more personal direction by pointing out that each person has talents. Talents are handed out for God's work. The book advocated that each problem in life was a lesson for us to use later. She did not fully understand that concept more than why a good God allowed terrible things to happen. Connie's declaration that God had all power in heaven and earth and that he was an excellent God caused Nicki to revisit the book. Nicki kept replaying how Connie clarified the definition of good. Good does not include a time frame, like immediate. Good transcended all time, present, and future as if God owned time.

When Nicki would pass Ranger Craig, she would wave, and he would respond with a half-wave and no emotion. Niki knew he would turn her in one day, and it caused acid in her stomach. Today, on her way to drop off some cookies to Taylor, she would have to come to terms with Ranger Craig one way or another. There is no way of avoiding it.

Nicki enjoyed watching Taylor work on his bikes and tell stories; she never knew if they were real, but he once lived lavishly. Nicki became infatuated with Taylor Samms. She could not help but ask questions about his economics background and publishing career. His knowledge of history and how to influence people kept her coming back.

Early October had changed into late November. The first two weeks of the month were warm. Like clockwork, the seasons changed at the beginning of the third week. The wind shifted no longer gentle east breezes but Northeasters with gray skies and howling winds. The ocean churned like victory at sea. The days were dark and wet. The foliage on the Island weakened one level of green, and the deciduous trees dropped their leaves. Nicki became melancholy as Thanksgiving was one week away. The tradition was to have a Thanksgiving Picnic on the back lawn of Mrs. Lucy's castle, weather permitting. It would have been a dream scene from an epic movie if children on the Island were flying kites and running around the meadow.

They gathered on the expansive green lawn between the fountain and the river on Thanksgiving Thursday. They laid blankets on the ground and used tree stumps and sea walls for seats. Connie, Evelyn, Taylor Samms, The Franks, Ranger Craig, Beth, and Charlie moved back and forth in a slow, sweet dance of fellowship, ten prisoners of a kindred spirit. They bowed as Dr. Maker prayed a prayer of Thanksgiving and for being imprisoned on the Island. He delighted in his designation as this is the place of preparation for future great works. Nicki recognized the words as content from the final chapters of her well-hated book. The concluding sections showed clearly how the sovereignty of God's actions was like seeds in a field, multiplying his purpose. Circumstances were the sharpening of skills for victory in the more significant battle. These chapters had throttled back Nicki's fits of anger in her second reading. Dr. Maker's prayer was remarkable. The Thanksgiving Picnic became imprinted on Nicki's soul like a new Christmas bike for a six-year-old. Nicki slowly sauntered toward Dr. Maker with an apology. He well received it and invited her to his house the next day.

She was isolated on the island for two months and had seven five-minute conversations with her father. He had recorded several conversations with Nicki and Thomas White. Bobby Boaz told Thomas they were left on his voicemail, and he didn't know how to reach her. In her messages to Thomas, Nicki wanted to be romantic and loving, but she could only be casual instead of love talk.

Nicki had learned that things grew worse for her dad and the country. The government had nationalized all news, books, newspapers, and TV distribution. It had gained control over the internet and its contents, labeling it a public utility. Large businesses started leaving the country, and unemployment grew to the point where you either worked for the government or did not work. The government had convinced everyone that it was their savior. Nicki's Dad was pressured to turn over his Boaz Power business to the government for the public good. He and a few of his business friends had enough public presence to keep them at bay, but not for long. For most CEOs, It had become time for fight or flight.

Thomas White, Vice President of Boaz Power, made several trips to Washington in October and November to lobby for the continuation of private ownership of the company. Robert Boaz, who replaced Nicki in the San Francisco headquarters, would accompany him on certain occasions. Robert's Dad's faith in Thomas had waned. He had become somebody in Washington as the powers wined, dined him, and indulged him in all that would make him feel important. It worked. The Prelate invited Thomas to a November dinner at Francis Vile's home. It took only seconds for her to dominate Thomas White's soul. With Thomas's newfound allegiance to The Prelate's cause, he inquired about the whereabouts of Thomas's fiancé. As eager as he was to give them any information, he did not know where she was.

Nicki's distress about being on the Island had notched down a level. As the hot summer turned to fall, the leaves of restlessness fell from her soul. Her feelings for the Island became permanent. Humidity-laden fresh salt air became her fuel for living.

Making peace with Dr. Maker, she accepted his invitation to take the program he was developing for Christian Counseling. A Doctorate class that would help pastors encourage their hurting people. Dr. Maker was dedicated to serving the country after his release or training a disciple to carry forth upon his death. Mondays and Wednesdays, she spent the day at the Stafford House at the feet of Dr. Maker.

On Tuesdays and Thursdays, Nicki would show up at Taylor Samms and sit at a workbench on a mechanics stool. Taylor laid out how she could best think like an economist and included the skills of publishing a newspaper. Mr. Samms was also a decent American Historian, and Nicki found all the topics stimulating.

On Saturday mornings, she would visit Connie and Evelyn for friendly conversation. The topic would end up focusing on faith and attitude.

Sunday was the best. Sitting at the picnic table overlooking the creek, the blue sky and the marsh crispness made the sweater mornings a dream. Hot, fragrant coffee streamed from the cup while the cool breeze blew the moss. Thoughts of her mom dominated her. Her dedication to completing her mom's plan grew in her heart each first day of the week. Nicki Boaz would smile as she felt like she knew what communion meant.

Sunday afternoons were restful with Joe and Evonne on the plantation porch. Joe did not work on Sundays, whatever that meant. Nicki enjoyed hearing stories of her mom and Grandmother and the supernatural events. Nicki was spellbound because Joe and Evonne were eyewitnesses.

Christmas came swiftly, and the weather was sweet and chilly, with bright skies. Somehow, the weather added senses that caused Nicki to fall in love with the Island. Christmas was a formal affair at the Plum Orchard Plantation. Darkness arrived at 5:45 PM, and the social hour began at 6:00. It was a reenactment of the privileged days of the Gilded Era, with beautiful China, elegant tablecloths, pine needle wreaths, and candles. The turkey was a gift from Ranger Craig, and the vegetables were out of Connie's garden. All the decorations were thanks to Mrs. Lucy's daughter. There was a deep love for one another and the Christmas Story for all the formality. As the outside world celebrated a holiday season or no season, the focus in Plum Orchard was powerful and meaningful for all in the room that night. With joy and fellowship came courage and a bond to an important cause.

Charlie and Beth had announced that on January 2nd, a party of four, plus security, was arriving for a three-day hunting trip. Ranger Craig would lead the expedition. The Franks gave Nicki strict orders for those three days. She would remain locked in her room with the curtains closed. Mrs. Frank would prepare several days of food. Nicki knew there would be a problem; the spring tide was just before sunrise on the second day of their trip. Nicki did not mention it to Joe because she already knew his answer. Nicki needed to talk to her dad. She believed she could reach her spot, speak to her dad, and safely return to Plum Orchard. Her biggest fear was Ranger Craig turning her over.

On January 2nd, Nicki was sequestered in her room. She had a book holding the curtain open at a slight angle to see out and not make the curtains move. She had plenty of reading material from Dr. Maker. Although she didn't understand everything, she kept studying, hoping the bell would go off for full enlightenment.

Nicki rose at 4:45 AM the following day and dressed in her darkest clothes. Checking the window, she tiptoed barefooted to the back stairs. As she reached the porch, she slipped on her shoes and crossed over the car ruts behind the house. She crept into the bush between the creek and the home. The hunters would first go to the fenced lot at the Plum Orchard property. She could see no activity, so she slowly walked through the bushes toward the side of the house and out to the main road. She stayed on the main road because it was quiet and could see in either direction. She hurried to her Drum Island location. It remained dark until 6:30 AM, so Nicki was confident she could reach her site and then get to the small platform hidden by a screen of trees. Her high tide mark was 5:45 AM. She knew she could hear the hunting four-wheelers if they departed Plum Orchard. She was fearful but also confident that this was her island. She understood the lay of the land. At 5:40, her dad's voice came boldly out of the tiny device. Cupping her hands to reduce the noise, she talked into her hands. Not one word of her dad's words was good. In four weeks, he and Thomas White would go to Washington for the National Prayer Breakfast, and he would have greater detail on what seemed like the end of democracy. Nicki wanted to hear more, but time was up. Her I love you was cut off, and the red light appeared. She sat on the wooden platform, head hanging down. It was 6:00 AM, still dark, but the light was coming over from the east. She headed up to the main road, hoping she could get back the way she came.

Fifty steps heading north, she saw the lights of the two carts. Ducking into the bushes, she returned to the river and waited in the moist sand. She could hear them coming through the brush at only two feet high; it did not hide her very well, and the sun would be up soon. The four-wheelers stopped on the Main Road. After a long night of cards and drinking, the hunters stopped to relieve themselves.

Nicki's left foot sank into the wet sand and fell backward, grabbing the bush before her. The noise sounded like two bucks fighting in the trees. Once she caught herself, she headed North on the tide line, trying to stay in the wet sand. The hunters were on her trail, thinking a prize hog would soon be theirs. Nicki could hear them talking to the guide as they walked parallel to the river. Nicki stayed fifty yards ahead of them and twenty yards west.

She was west of the river trail, and the bushes got thicker between the road and the river. The wet sand ran out, and only leaves and washed-up branches were on the ground before her. She stopped. If she went forward, it would give away her position, and if she moved up from the river, she could run right into them. She looked at the river, the same river she floated onto the Island. If she dove in, she would be visible. She bit her lip and started running fast across the leaves and branches. She could feel the noise in every part of her body, and so did the hunters. She started sprinting, hoping to get to wet sand soon. The hunters, separated by twenty yards of brush, were ready to fire at any noise. They were not real hunters. They were politicians. Nicki hit wet sand again twenty feet later and poured on the silent speed. She knew she must be getting close to the icehouse, arms swinging, legs pumping. Nicki stopped like she had hit a wall, clotheslined across the waist, and went down. Someone's arm wrapped around her head, and a hand landed across her face, pulling her to the ground.

Panicked, she didn't understand what had happened. Now, she was being dragged away from the river; she fought, but the attacker was stronger. She felt helpless when she pulled onto a wooden floor and through a doorway. Her assailant opened a door, pushed her in, and followed her. Breaking loose, she elbowed him in the nose as the door shut. She decided she would scratch his eyes out when he came after her. She crawled across the small room. It was the bathroom, the bathroom at the icehouse. Nicki could hear the attacker lock the door. Nicki was ready for the attack; the temperature was in the mid-forties, but she was sweating like it was ninety.

"Nicki," a voice said.

"Nicki, it's Todd."

"I am getting tired of saving you."

Nicki slid down the wall, her hands over her eyes with relief.

"Just sit and be quiet. The hunters are looking for hogs, not people. They will pass soon."

"What are you doing out? I am sure the Franks told you to stay in."

"I had to talk to my Dad," she said lowly.

"I think you broke my nose."

"You deserve it, Todd."

Todd came over and sat on the floor next to Nicki.

"I saw you walk around the back of the house this morning. I followed you. I knew things might not turn out so well. You're so hard-headed."

"Well, Todd, maybe someday I will be able to thank you, but not today. I could have handled the hunters."

"Nicki, you are a pain."

"What did your dad have to say?"

"Things are bad. He and Thomas are going to Washington next month for some meetings. Thomas is my fiancé; Todd, do you get it, fiancé."

"I know Thomas, Nicki."

It got quiet in the bathroom of the icehouse. Todd's shoulder pressed against Nicki's, and she leaned her head on his shoulder.

"Todd, what are you doing here."

"I work for the State Department. I am responsible for the Southeast District and all the high-profile people that move in and out. I brought the Senators and their guide. I also bring men like Ernie and Taylor. My office is in Washington, but I work out of Atlanta."

Todd said thoughtfully, "You would be my responsibility if anyone knew you were here."

"Todd, you are a scumbag working for the state," she lifted her head and hurried away from Todd. Are you going to turn me in?"

"Think what you want, Nicki Boaz, but I see myself doing the Lord's work," he grinned.

"You are full of it. What are we going to do?"

"We will wait about fifteen minutes, then I will get my four-wheeler and come by, and you can get in the back, and I will cover you up with a tarp and take you back to the Franks."

"Then what?"

"What do you mean?"

"Todd, I mean, what is next?"

"Your Dad will tell you what is next."

"Do you ever talk to my dad?"

"Sometimes, he is a great man, powerful in our country, but they are moving in on him. Please don't give up on him. He leads a powerful movement."

"Todd, are you married?"

"No, Nicki, I am not. Just married to my work."

"What is that band on your finger if you are not married."

"Todd grinned; it was like a fraternity ring. He rolled it over to show Nicki two letters, Bs, back-to-back with a vertical line between the Bs and a horizontal line through the top of the two Bs.

"Married to your fun is more like it."

Todd was grinning big and poking fun at her, "You still care, don't you, Nicki?'

"Todd, I told you I am engaged."

"Ok," he grinned with his whole face.

Nicki gave him the finger sign.

It is daylight, and we can go. I will pull the 4-wheeler around, get in the back, and pull the tarp over yourself. I will drop you off at the end of the house.

Todd pulled her up with both hands, drawing her to his face. They stared at each other, then let their arms drop. His hands slid down Nicki's arms, then to her fingertips. Goosebumps appeared on her arms. Nicki started to say something, but Todd opened the door.

The trip was short, and Todd pulled around the back of Plum Orchard. Nicki came out from under the tarp. Joe Frank stood like a stern Father with his hands on his hips as she ran up the steps beside him without making eye contact. In her room, Nicki thought about her narrow escape from the hunters. But she relished the rendezvous in the bathroom.

CHAPTER 9

There is no such thing in anyone's life as an unimportant day.
Alexander Wolcott

Nicki remained in her room until the hunters departed. Todd left with them. During her isolation, she decided to learn as much as possible from Dr. Maker, Taylor Samms, Connie, and Evelyn. It was like college again: profoundly serious with Dr. Maker, lots of fun with Taylor, and real-world aggravating lessons with Connie and Evelyn. The two older women seldom treated her comfortably, forcing her to accept personal accountability and responsibility. Trusting God was their tagline, and they drove it home with a ten-pound hammer.

In January, the remaining days and weeks were intense, schooling with Dr. Maker from 8 until 12 and Taylor Samms from 1 to 5. Saturday mornings, she would spend with Connie and Evelyn. It was demanding because it was personal. Nicki would study Bernie's and Taylor's notes and Connie's insightful proverbs. Nicki reads three books weekly, thinking *this is more work than graduate school.*

Bobby Boaz, Thomas White, and Robert Boaz met in Dallas for a direct flight to Washington, DC, for the weeklong National Prayer Breakfast. Arriving Sunday afternoon, they checked in as VIPs to the Washington Hilton on Connecticut Ave.

Nicki's Dad was a close associate of the sponsors. The actual

96

breakfast was Thursday, but some three thousand people came from all over the world to agree and disagree on many topics. Bobby's job was to format a relationship with the influential attendees, some old friends, and some foes. Thomas's job was to hobnob with the government officials pushing hard to take possession of Boaz Power's patents. The Government was moving in on them from a monopoly standpoint. Robert's job was to watch Thomas.

The political overtone outweighed the prayer aspect in the first part of the week, but they would become holy on Thursday. The Prelate strutted around like a peacock, holding out his ring finger to see if anyone would kiss up to him.

Undercurrents circling the meeting were that there was a secret rebellious grassroots group gaining power and supporters. The group was called Billy's Boys, and they were well-organized and well-disciplined. The Government had not been able to ferret the group out. They saw them as a weak religious group and claimed the uprisings were fragmented.

The big talk was that the Prelate had invited Francis Vile to breakfast. Even the worst of the group found disdain for Francis Vile at this religious event. The Prelate was smiling, promoting his guest. Everyone stayed far away, suspecting God would send a lightning bolt to fry the little demon lover. Bishop Toyer could see that The Prelate had turned from worshiping God to Francis Vile.

Francis Vile's beauty and enticing personality made it easy for her to draw many powerful men into her conversations. She would say something personal as she reached both hands to shake with any relevant person. The mighty men melted like butter into her bowl.

The room became crowded just before the group was to sit down. Small groups milled around the room, glad-handing and lying to each other. As the groups bounced into each other, Francis Vile and Bobby Boaz came face to face. The crowds stepped back, leaving an empty circle around them, and the room became hushed. Their eyes met, and there was a low-pitched hum. Bobby Boaz spoke first," Good to see you, Francis."

"I was sorry to hear about Carrie," she said, tilting her head to the side.

He perceived she was slightly smiling. He clenched his fist and shuffled forward.

Robert Boaz slipped his arm around his dad and said, "Dad, let's go. I need you to meet someone." Standing erect and broad-chested, Bobby Boaz gritted his teeth and said, "God Bless you, Francis." The whole room could feel the disgust.

Later in the month, it became clear that the State had successfully gained power at the Prayer Breakfast. Bobby Boaz and his brother Tim had decided they would rather destroy their business than turn it over to the State. Tim began preparations for building a factory in South America. It also became clear that Thomas White was friendly to the State, reporting Boaz Powers' every move. He had also promised to deliver Nicki Boaz to the State within the month.

Francis Vile became more visible in state affairs; her influence extended from the government to the people, like some old horror movie where the people were in a trance. Power flowed to her like a river surging into the sea. In his short conversations with Nicki, her dad reported the happenings but was not distressed. He, like Connie, talked about all power belonging to God; even his voice believed it. He spoke more about the underground movement and the tipping point he thought was nearby. The people were waking up to being enslaved in a land of plenty. And that their masters were evil. For the first time, her dad mentioned the leader of the underground group. He didn't call him by name but told her he was hiding in some remote command center. Things were happening like lava flowing from a volcano. Nicki was sorry to be on the sidelines.

〜

February in Cumberland Island combines sunny, warm days and cold, wet Northeasters. Nicki treasured the bright blue skies after a weeklong gale. It could be a jacket and pants for one week and shorts and a tee shirt for the next. Nicki's love for this remote Island had grown intense. It was her Island. She spent early February working with Dr. Maker, studying God's law and man's heart.

When Dr. Maker started teaching about sin, Nicki pushed back hard. She didn't like the word. She laughed, grinned, and said, "Bernie, nobody uses that word. It is offensive." To the people of the day, everything was a disease and had medical causes or physiologically the fault of your family or society.

The thought that a person was responsible for his actions was revolting. Dr. Maker pointed out how the general population well-received this teaching that started in the seventies. The word sin disappeared as some forgotten artifact as the hearts of men grew darker. People did what they wanted without discipline or remorse. The law meant nothing. The only thing that moved people was their desires. Many of Nicki's peers had never even heard the word sin. Dr. Maker focused on sin and how it was the root of man's heartache and dilemmas. It was hard for Nicki to buy into his teaching. She knew that the world did not have the faintest belief in what Dr. Maker taught. He made plain the consequences of the; *I am not a responsible movement.* No law and no discipline equaled no trust and no growth. Everything died like a plant without water. What Dr. Maker taught would make you feel bad about yourself. The current culture is all about feeling good. But Nicki perceived he was invested in every word he spoke. It mystified her.

Nicki, at best, learned to accept the sovereignty of God at face value. Somedays, it still made her mad, but she could practice Connie's mantra that God holds all power in heaven and earth, and God is good. Nicki felt her lessons might be easier to understand if she had an accurate Bible. The State had long since destroyed paper books and replaced them with digital printing, which consistently changed to fit the doctrine of the State. They removed any power the Bible had once proclaimed as they nationalized the printing and news businesses. Nonetheless, Dr. Maker's wisdom would transform Nicki.

Dr. Maker was a brilliant teacher. He had a deep understanding of God's word and work. He would often paraphrase powerful verses that Nicki had never heard.

One verse was so on the mark that she had been stunned when Dr. Maker casually cast her way, "Claiming to be wise, they became fools. They did not bother to acknowledge God. They knew perfectly well; they spat in God's face and did not care. Worse, they handed out prizes to those who did the worst." He had memorized the verse from a version called The Message. He said it was from a book called Romans, chapter 1, verse 32.

Nicki was somewhat confused, "Dr. Maker, how could a two-thousand-year-old verse be so correct today?"

Dr. Maker taught Nicki as if he could see the deficits in her wisdom. He was vested in her consumption of powerful schooling, knowing she would need it for the future. She leaned in as he taught. It was challenging work for them both. In and out of the Old Testament, up and down the new, all with detailed history. In-depth results of the actions of God and his followers. Nicki became friends with Abraham, David, Jesus, Peter, James, John, and Paul. The work was all-consuming. The instruction slowly changed her heart, yet she always carried a chip on her shoulder.

Dr. Maker, sensitive to Nicki's difficulty with the sovereignty of God, told Nicki a story.

"Mary, Martha, and their brother Lazarus were friends of Jesus. Yes, Jesus had backslapping, belly-laughing friends as we do. They were remarkably close. Jesus was in a town several miles away when Lazarus got sick. The girls knew Jesus would come quickly to help his friend, so they sent word. Expecting Jesus to come that afternoon, they were disappointed when he did not show up for the next two days. Well, Nicki, guess what happened? Lazarus died."

A little anxious, Nicki asks, "Really, Dr. Maker, why didn't Jesus come to help him if they were such good friends."

"When he arrived, the girls were upset. Martha, bold with

toughness, greeted Jesus, "If you had been here, my brother would not have died." Sweet, loving, and humble Mary also went to see Jesus, fell at his feet, and asked the same question, "If you had been here, my brother, your friend would not have died. You could have saved him."

Jesus cried.

"Nicki, you ask the same question to Jesus. Why didn't you come and help my mother? She was your friend?"

"He could have, Dr. Maker. He should have."

"Nicki, He cried for your mom. Jesus knew Lazarus was dead before he ever left his location. He knew he would die well in advance. He allowed it, the sovereignty of God."

"Jesus so deeply touched raised Lazarus from the dead. He was four days dead, and it happened in front of many people. Nicki, it changed everything. A huge crowd witnessed the event. The talk was so big that it set the city into a commotion. The finale of Jesus's mission rose to action. This event set his purpose on fire."

"Your Mom's death was known to God well in advance, and it set into motion events moving God's plan forward, all for the good of his people.

Nicki was still, "He could have raised my mom."

"Nicki, Lazarus did eventually die, as we all will. Your Mom is honored by those who heard her voice, watched her life, and took courage in her faith. The enemy is more afraid of your mom dead than when she was alive."

A scowl came on Nicki's face, and her shoulders slumped, "I have to go."

In the soothing coolness of the late February morning, Nicki walked back to Plum Orchard, careful to stay out of the woods and on Main Rd. Her walking was deeply reflective. She was not angry, not sad. Instead, she was blank. What was all of this about? Her Mom's death, her arrival on this Island, these people, her future. Moving toward a nearby tree stump, she sat, her feet a few inches off the ground, her arms hanging limp. She tried her hardest to deliver a speech to God. An oration of her lack of understanding, anger, lack of faith, and total desperation about what to do. As her breath ran out, she mumbled the softest prayer of helplessness. She concluded with, "Help me, LORD."

Feeling a little lighter, she hopped off the stump and grabbed a 4-wheeler for the ride to the Settlement and her class with Taylor Samms.

Taylor Samms had introduced Nicki to one of his favorite teachers from his graduate class, Professor Randall Bartlett. He had a thumb drive with the Professor's course, *Thinking Like an Economist, a guide to rational decision-making.* Taylor had used Professor Bartlett's method in several of his classes and found it fun and valuable. Taylor Samms loved fun. The purpose of the course was to learn to ask the questions necessary to analyze and reason your way to an important decision. The guide separated the system into six sections.

1. People respond to incentives.
2. There is no such thing as a free lunch.
3. No thing is just one thing
4. The law of unanticipated influence
5. The law of unintended consequences
6. No one person is, and no one person can be in complete control.

Nicki loved the course. She could understand this information; she could use it today. Listening intently, Nicki could not wait until the conclusion. They discussed the topics, and Nicki headed home to do her homework.

At Dr. Maker's the following day, Nicki was straightforward with her questions. Dr. Maker, what can change things? What was my mother working on that could make a difference? And please do not talk to me like a Preacher.

Nicki, "I am a Preacher. Come sit."

They sat on the concrete steps of the front door. Looking to their left, they could see the cotton plants. Dr. Maker was the father of six children, and he could feel Nicki's plea for help.

"I am not sure exactly what your mother was working on, but there is an answer. It is called repentance."

"Watch it with the preacher's words."

"Nicki, repentance simply means I am sorry for what I did and will change. History is full of civilizations that went off on their own opposing God, always ending in destruction. The Jewish people were among the few to learn repentance. God restored their culture, country, and lives at their repentance many times. The great Roman civilization that the United States loved to idolize could not return to God or give up its higher thinking. It ended in destruction. Long before we had States or a Constitution, people arrived in our country with pennant hearts. Nicki, it is straightforward once you understand. Repentance is a big part of marriage, raising children, or dealing with friends. It is a relationship word that allows the bond to grow. It is the same with God.

Nicki quickly leaned in and asked, "Does everyone have to repent?"

"God uses a word called a remnant, such as a fragment or a scrap. Even in small groups, he hears and is moved to action by their pleas. I am one of that group. That is why I am here. I will not bow down to the Government in worship. I publicly ask God to forgive us. There is a remnant. There is always a remnant, and that group grows in power through prayers and faith.

"Who are they, Dr. Maker?"

"Brave men and women who know the truth. People like you, Nicki, who want to know why and what to do."

Dr. Maker put his arm around Nicki and said, "Let's return to class. There is much for you to know in a short time."

The short February days turned a little longer and brighter. Nicki's work with Dr. Maker was intense. She wanted complete understanding, but it was elusive. Her knowledge was impressive, but she could not put it to work. She so wanted to be at the level her mother had obtained.

Nicki had dedicated the first week of March to Taylor Samms and his teaching and history lessons. She wanted to learn the secret of how to make decisions using the power of economics. She was determined to fill her cup with learning that could give her strength and the upper hand.

Nicki's Saturday mornings at Connie's and Evelyn's had turned into an all-day affair. Connie's love and belief were Nicki's revelations. Connie taught from experience. You would have thought Jesus was her best friend. Her views had become facts, not through study and instruction like Dr. Maker but through concern and relationship. The classroom was a card table with a domino and a game of Mexican Trains, such fun.

She had finished Taylor's course and was ready to discuss it and dig deep into several topics. Full of excitement when she arrived, she was prepared to address the issues she had learned. Mr. Samms met her at the front of the garage with a purple folder labeled Venezuela. He handed her a thick folder of newspaper articles, handwritten notes, and official government documents. He said this is homework for tonight. We will discuss it tomorrow.

"But Taylor"

"No, butts Nicki. Head home and start studying."

"But Taylor, I have…"

"Not today, Nicki. I have a lot to do. See you at nine in the morning. Be prepared."

"Yes, sir."

Nicki and her hurt feelings decided to take the beach home. She drove the 4-wheeler slowly and looked over the mesmerizing teal water folding into the blue and white sky. Her mother came to her mind. Nicki spoke aloud to her mother's memory. She never heard a voice, but she got an insight and knew what to do. She headed back to Plum Orchard and opened her mom's file. She had told Connie that she couldn't find anything on which to act. But Connie would not accept Nicki's giving up. She insisted Nicki try again and again.

Nicki retrieved the folder from her room and headed to the picnic bench to study. After four hours, she still did not have one insight. Nicki did notice something she had missed. She remembered passing over it because it was in pencil; to Nicki, things in pencil were not essential but temporary. The words were written vertically on the second page at the edge of the paper, beautifully scribed in her mom's best cursive, *In the Sully on the Hill.* Nicki could not tell if it was a clue or a random thought like the rest of the words on her mom's notes.

She felt everything she sought was there but couldn't put the pieces together. Nicki put her bent finger in her mouth and bit it as she shook her head. *Feelings always make me irrational. I need the facts, not feelings.* She had to set her tantrum aside to study for Taylor Samms's meeting tomorrow. The purple folder was more detailed than she had imagined. It would take her days to go through his material. She made a quick sandwich and went up to her room.

Early the following day, in the kitchen on the porch, Nicki saw Joe making a cup of coffee.

"Good Morning, Nicki. How are you doing with the Island prisoners?"

"Mr. Frank, those guys are smart, well beyond my ability. I am off to see Taylor Samms. It's a shame they are stuck on this Island. They could be making a difference."

"Miss Nicki, I know they are making a big difference."

"Well, off to work now."

"Joe, this is an Island with ten people. Where do you go to work?"

"Nicki, I have to talk to some people who run a railroad."

"Joe, I don't understand."

"Nicki, stop by and see Charlie and Beth this afternoon. They are going to Jekyll Island, and I would like you to go with them."

"Will I get caught?"

"Don't worry. You will be with the Tenders. They will take care of you. It will do you good to get off the Island and have a little fun."

Nicki loved the ride to the Settlement. The North end had once been a tourist spot with big hotels and hundreds of vacationers. Everything had long been destroyed or decayed back to the moist, fertile soil. She parked behind Taylor's house in front of the little Church, and it always made Nicki smile when she turned the unlocked door handle and walked in. She sat in the front row and gazed over the bare walls, floors, and empty pews. There was nothing in here except old benches and a podium.

Nicki went through the back gate to Taylor's garage. "Mr. Samms," calling loudly. She carried her purple folder and notes from her Economics class.

"Come in, Nicki, come in."

Taylor Samms looked serious for the second day in a row.

"Mr. Samms, are you ok?"

"No, Nicki, I am not."

"Things on the Mainland are far worse than I thought. The country is at risk of losing its freedom. The Government has long been unable to deliver results to its citizens because of the political system. When that happens over a long period, the people will trade their Representative Republic for the strong arm of an authoritarian leader. They will turn their backs on the laws that have prospered them and settle for any promise of love. They will even choose to love evil in the face of unreciprocated affection."

"Is that why you gave me the Venezuela file."

"Yes"

"Mr. Samms, it is so obvious. How could it happen that a beautiful, prosperous democracy turns into a land of crime, poverty, and economic chaos."

"It is all there, Nicki, the politicians, representatives of the people, taking from them and giving to themselves. Failing to do anything for the people except talk big, never delivering the good results they promise. The angry people start looking for a voice. There is always a voice, a strong authoritarian voice screaming and shaking a granite fist, promising to fix things. They promise prosperity by taking from the rich and giving to the people. It never works. The populist leaders take everything for themselves and rape the land. Call the police in Venezuela, Nicki, and it may be days if they show up. The populist leaders trade away the country's assets to the big global powers for more gold in their pockets. The foreign governments strip the land for their own good, leaving it a barren desert. The only thing lacking for the fall of our country is the voice."

"Taylor, my dad says that voice is The Prelate."

"The body may be The Prelate's, but the voice within him is dark, evil, and cunning."

Taylor, "Do you know who the power is?"

"The Devil never does his bidding, Nicki."

"What should we do?"

"Finish our discussion on Venezuela today and spend the rest of the week on the six topics for better decision-making."

On the Main Rd. returning to Plum Orchard, Nicki turned right into the Greyfield Inn. Nicki parked on the south side of the Mansion and bounced up the stairs to the long, wide porch.

Charlie was coming out of the screen doors with a black bag.

"Hey Charlie, Mr. Frank told me to stop by and see you."

"Beth and I would like you to ride to Jekyll Island. We will leave in thirty minutes and return in two hours."

"Sure, if it will be safe. I have never been to Jekyll but have heard much about the island, the home of millionaires."

"Great, go inside. Beth will get you outfitted, and we will leave soon."

Beth opened a big black zippered bag, and Nicki scrunched in. Beth zippered it three-quarters closed and dragged the bag with Nicki onto the front porch with several other bags. Charlie loaded the bags on the cart and then onto the boat—business as usual.

CHAPTER 10

Long is not forever.
German Proverb

The boat advanced onto the Cumberland River across the St. Andrews Sound and into the Jekyll River. Ten minutes into the ride, Nicki sat in the bag but still below the rail height. What are we going to do at Jekyll Island.?"

"Go to the club."

"Wow, sounds nice."

Nicki asked Beth and Charlie about their work with the girls. Beth moved back near Nicki because of the noise. Beth smiled as she talked. She and other women went inside strip clubs, spoke to the girls, and offered them an alternative life. The girls made big money at one time, but now they were forced into these jobs by the State. Called essential duties, they were now captives. Charlie would wait outside with two other guys. Beth was a fantastic salesperson who always left with a girl in her bag. They would bring them back to Greyfield Inn, feed and love them. After a short stay, they returned to the mainland with a new identity and off to the underground and the Boys.

This afternoon, they were to meet with a group from Atlanta to plan for an expansion program. In addition to workers, Charlie and Beth were essential funders of the program. Beth explained to Nicki that they were friends of many influential government officials and spent time in Washington. Beth said there are a few good guys left in Congress. The congressmen and women liked Beth and Charlie because of their social influence and pedigree.

Arriving at the Jekyll dock, Nicki tried to slide back into the bag, but Charlie reached for her hand to pull her out. Nicki, we are in a public space; you will blend in with the crowd when we get off at the dock. The dock was more than a boat dock. It was a beautiful restaurant with fantastic sunset views. Many huge flower arrangements adorned the walkway to the club. The pier leads to the club's driveway, an extraordinary entrance with large oaks on both sides, like a perfect Gilded Age portrait, and a sprawling croquet court to the right. The grass was manicured, and the green contrasted brightly with the white uniforms of the players. Nicki jerked her head back and forth, admiring the sophistication.

Charlie explained the Club's historical value, the Federal Reserve's founding place, and the Central Bank. In 1910, six men secretly met at the Club to reform the nation's banking system. He said that the homes on Millionaire's Row belonged to a group of men that controlled one-sixth of the world's money. Nicki's eyes grew as they walked onto the gray-painted porch. A long row of white wicker rockers was on her right that overlooked the croquet field. The view held her silent and captivated.

Charlie and Beth held the double doors open, and Nicki looked down the long hall flanked by floor-to-ceiling mirrors. Faded black and white pictures of J.P. Morgan, Joesph Pulitzer, William Rockefeller, and The Goodyears hung on the wall. Even Lucy Carnegie would come to dinner with her rich friends at the Club.

Charlie stopped as the Grand Dining Room came into view. He paused in front of a door labeled the Aldrich Room. He opened the door and asked Nicki to wait in this room. Beth and I will handle our business and return in a few minutes. Nicki walked into a bright, sun-filled room. It looked like a library with a view of the river. The shelves climbed to the ceiling. She took a book from the shelf and knew these were the originals, the first-run copies. Big leather wingback chairs were in groups of four, two facing each other with a table in between. There were three sets of four chairs. Nicki strolled around the room, touching every piece of the treasure.

A voice bellowed from the end of the room, "Put that down."

She looked but couldn't see anyone.

Again, "Get your hands off the valuables."

Nicki ran around the chairs as fast as she could, threw her arms over the top of the farthest chair, and whispered," Dad, I love you."

Around the front of the chair, her dad stood for a hug of the most profound relief.

"Sit, Nicki. I only have a few minutes. I am meeting with the boys, and I have a boat waiting. Nicki, you look good. I miss you so much."

"Dad, can I go with you?"

"No."

"The Prelate has created this false story about you and your mother. They want you more than ever. It's just not safe now. We are making progress with the underground.

On the other hand, the forces of evil are reaching a new pinnacle. It is hard to tell which way things will go. The election in November will tell the story. If we should lose, I will come back for you. Robert, Tracey, your grandfather, and your aunt will leave the country. Tim has been building our new home.

"How about Thomas? Can he go?"

"I must go, sweetie. I love you. You are in the company of some great people. It will work out, I promise."

"By the way, Nicki, Todd says hello."

She buried her head in his chest and cried like a child. She gripped him so tight he could barely breathe. Lowering his head, he kissed his sweet daughter on the head, breathing in the heavenly scent of her mother. Bobby Boaz cried.

"I have to go."

Nicki held tight, not about to let go.

Still well-built and robust, Bobby Boaz picked up his only daughter and set her in the chair like he did when she was six. She pouted. He kissed her head again and said, "You can trust me, girl."

"I see your mom's charm around your neck. Nicki, you know it represents faith. But it has some power that only Aunt Maggie and your mom could access. It came from her parents, who were missionaries in South America. They were killed in a plane crash. Occasionally, someone will comment on that piece of see-through metal. If they do, they are trustworthy. Her dad smiled, "Your mom would rub that charm like she would wear it away."

He quietly left the room, and she sat happy and sad.

The door reopened, and she stood, hoping the dad had come back for her, but it was Beth and Charlie.

"Come to rescue a lost girl," Nicki said.

"You bet," Charlie replied with a huge smile.

Charlie allowed Nicki to sit up front until they were within ten minutes of the pier on the way back.

Nicki's new posture was still and quiet. She knew less now than before about how she got on this Island. Beth put her in the bag. Charlie got her into the house, and after hugs, she was in the 4-wheeler to Plum Orchard. She was exhausted and fell asleep before dark, thinking March was one day away. March was freedom. March was hope for more extended daylight and warmer days. New life would come with March.

Nicki headed to Taylor's to finish her two days of history and economics. Taylor was in a great mood, back to his old outlandish self. Nicki started with a question she had been waiting to ask.

"Taylor, how did you get into the publishing business?"

"While in college, I worked for a local weekly newspaper and immensely enjoyed it. I made an excellent friend, and he purchased the paper after I left. Along with one other friend, I became an investor in his company. Things changed over time, and I moved to manage the newspaper actively. I loved the work. It was all about people. Everything is about people. Even your friend Dr. Maker will tell you that everything his God does is for people.

"Are you a believer, Taylor?"

"Yes and no."

"I am not a Bible beater or Churchgoer, but I believe there is a greater power than man. I am always confused about God and good, but I think life is a battle between good and evil. If you must choose a side to be on, I will choose God's side.

He quickly changed the subject, "Let's work on the things I know, our six principles, and our case study of Venezuela. Nicki, it would be best to make good economic and political decisions. Sometimes, the wrong way is appealing, like Eve's apple."

"Really, Taylor, a Bible story. I am impressed."

"Very funny, but like that story. No matter how things appear on the surface, a leader is always manipulating the people, wooing them to their side. They are never fully exposed. In your Eve story, Satan dressed up like a snake. Your Eve would have never believed in a fully exposed Devil. Call them Satanists, dictators, kingmakers, and Politicians. You must see past the candy they hold out in their hand and see the one making the offering. You can rest assured that they always offer an easy and no-cost ride. Nicki, there is no free ride, but many want to be free riders."

"It happened in Venezuela during the economic heyday. Prominent, bold voices said they would take from the rich and give to the poor. It didn't take long for riots and revolutions to take place. The Marxist manifesto is revolution. Socialism is the next step and then the final step to communism. The social programs overflowed, and everything became free for everyone. Oil was the front-facing power of the good life in Venezuela. It was given and traded for prestige and resources. Foreign countries took it all. It was rape. When the incentives change, people change with them. When the incentive for hard work was success and income, people worked. When you received everything for free, the work stops. As they gave up jobs, the Government took over the people's freedoms. They took control of communication, the press, and T.V. The government nationalized education and closed Churches. The growth in the country was astounding on the surface. It was beautiful, like Eve's apple, but it was not homegrown. Doctors and professionals were the gifts other powers donated for the precious natural resources. Venezuela's balance sheet was run dry by the smiling countries with their hands in the cookie jar, and now others were making the cookies. No thing is just one thing. After several smart moves, the other countries wanted ownership of the oil. Unexpectedly, oil prices dropped. The rich countries pulled out, leaving Venezuela naked and destitute. Unanticipated consequences, whoever would think oil prices would fall. The social programs were in danger. The country became poor almost overnight. The leaders took rule by decree, arrested any opposition, and shut down their Congress. The major Democratic countries put sanctions on Venezuela because of their treatment of their people. Life sucked out of the country in a few decades. The land and the people suffered so much with the unintended consequences.

"Wow, Taylor, is there any hope?"

"There is always hope, Nicki. Your friend Dr. Maker will be happy to know that Venezuela is trying to reestablish religious activity and the Church as their base to recovery."

Nicki understood every word Taylor spoke. It would make an excellent addition to her skills as a Lawyer if she used his tools.

Nicki spent a few more hours a week with Taylor and Dr. Maker because she enjoyed their company and their concern for her. They had moved on from the formal lessons; every day was a Q&A.

Saturdays still belonged to Connie and Evelyn, the Train Masters. Nicki had progressed in her skills, but Connie always seemed to beat her. Nicki wanted to win, but the rules were flexible in Connie's favor. It was fun.

There wasn't a beneficial view out the kitchen window at the white house, just an empty lot, scrub oaks, and wild palmettos. But that is where the serious conversation took place.

"Nicki, I haven't seen you wear your necklace lately."

"I have it in safekeeping since I talked to my dad. I am afraid to wear it on the Island."

"Remember how special it is and what that blank charm means when you put it on again. It is important."

"What do you mean, Connie."

"Always asking why, child. You should know you can trust God by now. And I want you to stop worrying and wait. The right thing to do is watch what God does, and then you do the same thing. But mostly what he does is love people."

"Connie, this is pretty deep stuff for a Saturday afternoon."

Connie walked around the small kitchen area with a stern face and pointed her finger back at Nicki, "You like the word courage?"

"I love the word."

"Think you would like to be known as courageous?"

"Of Course."

"Well, Nicki, you must wrap your arms around fear. There is no courage without terror. Fear is the subject of the sentence in the definition of courage. Please don't run from it, don't hide, and don't worry. Walk right up to it, wrap your arms around it, and crush the life out of it."

Nicki almost laughed, but she knew Connie was serious. Nicki knew that while she was hard to believe, she was to be considered.

"Now Nicki, I have a friend named Brunson who says, "Don't wrestle with a pig. You will both come out dirty, and the pig will be happy."

Nicki broke into a wild laugh and hugged Connie, for Nicki understood the pig story. But she did not understand the seriousness of the day.

⤳

At the World headquarters of Boaz Power, Thomas White looked over the San Francisco skyline as he talked on the phone.

He was noticeably disturbed by the call. He sat at his desk and then walked down the hall to the office of Robert Boaz Jr.

"Robert, you got a minute?"

"Sure, Thomas, what do you have?

"I have a new employee that has some serious troubles. Drinking and drug problems. I was hoping you could tell her your story to encourage her."

"Thomas, I normally don't share my story with just anyone. I must feel the need."

"It is important, Robert. How about we meet for dinner tonight, and you can meet her and then decide."

"Thomas, I am catching a plane back to Plentywood tonight to see Tracey."

"It will be a quick dinner, I promise, at Lolo, five fifteen?"

Robert had his duffle in the seat next to him. He was fidgeting as he waited. Facing the door, he saw Thomas arrive with someone shadowed by his profile. When Thomas got to the table, she moved from behind him. Robert was speechless. She may have been the most beautiful young lady he had ever seen. He knew the lump in his throat must have been visible. He stood up and stumbled through an introduction. Thomas asked her to sit, her sleeveless dress showing off her strong arms and her low-cut dress showing off everything else.

Thomas said, "Lisa works for me as an assistant."

Robert had been a single dad for some time. Lisa was out of his league even when he was a player. When he could gather his thoughts, he wondered what Thomas was doing with an assistant like Lisa.

Thomas described Lisa's problem and asked if Robert might tell his recovery. Robert had been a drop-dead alcoholic for many years and met thousands of alcoholics. He had never seen a drinker look as flawless as Lisa.

The waitress got their orders of Tacos and grilled beef. Thomas and Lisa ordered water, and Robert ordered a Coke.

Robert had a plane to catch, so he started his story. He had decided that he would make it a short story.

"In high school and college days, I drank a lot. I was good at it. I married my high school sweetheart, who drank as much as I did. As my drinking disease progressed, I had to drop out of college in my junior year. My wife and I were drinking and drugging every day. We lived in a single-wide on the property of my dad's friend in Jacksonville, Florida. My sister had gone to college there, and my grandfather lived there. My wife became pregnant, and we had twins, Tracey and Tom.

Someone across the room called Robert's name. It was Paul from work waving for Robert to come over. Robert excused himself and stepped over to Paul.

Thomas reached into his inside pocket, opened a pill vile, and poured the contents into Robert's coke. He handed two other capsules to Lisa.

Robert returned quickly and started again. Lisa slowed the conversation with women's questions, asking about his wife and life. Robert looked at his watch and tried to speed up the story again. Lisa slowed it down.

Dinner arrived, and Lisa could add more of the capsule to his new Coke.

Thomas excused himself, citing an emergency meeting, leaving Robert alone with Lisa.

Robert's gaze sank onto Lisa's low-cut dress as he continued. "Our drunkenness continued even with our children. Our parents were on us, threatening to take the children away. We kept promising we would do better."

"One weekend, we asked my wife's sister to watch the kids while we went boating. We drank and drank. We arrived back at the beach, wasted. My wife wanted to play water volleyball with her friends. I went home, but she never did." Robert started to tear up.

"I went back to the beach and called her friends. Nobody had seen her since she was in the water at the beach. I called the police.

Two days later, they found her body. I was a wreck; I drank and drank and drank. My wife's sister kept the twins, but after five months, they sent Tracey to live with a family from her Church, who were childless."

"Two months later, Tom got out of the sliding glass door at my sisters-in-law and drowned in their pool. I drank myself to oblivion. My parents couldn't help me, my friends couldn't help, and God would not help me, and I didn't blame him. I wanted to die but couldn't kill myself. My Dad took me to Orlando for the Salvation Army program. I couldn't even make it from the bus to the facility. I was there for six months and got sober. I was out living with friends and went back over the ledge. I lived in the woods. "Robert was slurring, and his head was wobbling.

"After another two months, I returned to the program, thanks to my mom. I was to leave six months later but lacked confidence, so I stayed and worked for six more months."

"I moved back to Jacksonville, rented a room, and worked in a warehouse. I got drunk two weeks after I got there but was able to get sober again thanks to A.A. With the help of my mom and Dad, I was able to locate Tracey. The family had moved about seventy-five miles away to Palatka, Florida. The family had a large home on the outskirts of town. They loved Tracy. I planned to visit. I caught a Greyhound bus to Palatka, walked six miles to their house, and knocked on the door. They slammed it in my face. I stood there and cried." And Robert was crying now. "The worst was walking back without seeing my little girl. The walk gave me ample time to relive my disgusting life. It hurt bad."

"I worked at seeing Tracey. My wife's sister was of no help. She was still in shock from Tom's death. But there was no legal adoption. I worked harder and saved all my money. Each weekend, I would take the bus, walk the six miles, and knock on the door. One day, I saw Tracey in the background. I had been sober for twelve months, attending church and working in a twelve-step program. My Dad encouraged me to keep it up. My Dad helped me get a lawyer to start the process. I continued my program. The court case took six months of bitter confrontation, for they loved Tracy and hated me. I won the case and took Tracey back to my parent's home; I have remained sober, and I finished my law degree." Robert was stoned and slurring and stumbling as he reached out to hold Lisa's hand with his most admirable, "you're so pretty" slur.

Lisa was quick, "Robert, what about your sister Nicki? Did she live with you?"

"Sometimes, she was always working with my mom."

"Where is Nicki now, Robert."

Robert's slurs were long and slow, "I don't know where she is."

"Sure, you do. Your Dad wouldn't keep it from you. You and Nicki are close. She adores Tracey."

"She does."

"Robert, where is Tracey?" She reached her hand across the table, and her blouse opened."

Robert grinned a drunk grin.

"Robert, sweet Robert, Tracey would like to see Nicki. Where would she find her?"

"Robert shook his drunken head and smiled. Oh no, you don't. You can't trick me."

"Bobby, is that what your mom called you?"

"He shook his head."

"Bobby, let's take Tracey to see Nicki."

"Yes, let's take her."

"Where is she?"

"Cucumber Island in Georgia."

Robert's head hit the table with a thud. Lisa bolted out of her seat with her phone blazing. Robert never made it to the plane to Plentywood.

⌒

Nicki played cards with Connie and Evelyn when Mrs. Frank drove up, screaming and yelling Nicki's name. "Nicki, get in the cart now."

"What"

"Just get in."

Mrs. Frank headed south at full speed and stopped at the front of Carnegie's Graveyard. She reached behind a plant covering a post, and the Ivy-covered gates opened. They ran in. It was dark and cool, but as they went, deeper sunlight appeared. In the back corner was a concrete building with lights and antennas. Mrs. Frank opened the door to the building, and there sat Joe Frank with a headset talking into a microphone. His expression was a total shock as he looked at Nicki.

Mrs. Frank said, "The Prelates men are on the way. Nicki's Dad sent word through Nicki's communicator. I heard him speaking as I was cleaning Nicki's room. Nicki's brother gave away the location last night in San Francisco. We have maybe two hours to get off the Island."

Joe put his head in his hands. "I knew this day would come. We have a plan. Nicki take Mrs. Frank back to Plum Orchard. Stop and tell Dr. Maker to be ready to go in an hour. After dropping Mrs. Frank off, get Taylor Samms and tell him it's time. Stop and pick up one bag. All of you are in the front yard of Stafford's house, ready to go. I mean ready. Mrs. Frank will come back to me."

"Hurry now."

Within the hour, in the late morning sun, Doctor Bernie Maker, Mr. Taylor Samms, and Nicki Boaz stood in front of Stafford House, facing Main Rd. Each had one bag at their feet and a concerned look. Looking directly into Taylor Samm's eyes, Nicki whispered, "What's next?"

He removed his silly hat and rubbed his hand through his hair, "The law of unanticipated."

PART III

"Life's easier to take than you think. All that is necessary is to accept the impossible, do without the indispensable, and bear the intolerable."
Katheleen Norris

CHAPTER 11

Life shrinks or expands in proportion to one's courage.
Jane Austen

Nicki asked Dr. Maker, "Do you think they will catch me?"

"I am sure Joe has a plan. Joe always has a plan."

"What do you think the Prelate will do to me if he catches me?"

"Bill Malum is a friend of mine, ex-friend actually," Dr. Maker sighed.

Nicki asked, "Who is Bill Malum?"

"Prelate Malum. We were hunting buddies after seminary. We went to Montana several times to sharpen our skills. He is an amazing marksman. He can hit an elk from eight hundred yards."

"Really, two preachers crack shots. That doesn't sound deeply religious to me." Carrie said it hard.

"I don't know what to tell you, Nicki. We like to hunt, and Malum is a remarkable hunter. I am sure he has the best equipment his high-ranking position can afford. He deserves it. He had an odd and challenging childhood. His parents were murdered, and two occultist aunts raised him."

"What do you mean? Do you think he will shoot me?"

"I doubt he will shoot you." Dr. Maker grinned. "But I did hear your fiancé and the Prelate are hunting friends. Thomas White went hunting with him several times in North Dakota last fall."

"Ex-fiancé."

They could hear a loud noise from the other side of the Island, the roar of a big engine. It sounded as if it was coming from the cotton field. They could not see anything because the road was diagonal. After several minutes, the 60s Piper Comanche came into full view on Main Rd. The pilot turned the plane around and headed back toward the east.

The engine, still rumbling, the pilot opened the door and came around. The pilot was Ranger Craig.

"Oh, no," Nicki said, turning her head away, "He will deliver me into their hands. I am not going."

Ranger Craig approached the group and said, "It is time. Let's load up."

"I am not going," Nicki said.

Taylor Samms put his arm around her and said, "What gives?"

"I just don't like small planes."

"Nicki, this is all for you. Everyone is trying to save you, and you are going to be a problem?"

"Taylor, I do not trust Ranger Craig."

"Nicki, you can trust me, and I trust Craig. Let's go."

Taylor walked Nicki to the plane, and she and Dr. Maker got into the back of the four-seater.

Ranger Craig went through his checklist for the old aircraft. His procedures took a long time. After he finished, he did it again.

He told the group, "Normally, we take off to the west, but I will take off to the east and barely clear the trees. We will hug the ocean until I can turn over to St Simmon's airport. I have a cousin who will file a flight plan for us, so it will appear we are on a local plane. They will shoot us down if I take off to the west without a flight plan. I have never done this, so Pastor, pray."

The plane rumbled, roared, and struggled through the cotton field. The runway was smoother than Nicki had imagined, but it felt like the plane was falling apart. At 80 miles per hour, he lifted the aircraft off the ground but only to two hundred feet. They cleared the trees, increasing the airspeed as they climbed quickly. Then, he skillfully lowered the altitude to one hundred feet. St Simmons was thirty air miles away.

Her eyes closed, and Nicki shook profusely. Her hands were in the praying position. This was too much.

Ranger Craig turned the plane west and picked up the airport, and he faked a touchdown and took off with a flight plan locked into his equipment. He continued west and climbed to thirty-five hundred feet at 185 miles per hour.

"Over the loud engine noise, Nicki asks, "What happened to you and the Prelate."

"After seminary, we hunted a few times together in Virginia. I got a small Church in Southern Virginia, and Malum worked hard for a Washington, D.C. position. He was highly motivated to move up quickly. I had to hand it to him; he was a great speaker. He was intensely interested in his ability to influence people. We lost touch, but I heard he joined a political group. I don't think he ever had his own Church. He taught at a private University in the Capital. I would see him on T.V. from time to time dressed in his regalia, talking about secular matters. He rubbed shoulders with the Congressmen and Lobbyists. Over time, he became a Religious Celebrity. Nobody ever knew where he got his funding.

"Where do you think he got his power?"

"I don't know, Nicki, but I don't believe it was a gift from God."

"Where are we headed," Nicki asked, but nobody heard. She was in the seat behind Ranger Craig, so she leaned over to ask Dr. Maker to see if he could get Ranger Craig's information.

"Blairsville, Georgia, eta two and a half hours." Ranger Craig said.

"Blairsville, Georgia, what is there?"

"No idea," said Dr. Maker.

Ranger Craig turned the door handle on the top of the cabin from time to time. Other than that, it was a cramped but smooth and noisy ride.

Ranger Craig made voice contact with Blairsville Airport. Nicki could see the runway, and it looked small and short. Ranger Craig slowed the plane to eighty miles per hour, and the aircraft floated between the large numbers painted on the runway, 19/33.

There were five metal buildings at the airport. Ranger Craig taxied to the end of the runway and parked in the grass between two compact cars.

Shutting down the plane and opening the doors, Ranger Craig announced, last stop. Taylor Samms and Dr. Maker helped Craig tie down the aircraft. Putting their bags in the car to the left, Taylor walked over to Nicki and hugged her. Goodbye, we love you.

"Wait, what are you talking about? I am going with you."

"No, you have to go with Ranger Craig," Taylor said.

"No, I will go with you."

"Nicki, time is short, and things have blown up. We have much to do, and so do you. The election is months away, and if we don't change things, it will be the last election for our country. We will see each other soon.

Dr. Maker hugged her and said, "Please be careful. It will not serve a good purpose if you get caught."

"What do you want me to do?"

"Remember this: the answers do not come from within you. The solutions will come from the outside, from God. He is the main character of the story. He will mark your path well. Go with Craig, and it will be ok." Dr. Maker's eyes lowered as if he were pronouncing a benediction.

Dr. Maker and Taylor drove away in their little blue car and headed toward the airport hangers. Ranger Craig put a tarp over the windshield and pulled his bag out of the plane.

"Hop in the car, Nicki."

She knew he would drive her to the police station and turn her in. She could run, but to where?

Nicki threw her bag into the back seat and started to get in but changed her mind and sat in the front. Ranger Craig was tall for the small car, and his knees almost reached the dashboard. He drove along the runway and then between two metal buildings. They turned right at the four-way stop onto Blue Ridge St.

"Where are we going."

"Neels Gap."

"What is Neels Gap?"

"It is like a store."

"What do you mean like a store, and how far away is it?"

"Thirty minutes away, just sit back and enjoy the ride. You ask a lot of questions."

"I am a lawyer."

Ranger Craig turned the compact car tight into hairpin curves, first left, then right, and left again. He was driving the car hard. Nicki was holding on tighter than in the plane. She thought *This was too much for one day*. Ranger Craig was aggressively driving the car faster. Nicki became nauseated. Turn after turn, smashing into the door, then into Ranger Craig.

Ranger Craig powered the little car into a right curve thirty minutes later. Instead of turning back, he coasted into a paved parking lot and stopped. It was like when a roller coaster stopped. You are still, but your body feels like it is in motion.

In front of the car was a stone building. It looked like it was a large house at one time. Ranger Craig got out and opened her door.

"Let's go," he said.

Apprehensive to get out, she said, "Go where?"

"Up to the store."

Nicki turned her head around the side of the car, and she could see an open sign blinking on the front of the building.

"It is an outfitter rather than a store."

"What is an outfitter."

"An outfitter is a place that equips you with the stuff you will need for your expedition?"

"What expedition?"

"The Appalachian Trail."

"I am not getting out of this car. You can take me to the city."

"What city? There is no city around here, and I am sure they know Nicki Boaz is not on Cumberland Island by now. We have maybe two hours to get on the Trail, which is out of sight. Come on."

"No. Give me the keys, and I will drive myself out of here."

A frown appeared on Ranger Craig's face, "Better guess again, see the guy walking down the steps? He is going to take this car back to the rental company."

Ranger Craig tossed him the keys.

"I am not getting out."

"Ok, with me, he will take you back to Blairsville. I am sure the police are all over that plane by now."

"Ok, OK."

Nicki retrieved her one bag with two sets of clothes, her mom's folders, and the paperback *Salesman* book from her room. Her appearance was worse than her attitude. Over the six months on the Island, her hair had grown out. Always in a ponytail, her now blondish hair was unkempt. She huffed and puffed to show her great displeasure and followed Ranger Craig up the steps.

Neels Gap was a beautiful building out in the middle of nowhere. Nicki strode up the stone steps towards the front door. A patio to the right overlooked the mountains and the valleys. It was a view like in a travel magazine. Nicki stopped to survey the splendor. Ranger Craig continued in.

In ten minutes, he came out and called her. The store was large, with room for hiking gear, boots, jackets, pants, and backpacks. There were rooms with supplies and food. Nicki was astonished you could find so much merchandise this far out into the woods.

Craig said, "OK, let's get started with your boots. You will need three pairs."

"What boots."

"Boots for the trail."

"I am not going on any trail."

"Look, Miss Boaz, I am getting tired of you. I will leave you here, and whatever happens is up to you, but I am getting my stuff for the trail. Time is running out. You can stand before the Prelate and his henchman in a few hours. I don't care. You better get on the train if you are coming with me."

Nicki bent her index finger, bit down hard, and shook her head.

She took a deep breath, centered herself, and tried on several pairs of boots and hiking pants. Craig tossed several flannel shirts and undershirts her way. While she was in the dressing room, he gathered gloves, socks, a hat, and a beany. He piled her clothes on a shelf and then had her turn around for a fitting of her pack. Not your school backpack but a huge multi-compartment bag.

Ranger Craig paid for her clothes and bag and sent her to the overlook picnic table to pack. She carried her gear, threw it on the table, and sat.

Craig came several minutes later with sleeping bags, tents and tarps, dry bags, and trekking poles. He made one more trip inside for food, hydration bags, and cookware. It took an hour to pack both bags. Nicki didn't do any packing. She watched as Ranger Craig applied his skill. He put a three-foot pile of stuff in a two-foot-long backpack weighing 29 pounds. It would be like carrying a four-year-old child on your back as you climb mountains.

She wore nylon hiking pants, a base layer undershirt, a flannel shirt, a pullover wool sweater, and an Insulated Jacket. Her Dad would have never believed his couture Daughter could look like a mountain man.

The last pack was a small bag of books and electronic gadgets for navigation. Ranger Craig tightened a bulky Garmin Hiking watch on her left wrist.

Nicki's face had turned bright pink, and her strength had dropped to a minimal level. It had been a long day, and it was only 3:00 PM.

The Appalachian Trail passed through the Neels Gap property. Ranger Craig wanted to avoid starting walking from the building but wanted to walk a quarter of a mile up the road and take a spur to The Appalachian Trail. Walking along the highway, they crossed into an enchanted canopy of trees. The top of the trees touched the sky. There were several parking places and a few picnic tables.

They were at the Bryon Reese Trailhead that leads up to the Trail. Nicki gawked at the deep, dark woods in front of her. Immediately she started taking deep breaths, sucking air, trying to breathe. She turned red and started choking. Ranger Craig stood her up, put her hands over her head, and sat her down. Her backpack was causing her to wobble and then fall over.

Nicki finally gained her breath, sweating with her head lying on the picnic table. She moaned and groaned. Her heart rate appeared to be back to normal when Ranger Craig lifted her head and looked into her eyes, hoping to find some sign of a diabetic seizure. She looked good. He sat on the other side of the table while she laid her head on the dirty picnic table.

After twenty minutes, Ranger Craig asked Nicki, "Are you okay? Do you have asthma, allergies, or seizures? Do you have medicine?"

"No"

"No, what?"

"No, none of those."

"It was a panic attack."

"Over what?"

"The woods. I cannot go into the forest."

"Why?"

"I would rather die than go into the woods."

Ranger Craig contemplated his watch. They needed to disappear into the woods.

"Nicki was sitting up, and her red face had turned pale, her nose was running, and her eyelashes were wet from tears. Nicki slipped off her backpack. She cleaned her face with her sleeve. Taking several large gulps of air, she said once again. I cannot go into the forest."

"Nicki, we must. Can you tell me why you cannot go in?"

"I just cannot do it."

"We must move from this location. Anyone driving by could see us. Follow me. We will move just on the other side of the trailhead sign. It is just bushes, not a forest." He grabbed her backpack and pulled her by the hand. They sat on a rock just past the trail sign.

"That was quite a show. What is going on?"

"When I was a senior in high school, I was kidnapped. I was with a group on a trip to see Colleges and Universities. A disgusting man snatched me when I got off the plane in Jacksonville, Florida. This man had planned to get even with my mother by kidnapping me. He wanted both of us to come to support his organization. If we didn't, he would kill both of us. He took me to the woods and tied me to a tree for two days. It was horrifying. Animals came around me. A snake crawled over me. I had no way to get loose or go to the bathroom. A giant spider got on my head, and a Bobcat came within ten feet. I was terrified. I passed out twice. Finally, he returned and took me under a bridge over an Interstate Highway. My mother rushed to save me. Some unknown man with my mother killed the kidnapper. I cannot go in the woods, not now, not ever."

"How long ago was that, Nicki."

"Ten years ago, I have not gone near any woods."

Ranger Craig sat there silently. They had to go. They were running out of daylight and needed t to get to the summit shelter.

"Nicki, I am a National Park Ranger and have survival skills for hiking and climbing in the woods. You will be safe with me."

"I am not so sure. Why haven't you turned me in yet?"

"Pardon me?"

"I know you work for the state, and you will turn me in."

"Ranger Craig pulled off his backpack and removed his jacket, shirt, and undershirt."

"Nicki screamed. No."

"Cool your jets, Nicki," he showed her the tattoo inside his arm, two B's back-to-back with a cross through them, like Todd's.

He put back on his clothes and said, "We will have to go, but we will go slowly."

Nicki stood up, still whimpering, and put on her backpack. Its weight bent her over like an old lady.

"We only have to go a few miles this afternoon, but getting used to your pack will take a while."

Craig set her trekking poles to the correct height for uphill, and slowly, they headed up the Trail. The temperature was cold, and it could easily snow in Georgia. The climb started at a gradual incline, but about halfway up, the trail soared 1,800 feet straight up. Nicki struggled to stay within ten feet of Ranger Craig, who had tied his Black Diamond rope to Nicki's shoulder strap. The going was slow. Nicki gasped for air occasionally, and Ranger Craig stopped long enough for her to get calm. He set up his Garmin satellite communicator and locked onto the position, and they started again.

Nicki often twitched her head, looking around for danger. She continuously scanned the terrain and picked up on the white rectangles painted on trees and rocks. They were on both the front and the back of some trees. She wondered *who would paint patterns on trees in the woods. They seemed to appear regularly.*

As they got within sight of the top, the trees disappeared, and solid rock, like granite sheets, dominated the landscape. The view was breathtaking. Nicki was not afraid of heights, just woods. Nicki collapsed on the rocks a quarter mile from the top, a solid faceplant, and stayed down. After a few minutes, she pulled herself up. The climb was too much after such a long day. They rested and drank water as dark approached.

Nicki said, "I don't think I can go on."

"I am not sure you can either. You are a wimp." Ranger Craig said.

Craig hurt Nicki's feelings. She was looking for some encouragement, not hate talk.

As they sat, Nicki asked Ranger Craig about the white-painted marks.

"Blazes," he said.

"What is a Blaze?"

"It is a trail marker. There are no street signs in the woods, but you have blazes. There are white Blazes on the Trail from Georgia to Maine. Some trails have blue blazes, some yellow. If you get lost, you can find your way no matter your direction because of the blazes on both sides of a tree or a rock.

"Who would go to that much work?"

"There are people who love this trail, and hiking clubs keep the trail maintained."

Nicki thought, *who would have imagined*?

They stood; although she was shaky, they finished the last quarter mile, with Craig reluctantly carrying her pack. Arriving at the shelter, Ranger Craig looked in, and there were two hiking parties already settled in for the night. He knew Nicki could not make a camp and put up a tent tonight, so he found a space in the backroom. As they unrolled their sleeping bags, Ranger Craig handed Nicki a small flashlight, only about half the length of her index finger. He passed her six unusual batteries, not the standard AAA batteries but short and stubby. Craig said, "It is small, but it will take good care of you. It will light up a mountain a quarter mile away. Hook it to your shoulder strap.

It would be cold even though they were in a building. The doors and windows were missing. Hikers had burned them long ago for winter warmth.

Nicki used a tree stand latrine before eating a pack of crackers. She quickly climbed into her sleeping bag. They slept end to end with their feet touching. She trembled at the thought of being in the woods. At least she was in a building if that is what you called it. Nicki had perceived that no day would be as bad as the days of her kidnapping. But today was similarly unforgiving.

Nicki woke up looking through heavily crusted eyes. The backroom had added two other hikers overnight. Ranger Craig was gone. His rolled-up sleeping bag was still next to Nicki's feet. She was tiptoeing out through the main room and outside. Ranger Craig had made a pot of coffee on a small fire. She used the outhouse and returned. They climbed up to the overlook rock and drank their coffee in the perfect quiet of a mountain morning. It smelled perfect, like fresh linens dried in the sunshine. An ever-so-slight breeze was blowing into Nicki's face, crisp with no humidity. She closed her eyes and remembered the soft breeze at the picnic table at Plum Orchard, warm and moisture-laden. Nicki said to Ranger Craig, "This isn't so bad."

He smiled, "This is as good as it gets."

Sitting having coffee, she asked, "What is your first name."

"Craig," he said.

"Oh, I thought it was your last name, like in Officer Craig."

"No, just Craig."

"Do you mind if I call you Craig?"

"No."

"We better get going. We might get a dusty snow today."

"Craig, I don't think I can make it. She pulled her coffee cup close to her chest. Cumberland Island is flat. The highest elevation is an anthill. I am not prepared for this. I can follow the trail back down."

"Nicki, I am going forward. There is nothing back down this mountain but trouble for you. But it is up to you. I told them I didn't think you could make it anyway."

He headed out.

CHAPTER 12

We generally change for one of two reasons:
inspiration or desperation.
Jim Rohn

Nicki did not reply or move. She had a quick, arrogant thought as she puffed out her chest. *I am the boss of myself, and I can do what I want. Ranger Craig isn't my superior.* Then her next thought was, *I am a fugitive running for my life,* and she shrank back down. Yesterday morning, she rested in bed on their Cumberland Island paradise. By midmorning, she had escaped the island in a small, clandestine plane ride. They rode a rollercoaster up a mountain, bought clothes, built heavy backpacks, and climbed mountains. That same night, they slept in a shelter with many people. It was a lot for one day. Nicki did not realize the significance of running for her life, but Craig knew she would soon discover her peril.

At 4,500 feet, almost a mile high, they started north. Little snowflakes fell in the morning and disappeared as the sun rose in the cold, fresh sky. The faster they walked, the warmer they stayed. Nicki could see Craig's impressive strength and skill as he led.

They took an early break for a snack and ate lunch at 1:00. After a can of Vienna sausage and saltines, the question came. "Where are we going? How long will it be?"

Craig took a deep breath. I will deliver you to Harpers Ferry, West Virginia, by early September.

Nicki's eyes rolled backward like she was going to faint. She leaned forward with a beet-red face and spit two questions. "Aren't we in Georgia, and isn't it the second week of March?"

"Yes."

Nicki's voice reached her highest octave, "Are you suggesting we hike for seven months and God knows how many hundreds of miles?"

"Yes"

The veins in her neck popped out, "Nobody does that."

"Happens all the time. The Appalachian Trail goes on for 2,100 miles north to Maine, and people do it yearly."

"I cannot do that."

"Nicki, let's not start this all over."

"Whose plan is this?"

"Charlie and Beth and the Boys."

"I don't know the Boys."

"You can trust them. That is what they do: move people around the country. You are a VIP, destined for something special. You are going to have to get over it. You're a crybaby."

She threw her empty can of Vienna sausage at him. For the first time, he laughed.

"Not going to happen. You better get in touch with your Boys and get a change of plans."

"Right, I will call them. Important people prepared this expedition for you. It is no afterthought. It would be best if you reached your destination safely. For some reason, they think you have special powers or something."

"Why did they choose you?"

"I have completed the trail twice, once south to north and then north to south."

Softly, she said, "Pretty impressive."

"Yes, it is. We will have to make camp tonight, and it will take you some time to get the procedure down."

"Think so."

"I know so."

On their first day, they were only able to go five miles. Nicki was slow and tentative, always considering how she could go back, her eyes moving back and forth, watching the woods. They needed to average eleven miles per day, some days more. The trees were so thick you could not tell where you were by looking to the left or right. You could only see what was before you and could not always know if you were going up or down. Nicki could cope if Craig were within ten feet, and she remained tethered to his rope.

Close to Tray Mountain, Craig found a nice campground. There will be a freeze tonight, but no snow. A freezing night in a sleeping bag would be a new test for Nicki. They started the unpacking ritual. The tent building instructions were followed.

Craig scouted the area for level ground and showed Nicki how to maximize weather protection. He showed her how to watch for trenches, dead limbs, and wind alleys. Craig recommended staying back from streams and lakes. He found a clearing, and they picked up a few branches and rocks to make it smooth. Nicki was attentive and quiet.

He showed Nicki how to build her tent by laying out his. She would copy him.

On his knees, laying out his tent, he said, "I have a gift for you," with a big smile, he reached into the side pocket of his vest and tossed her a box, seven inches long by two inches square. She caught it and looked at the Kershaw 1605 3.1-inch blade-assisted knife box. Nicki smiled, "a switchblade," she said out loud.

"Blade assisted," Craig replied.

Nicki twisted it over and around, but she couldn't open it. Craig showed her how to hold it with her thumb and pointing finger. The blade sprang open with her finger pushing on the metal sticking up. She swung it around like a pirate. Nicki liked it. She tried to close it but could not find any buttons. She attempted folding it, but it wouldn't budge. She was afraid she would cut herself. Craig turned the knife over and showed her how to slide the metal piece toward her, the blade smoothly folded. What a great knife, thank you. He showed her how to use the clip-on in her pocket to retrieve it quickly with one hand.

Craig continued with tent school. He was laying out the ground cloth footprint. Putting the tent on top of the footprint, Craig suggested facing the tent's strong side toward the wind. He assembled the poles, inserting them into the grommets. Clipping the tent to the poles, he located the stakes. Finally, he placed the rainfly over the canopy and attached it to the body and the stakes. He talked about guy lines but didn't think they would need them tonight. Nicki followed the procedure, and her tent remained standing to both their surprises. She clapped. Then she remembered she was in the woods with a guy who detested her and that it would freeze tonight. Her face changed to an ugly contortion.

After a canned dinner and a few pieces of jerky, she retired early to her freshly assembled tent.

Woods are spooky, especially at night, she thought. You feel small in the forest with trees surrounding you. The crickets are so loud it is like New York traffic. You are defenseless; you know those insects and large animals are watching you. The deep aroma of the decaying leaves on the forest floor was like a magnetizing perfume. Lying still for an hour, she couldn't sleep, hearing distant shuffling noises. The noise got closer and louder. It was footsteps, bear steps, monsters' steps, she wasn't sure, but she was sure they were in the camp. They were slow, shuffling, and deliberate; they would stop and start. She could see a dispersed light shine through the rainfly of her tent. She reached into her pocket and pulled out her knife, and the blade swished open.

The light shined directly on her tent.

CHAPTER 13

It is discouraging to think how many people are
shocked by honesty and how few by deceit.
Noel Coward

"Who goes there," she heard Craig say in a strong, in charge voice.

"Howard Youngblood, here, good evening," Nicki could hear the voices come closer.

"What brings you here?"

"I started a few days ago at Springer Mountain. I had a slow start and am trying to compensate for some lost time. I shouldn't be trekking at dusk, but I have seen the blazes." Howard said with a slightly fake British accent. I am a thorough hiker from Baltimore. I am on my second attempt on the Appalachian Trail. My brother Bill lives in Sarasota and is a Judge. My sister lives in Phoenix, and they make fun of me because I like to hike. His arms flapped out in front of him, and his head moved back and forth faster than his words.

"Slow down," said Craig, "Step into the camp."

"Nicki lay in her tent as stiff as a board with her blade-assisted knife in her sweaty hand.

Howard stepped into the light of the campfire. He looked like a Boy Scout Leader in a Kaki shirt, pants, a triangled scarf, and a felt campaign hat. His Jacket was dark brown leather and looked expensive. The hat looked like the hat worn by the Royal Canadian

Mounted Police. A high crown with four pinched points, a full leather band at the brim, and the cap's meeting. Howard's outfit appeared pressed and starched. His round, extra-thick glasses made Howard look like the perfect geek. He had the most unusual smile. It was crooked.

Howard said, "I am sorry to disturb you. I was hoping for a spot of tea and company. I have a kettle and real cups."

"We don't have any tea, but you can sit for a while."

"I have tea if I may use your fire."

"Of course."

Nicki got up to her knees and peeked out of her tent. She could see Craig listening and Howard speaking. It seemed safe. She rolled out with a big, "Hi, I am Nicki."

He stood and tipped his hat, revealing a full head of dark curly hair. "Good evening, Nicki. I am Howard Youngblood from Baltimore, Maryland. I work in Washington."

Howard knew everything about hiking and the equipment. He also knew everything about any topic you could bring up. Politics was his specialty. He was polite but authoritarian. The oratory lasted hours. He asked if he could pitch his tent in a clearing thirty yards north of their spot. Craig agreed.

Early the following day, Howard was up and cooking oatmeal and coffee. Pleased to be serving, he offered Craig and Nicki bowls.

Howard felt grateful for the companionship. He headed out first, signaling goodbye with a half-turn of his hand in the perpendicular position. Nicki thought, *Howard, you are a nerd.*

Nicki packed her tent with oversight by Craig, and they left forty-five minutes later.

Nicki said, "It has been a busy two days, and I never asked, what happened to Joe and Yvonne?"

"There is a back entrance into Lucy's Cemetery, and a creek flows up to a dock. Joe arranged for Jim Rowell to send a small boat and load his equipment. Joe's equipment is connected to Jim's office electronics on the pier."

"Evelyn and Connie?"

"They will be fine. Charlie and Beth will be back soon. Nobody is after them."

"Nicki said despondently, "I will miss that Island and the people."

Nicki changed the subject quickly, "What do you make of Howard?".

"I don't know. You meet all kinds on the Trail. Remember who you are dealing with: people dedicated to hiking, living in a tent for months, and walking 2,000 miles. It is not for everyone. I am sure he is harmless. Over the months, we will cross paths with him and others. Most people are okay."

⌒

Bobby Boaz flew to San Francisco to attend to his son. Robert could not stop apologizing to his dad. His Dad confirmed that Nicki was safe and in good hands. Bobby Boaz went to Thomas White's office to fire him, but he was gone. His secretary reported he had taken a state job in Washington. Bob wanted Robert to return to Plentywood, but Robert wanted to stay. Bobby called his brother Tim in South America to return to help Robert run the behemoth Boaz Power. He was sure the government's efforts to take over his company would continue. Tim and Robert would make a strong team.

On March 31, Bobby Boaz traveled to Washington to meet with other like-minded Industrialists. They intended to bring a request to President Bill Smith. He knew their efforts were in vain; Bill Smith didn't run the country, and his cabinet had no power. But he owed it to the system to play by the rules until they wouldn't play. The power was with the Prelate; he was Francis Vile's puppet. Francis Vile had a personal problem with the Boaz family. The grudge she held was not easily satisfied with mere political persecution.

Bobby Boaz and his industrialists met in Georgetown days after meeting with the president. It was a do-or-die planning session for when the country fell. They had a detailed plan of when and where the country's largest companies' assets would be relocated. The government had already nationalized the newspapers, T.V., Internet, and publishing businesses. The men at the meeting and their companies still commanded great power and hordes of cash. Also invited were the Ambassadors from the countries that would gratefully accept these large American companies. At the meeting, they helped plan facilities and logistics. Bobby Boaz and his friends believed it was plausible that democracy and capitalism could be re-created on a platform outside the United States. Bobby Boaz personally acknowledged each man with an in-depth look into their eyes as they left the meeting.

He targeted five men to meet privately at Compass Coffee on Wisconsin N.W.

At the round table, the six men committed to giving up the leadership of their companies. They each would appoint men to execute the departure of their companies out of the country. But the leaders would not go. They would fight to the end, even if they had to die on the Capital steps like Bobby's wife. Bobby introduced them to the organization, Billy's Boys, and the excellent work they had been doing. Most of them were familiar in some way with their power and influence. He asked for their support for this underground group. Then, he invited them to join the movement personally. The plan's simple catchphrase was, *Return to the Promised Land*. They agreed to give it their all, even if the worn-down citizens gave up. He then anointed them as *The Federalist Five*. Bobby informed them that the Boys' head and his lieutenant had just exited a cab at P Street. They will be here to detail the organization and its plans in a few minutes. As they continued the conversation for freedom, two men came through the door, one young and one old.

The men at the table beamed and reached out their hands to greet the two men.

⌐

Craig and Nicki had dragged forward through a week of light snow that turned into a full-blown snowstorm. For a day, they were waist-high in snow, wet and exhausted. They wore their rain gear, and through the silence of the blanket of snow, you could hear the plastic rubbing together. They had spent the night in a three-sided wooden shelter with another couple, John and Debbie, weekend hikers from Florida. They used their tent cloth to make the fourth side the shelter. The plastic whipped and flapped but kept the snow out. John and Debbie had all the niceties of day hikers and shared their bounty freely with Nicki and Craig. Debbie cooked a warm meal and comforted them with kind words. Nicki needed help understanding the theory of heading north in the face of cold weather. "We should be heading south."

But as Craig would remind her, their mission was north. Often, Craig would say, "Nicki, I don't think you have a chance to complete your speaking mission. You don't know what you will say, where you will say it, or to whom. Even if you did, you couldn't get the state to let you say a word in public. Sounds like fairy dust to me."

Nicki would take in his failure talk, and she even started believing it herself. Her mission, on a national level, did sound impossible.

The distance to Harpers Ferry is less than six hundred miles on a map. It is six hundred miles up, six hundred miles around, and six hundred miles down on the trail. You could see up but never get there—day after day, up and down, about, and back. Put up your tent and take it down. It was tedious work. But as the days passed, it had turned warmer, not warm but warmer, as March turned into April. She would have lost her mind without the occasional breaks at the stores and homegrown restaurants along the backroads. They continued to come across Howard every few days. Sometimes, he came from behind; other days, he was out in front. He was a nerd, but he was indeed an expert hiker. Nicki came to look forward to his nerdy conversations. His political satires were hilarious. Through April, their pace remained below their needed average. Nicki had become a much better hiker but still no match for Ranger Craig.

Nicki would talk about her dad, Robert, Tracey, and Todd Miller at evening camp. She spoke about Todd as if she hated him, but she always liked to talk about him. While in Northern Georgia, her dad got through on the communicator. He explained what had happened to Robert and who had set it up. Nicki couldn't believe Thomas could do such a thing, but her dad assured her he did. As they moved further north, the communicator never turned red or green. It made Nicki uneasy. Although Craig had a satellite communicator, she thought it was just a receiver for weather and locations.

Craig had little to say. His dad was a high-ranking Naval officer, and his mother lived in Florida. He loved the outdoors, skiing, biking, surfing, diving, fishing, and sailing. If it was a sport, he did it with gusto. He couldn't sit still for a minute. He was always ready to go. In the woods, his skills were extraordinary. He was married and had one son. He told Nicki that his mom took his son to Church every week.

"Nicki asked, how do you and your wife feel about your mom taking your son to Church?"

"My Mom loves taking him. It is a dream come true for her. The truth is I should take him. I sometimes feel guilty. I believe in God. I am just unfaithful in giving my time. I give more to my government job. I am aware that there has been no government that has ever outlasted the Church. You would think that knowing the strength of the Church, I would do better. I stay conflicted between my dad's loyalty to the government and my mom's love of God. It was my mom that introduced me to Joe Frank. But I am grateful my son learns about God."

Breaking camp in the morning was Nicki's best part of the day. It was a new joy, a sensation of a birth. The crispness of the morning, the still-warm embers of last night's fire, the smell of fresh coffee, and the early dew of the day were like a drug. Some mornings brought stiff muscles and aches; other days were like new strength had grown overnight. Nicki never went far away from Craig. Even with her little orange shovel, she stayed within range of his voice. Craig told Nicki stories about bears most nights. No Grizzlies are on this side of the Mississippi, but plenty of Black Bears exist. They were not the size nor the ferocity of the Grizzly, but they were still dangerous. He loved scaring Nicki; her fear of the woods made it a double delight. Nicki carried her walking stick like a baseball bat in the late afternoon, ready to club any approaching black furry mammal. At night, Craig tied the food up in a tree.

The weather had warmed over the weeks as April had turned to May. Their daily mileage was still half of what Craig wanted. Their course often changed from south to north, east to west, and then back. Somedays, Nicki could do ten miles; on others, it was ten miles straight up with no forward mileage to measure. Nicki had grown strong. Carrying her backpack and moving uphill had bulked muscles they had never mentioned in yoga class. She could take down her tent, pack a bag, and march out to the Trail without effort. She looked like a wild mountain woman, with broad shoulders, chiseled arms, and her hair a mess, long and scraggly. In sixty days, they marched through three states: Georgia, South Carolina, skirting Tennessee and North Carolina. They would find a side trail leading to a highway store or motel every ten days.

They had been gone so long that Nicki forgot she was a desperado. In addition to Howard Youngblood, they hiked immediately with several other through-hikers. Occasionally, Nicki felt like someone was following them. Starting at Springer Mountain, all the hikers' attitudes were as high as a kite, and everyone was invincible. Months into the wilderness, attitudes waned. It was nice to have occasional company. New people added flavor to the repetitiveness of the trail.

The Smokie Mountains were magnificent, breathtaking towering heights with dense plant and animal life. Several of the highest mountains on the AT were in the Smokies. But the bear population was considerably larger. Because of growing tourism in the Rockies, the large animals were not afraid of humans and knew they brought food, which they loved to share with the bears. Nicki's first sight of the Smokies from a distance was mesmerizing. The deep blue mist and rocky cliffs created an image that showered delight in her heart. They had hiked over Clingmans Dome through the Great Smokies National Park and across the Broad River, which ran east to the Biltmore Estate in Asheville. Moving on to Spivey Gap, they hiked into The Pisgah National Forest. They were just west of Mt. Mitchell, the highest mountain in the eastern states. Nicki had become accustomed to the grand views, but sometimes, sitting on a ledge with her legs dangling off at night, a full moon surrounded by white clouds would bring peace to her worried soul. The moon's reflection off the clouds would light up the mountains like nothing she had ever seen. The shadows transformed in the diffusion as they slowly moved. It was like God shining a flashlight into the crevices, looking for her.

The morning hike's start was holy, and often, a light breeze accompanied the silence of the daybreak. Closing her eyes, she would rub the charm on her necklace and speak to her mom about the miracle of a new day. Nicki's terror of the woods had diminished but not gone away. The fear came at provocation and did not reside on her outsides like it once did. As the sunrise danced across the eastern sky, Nicki would repeat an old saying, "Red sky in morning sailors take warning, red sky in night sailors delight." It was so dependable that she would unpack her rain gear on red mornings. Nicki hated wet boots. She stayed out of the streams and took off her shoes if she needed to ford a shallow creek.

Her hair was wet hundreds of times, and her baseball cap looked ten years old. She shivered even in warm weather. Her clothes were well worn, and on some days, they smelled. She was in her second set of boots, which looked like they had traveled a thousand miles. She was thankful Craig bought her three pairs at Neels Gap. Nicki had not looked like a girl since her Mother's Memorial Service. It had been long since she wore $2,500 business suits and three-hundred-dollar hairdos. She could no longer cross the *I can remember* barrier. Her expensive briefcase now was a blade-assisted knife. She could pull the knife from her pocket, spring the blade open, and lock it faster than a street thug.

Craig, a type A, was generally patient with Nicki's speed and questions. They had become workmates. Craig had turned Nicki into a Naturalist. Her forest skills, while not excellent, were ok. For a girl with panic attacks just thinking of the forest, she accepted her circumstances. Her acceptance was conditional on Craig being in sight, even if she could not discern if he were a friend or foe.

On an overcast morning, Nicki was lagging Craig about a hundred yards. The path turned into rock walls and giant boulders thirty feet high. The blaze was in the middle of the boulder, directly in front of Nicki. With boulders, there are no well-worn paths. It didn't appear that the route went up. She approached the boulders to the right along a grassy way. Nicki couldn't see Craig, but she felt confident following the trail. After stepping out one hundred feet, the foliage became thick. She started to sweat, and she recoiled into a panic. Nicki sped up and kept moving forward, nervously looking for a blaze. She had walked out for twenty minutes without Craig, blazes, or path. She turned around, but the trail was not clear going back. The grass had a strange, unrecognizable bent. Turning around, she kept tight to the wall of rocks.

Nicki was only a cat's hair from a full-blown breakdown. She made sure her knife was in her pocket and slowly walked low. Nicki was not able to recognize if she had passed this way. The uncertainty flamed her anxiety. She passed a switchback but didn't remember using it on her way out. Then, up in the air, she heard some voices, men talking like they were in the trees. Nicki stepped into a small clearing, and Craig and two men were at the top of the boulders. He smiled and waved at Nicki. Wet with sweat, she lay face down over the boulder in mental exhaustion. The forest still oppressed her.

Nicki often lay outside her tent at night and looked at the stars. They were magnificent in clarity and brightness. She would shine her flashlight into the heavens, looking for her mom as Craig explained the constellations. She would use the low-beam light to study her mom's notes on other nights. It was silent in the woods at night, a quiet she had never heard in San Francisco. On some nights, the silence would change into a chorus. Tree crickets would start at the top of the trees with loud and deep screeches. Next, in the middle of the trees, the choir became surround sound as the high-pitched crickets started to sing, and then filling in the symphony were the frogs low to the ground. The three-dimensional sound would start small, build a loud frenzy, and then instantly stop, back to dead silence. Then it would start again in another wave of rising and falling volume and then back to silence.

After a long day of uphills and switchbacks at camp, they sat on logs facing each other. Craig reminded Nicki that she was still in hiding and that the trail provided plenty of time and space to get lost and allow The Prelate and his thugs to forget about her. But Craig would occasionally say," I think it is somebody more potent after you. I am not sure you are up to whatever you are supposed to accomplish."

On this night, Nicki froze at his words. She spun around and faced the opposite direction, her back to him. Heat rushed to her cheeks. She gazed down at her open backpack and saw her Greatest Salesman book's white and red cover.

Words rushed into her mind, along with an angry power. She stood straight up, turned to Ranger Craig, and took two decisive steps toward him as he sat on his log.

In a loud tenor voice and penetrating eyes, she broadcast, "I was not delivered into this world in defeat, nor does failure course in my blood." She took two more aggressive steps toward Craig, stunned by the outburst. She drew her knife, laid the blade's flat side on his chest, and said, "I am not a sheep waiting to be prodded by my shepherd. I am a lion, and I refuse to talk and walk and sleep with the sheep. I will persist until I succeed." Then she yelled again, "I will persist until I succeed. You got that, Ranger Craig?"

The camp fell back to silence, then Craig unfolded his three-foot-long trail map that showed they were only 1/3 of the way to

Harpers Ferry. Most people would be closer by now. Craig asked Nicki to increase their daily mileage. The terrain was not as rugged as the Rockies, and the weather should help pick up the pace. There would be an extra hour and ½ of daylight.

Nicki said, "I could pick up my pace. What happens at Harpers Ferry?"

"I don't know. My job is to deliver you by the first week of September."

"Really, you know more, don't you?"

"I know that it is my job to deliver you safely. That is all I know. It is going to be a nice day, Nicki. Let's shoot for twelve miles to Roan Mountain. We can do it. Are you ready?"

"Craig, are you for me or against me?"

"I am not sure."

After a hundred days, Nicki looked like Grizzly Adams and had the strength of two men. She carried her pack efficiently, and her steps were intense and prolonged. She could eat corn beef hash, deviled ham, and spam right out of the can. She could even take Craig's putdowns and bounce them back at him. Today, she even hummed an Elvis song, Return to Sender; she had heard it at the last general store, and it would not leave her head. She wasn't even sure who Elvis was, maybe her grandmother's favorite.

As Nicki picked up the pace, Craig was in a good mood. The Trail turned west just north of Spivey Gap and then slightly east to Roan Mountain. The days were long as late June approached, and they pushed toward their goal. Still enthusiastic, they found a campsite and celebrated their best day ever, 15 miles.

They quickly set up their tents. Now an expert, Nicki found a spot on a medium rise about forty feet wide, circled by a ravine. Craig was twenty feet directly across from her. There was a tree on the flat for stowing the food. An open space between them allowed room for a fire. Tonight was the big night they were going to fry some canned spam. Craig started the fire and placed the small frying pan on the coals, and in just a few minutes, the spam was a golden brown. They both agreed that it was a perfect finish to a perfect day. Craig was convinced Nicki had become more assertive. They decided they could regain some of the time they initially gave away.

They retired to their tents at about ten. Craig took care of the fire, tossed the food bag over the tree limb, and tied it off. Sometime in the middle of the night, Nicki heard a noise in the camp and the rustle of leaves. She thought it was big raindrops. Twenty minutes later, something heavy and oversized was in the camp. It was weighty and snorting next to her tent so loud she could feel it. A bear's hot breath, she thought. Her hands and head shook violently. She pressed down into the bottom of the tent. Monster claws swiped through her tent with speed and power, ripping it and causing it to collapse. Nicki and the tent fell back over the edge and into the ravine. The snorting turned into growling. The collapsed tent entangled Nicki as she slid down five feet. Nicki could hear the Bear run across the camp towards Craig's tent. Snorting and grunting, followed by noises like things thrown over the camp, pans, rocks, and leaves.

Craig shouted, "Run, Nicki," as he rattled cups together, his voice drifted off like he was disappearing into the distance. Nicki lay still in her collapsed tent. Things were happening so fast that she could not think clearly.

Thirty minutes later, dirty and wet, Nicki found a way out of her tent and crawled to the top of the gulley; peeking over the ravine's edge, the scattered fire embers revealed Craig's tent destroyed. A wrecked camp lay before her. Nicki whispered, "Craig, Craig." She received no reply. She stayed for another ten minutes and then crawled onto the flat. She looked in all directions, but no sign of Craig. They had never had any contact with a bear or seen one from a distance. She stood, walked to the other side of the flat space, and looked over the drop-off. She saw nothing. She shined her flashlight into the woods and called in a normal voice, "Craig."

No Reply.

She ran her hand over her head to see if she was bleeding. *Should I follow into the dark woods?* She thought. She shined the light in the trees to the left and the right, looking for anything revealing Craig. *What would Craig do?*

She could not hear any noises, no crickets or frogs. It was dead silent. Would the bear come back? Was Craig alive and needing help? What should she do? Lowering her head, she returned to the gulley, pulled the tent over her head, and lay still.

⤚

The Prelate's summons to Francis Vile's home disturbed him. He knew this day was coming and hoped he could deliver his promise. Believing this might be his last day, he felt slightly nauseous. His car pulled into the round driveway, and he looked out the window to see if anyone else was there. He clicked his fingernails. His driver opened the door and moved out slowly; as he headed for the steps, a boy of six or seven walked toward him and stared at him. The boy had a cat in his hand, held by the neck. The Prelate said, "Young man, let the cat go."

The boy smiled and squeezed the cat even harder. You could see the extra effort showing on the boy's face as it turned red, and the knuckles of his dirty hands turned white.

The Prelate hurried up the steps and into the foyer. He didn't have to wait. Francis Vile was waiting in the hall as always; she was radiant, the most beautiful woman in the world. She was not smiling. "Prelate, you have not made good on your promise. It has been two months since you told me you had her."

"Miss Vile, someone tipped her off, someone in our group."

"I understand you let my prized prisoners, Dr. Maker and Taylor Samms, escape."

"You are correct, mistress." She swirled around the room in anger. Like a tail, the train of her dress knocked over the furniture. Stopping after a full circle, she glared a powerful stare at the Prelate, who held his arms up over his face.

"How do you intend to solve our problem, Prelate? I need Nicki

Boaz dead before the election and to see her face-to-face before she dies. I would kill you today, but I will not have a leader for my election victory."

"I have every agency looking for her. She disappeared into thin air, protected by a powerful underground group," the Prelate cowered.

"You have sixty days. I want Maker and Samms arrested and in a real prison. Start executing Nicki Boaz's family in public until she shows herself. Do you hear me?" She screamed at The Prelate with such force he could feel the air blow by. I want their Church defiled. I command the statues and altars torn down and windows destroyed. Strip it of all reference to their God. Complete this a week before the election. We will rename it the Church of Reason, and after the election, you will set me up as the Supreme Leader and my throne shall be in their God's Church. See to it, Prelate." She put her arm around the dirty little boy standing to her right, "Or you will be like this cat. And get rid of that, Thomas White. He irritates me."

"Yes, mistress."

⌇

At first light, Nicki heard leaves rustle in the camp. She inched up to the ledge and peered over the leaves on the ground. Frank, a through hiker they met in passing four days ago, shuffled into the camp. Craig felt uncomfortable with him because he asked unusual questions about them. He looked around the camp, moving the trash with his hiking pole. Nicki had no choice. She needed help. She climbed the small ledge and walked humped over and slowly toward the hiker.

He was surprised to see Nicki. "Miss, are you okay?"

Panicked, she said, "No, I am not ok. My friend Craig is missing. I fear being killed by a bear."

"Are you sure he is dead?"

"No, I am not sure. I need help."

He took off his backpack, bent forward, laid it on the ground, and in slow motion, he pulled a revolver out of the waistband of his pants and pointed it at Nicki's head."

Before he could say a word, Nicki heard a dull bell ringing sound. Frank's eyes rolled back in his head, and he fell forward face first. Standing behind him was Howard Youngblood, holding a folding camp shovel. With a baseball-like swing, he had smashed the man's head with the flat side of the shovel.

Nicki ran and threw herself around Howard Youngblood.

Howard, surprised, had immediately noticed the camp. He calmed Nicki while he looked around. Nicki could not stop talking at twice the average speed and level. Howard walked to the woods on the other side of Craig's tent and saw blood on the broken bushes. It did not look good.

"Nicki," he said in his proper voice, "how did all these candy bars get here?" She looked around, and there were twenty small Snickers bars. Some sealed, some opened. They were all around Craig's tent. Howard looked over at Nicki's tent, which was the same scene.

Nicki hysterically yelled, "We didn't have any candy bars. I swear we didn't."

"Did you see anyone else on the trail yesterday," Howard asked. "No."

Nicki cried in an earsplitting scream, "Craig is dead."

Howard embraced her. Calming her down, he said, "It was a bear. Craig has much experience, and nobody would have a better chance than him. Give me ten minutes to follow the Trail."

"No, don't leave me. What if this guy wakes up?"

"I will tie him, but he may never wake up."

"It wouldn't be good if we both startled a bear with its capture. Just wait here."

Nicki was shaking and crying as Howard was gone longer than ten minutes. "I couldn't find anything. But I also could not find much blood or confirmation the bear had torn any flesh."

Nicki, we must get out of here and call the police. "All these candy bars came from somewhere for some reason. I also think this Frank may not be by himself."

"Howard, I cannot get involved with the police." With the least amount of detail, she described her situation.

Nicki wobbled as she spilled her story. She thought *Howard may have been involved. Would he kill me, too? Was he in cahoots with the man with the gun?*

CHAPTER 14

Our primary obligation is not to mistake slogans for solutions.
Edward R. Murrow

Howard was severe and in command, "Get your pack, and let's go."

"Howard, I cannot go with you."

Howard sat on a rock and pulled down his right sock to reveal a tattoo outside his ankle. Two Bs back-to-back with a cross through the Bs. "Craig was a brother."

Nicki's head fell in relief.

"Let's go."

Nicki and Howard headed north past Roan Mountain to the three Bald Mountains. At the top of Grassy Bald, Nicki could see Jane Bald and Round Bald off two and a half miles in the distance. The view reminded her of her life, up and down, up and down, up and down. She has had an upward struggle for the last year, losing her mom, her Fiancée, and her brother betraying her. Her dad was hiding, and a bear killed her friend Craig because of her. Nicki thought, *my life is as far from a San Francisco lawyer as possible.* On the rocky path, she walked flat-footed with her arms hanging down. Her feet would slide on the winding downhills. She wanted some joy, some resolution, some beauty in her life. At the top of Jane Bald, Howard clutched her gently by the arm and said, "Nicki, stop and raise your head. In your entire life, you may never come his way again. I know things are tough, but you are standing at one of the country's most beautiful spots. Look in every direction and see the largeness of this place. It's magnificent. Feel the cool breeze blow against your face as the warm sun fills you with life. You can see how the small path travels up and down and meanders around. You have been on this trail for a while, and over that last mountain will be your finish; savor your last steps and let go of your distress. There is beauty in every journey."

Still dazed, Nicki thought, *what an unusual speech for a bad day*—a day when a man died for her. But the Balds provided the most expansive views in the hiking world. Nicki could see the hills and the valleys for miles. The property owned and farmed in the valleys was carved out in perfect color and squares, like a brushstroke of green in a painting. She saw the path flowing down the mountain, winding like a squiggly line. She continued her line of sight up the next mountain to the bald. She became aware that she had seen this view in hundreds of advertisements. As Howard had said, it was beyond breathtaking. They headed down the mountain to Round Bald, then to Carvers Gap. They could see the parking lot a half-mile away from the height of halfway down the Bald. Howard told Nicki he had to get back to look for Craig and that she should head down to the parking lot and stand in front of the small restroom slightly to the right. Howard sent a message on his GPS. He said, "Someone would be there to pick you up. I am sending you to a retreat thirty miles away. The driver will ask for you by name. I will call some of the boys and go back into the woods to take care of your gun-toting friend and see what we can find of Craig. It will be ok, Nicki. When you get there, ask for Jobi Jones."

"Nicki was exhausted, confused, and frightened. All she could do was nod her head. She politely offered her goodbye to the Appalachian Trail, once a monster to her soul, now a teacher and friend.

She passed through a hundred yards of the small forest canopy. Sitting on a rock crying was a young lady holding her ankle and a three-year-old child. Nicki stopped and asked whether she was all right.

The young lady said her husband had already gone down the mountain with their eighteen-month-old son, and she twisted her ankle, stepping over a rock. She couldn't get herself and her daughter down because of the pain. The three-year-old had started to cry.

Nicki thought *this was not my problem. I am in a hurry.* She bent down and touched the lady's ankle. It was swollen twice the average size. Nicki gave the lady one of her hiking poles, pulled her up, and swung the three-year-old onto her hip. Exhibiting the strength of a mountain man, she headed down the last mile of the hill with the lady and the child attached.

The three disabled women made it down the hill. Nicki carried them across the road on the border of North Carolina and Tennessee. The hurt lady called out to her husband, resting in the back of his truck bed. The lady and her husband thanked Nicki profusely. She was wet from sweat inside her clothes, and she walked humped over as she found the restroom to the right. The parking lot was full and overflowing. She looked with trepidation at every car and every person that passed.

A dented and dirty white dually pickup truck pulled next to the bathroom, then back in front of Nicki. A tall lady exited the truck with it still running and held out her hand. "I am Sherry, and you must be Nicki?"

Nicki whispered, "Yes."

Sherry was sixty or so and looked forty, long, lean, with shiny dark hair down to her waist. She said, wearing jeans, boots, and a red flannel shirt, " Hop in, and we will get on our way. Don't mind the hay. It is for the horses."

Nicki tossed her bag in the back and noticed a Cowgirl Up decal on Sherry's back window.

"Are you a cowgirl?"

"Kind of. I have five horses. All my daughters and granddaughter's ride."

"Where are you taking me?"

"Little Switzerland."

"Really?"

"Yes, it might seem like a silly name for a place in North Carolina, but you will love it. It was a resort years ago, but a group bought it, and it is more like a private retreat used for meetings and conferences. Off the beaten path, most tourists would never encounter. An invitation is necessary to stay. It has one of the most beautiful evening views, a panorama of the mountains over a firepit."

"Am I invited? Will they know me?"

"I am sure. Howard would not send you without an introduction. Did he tell you to see Jobi?"

"Yes, Jobi Jones. Who is Howard anyway?"

"Just an old friend who loves hiking."

In twenty minutes, they were driving under an old stone overpass. The backdrop was moist and dark green foliage with contrasting vines and wildflowers.

After the underpass, Shery stopped. They faced two roads. Sherry said, "You can take either road to the left or the right. If you ever need to get out of here."

"The road went straight up, hugging a rock mountain wall. Nicki could feel the road circle in the sky as they headed up like a ride at Disney. They passed several old, closed lodges and a few vacation homes. As the circle continued, Sherry took a sharp right and left, and in front of them was the Switzerland Inn, old but lovely. The hotel buildings and a long line of low, neatly spaced shop buildings sat across the parking lot from the lodge.

Sherry drove under the overhang and said, "Here you are, Nicki. I will take you in and introduce you to Jobi Jones."

"Nicki ambled and bent over, and her pack was suddenly too heavy. She slid it off her back and into her right hand.

They entered through the wooden double doors, and to the right was a check-in desk. Sherry said, "Susan, is Jobi around?"

"I haven't seen her in a while."

"This is Nicki. Howard sent her."

Susan thought Nicki looked like she had been in a car accident and said, "Sit on the couch. I will find Jobi. You can leave her with me, Sherry."

"You look tired. Come with me," Susan carried Nicki's bag for her. Walking across the large lobby, then down a long hall to a room on the right. Susan opened the door, tossed Nicki's bag on the bed, and opened the curtains to allow sunshine to light up the room. "Take a load off, and I will tell Jobi you are here. After your rest, come to the front desk."

Nicki lay across the bed in her dirty, smelly clothes. Still fresh from sleeping in the compost of the wet mountain leaves. Her brain rushed, anticipating a bear eating her or expecting a kidnapper to kill her. Oh, how she longed for Craig to come walking over the ledge. What had happened was not a dream.

Nicki woke up to the daylight of an early July morning, still spring enough for chilly mornings yet sufficient summer for warm days. She walked across the room to the door that led to a small balcony. A mountain landscape lay before her. It was not unlike the views of sitting on a mountain ledge at dawn, but today, she could sit in a chair.

Nicki took a shower and put on her last clean hiking pants. She was exhausted but faithful to put her knife and flashlight in her pocket. She sat on the bed and tried to set things in order. It was months ago when she left Cumberland Island in the morning and slept in a shelter on Blood Mountain by evening. She gathered her thoughts enough to remember Susan at the desk.

"Good morning, Susan."

"Hi Nicki, did you enjoy your hibernation?"

"Pardon me."

"It has been two days since you arrived," Susan smiled slightly.

"Really, oh, I am not very stable. I have a hard time remembering everything that happened. I will find a cup of coffee and gather my thoughts." She went to the Keurig machine, brewed a cup, and walked out the side door to the firepit and mountain view. Sitting in a rocking chair, she started a repetitive motion and a low humming to match the rocker's cadence.

"Hi Nicki, how are you? I am Jobi Jones."

Nicki looked through her blurry eyes to see a short lady with beautiful long black hair and the most inviting smile ever worn by a human. Nicki's shoulders relaxed; she felt safe. "Hi, Jobi."

"What do you say we talk over breakfast? I know you haven't eaten in two days." Jobi offered out her hand and pulled her up. They turned to walk to the restaurant, and Nicki jerked back and stood straight up like she had received an electrical shock. Nicki perked up and smiled as she asked, "Who are those men shaking hands in front of the restaurant? One looks like Todd Miller."

Before Nicki could move, the men turned and walked away. Nicki started yelling, "Todd, Todd, it's Nicki, Todd." But the man turned and walked to the parking lot. Nicki could not run after them.

"You were right. That was Todd Miller."

"He arrived the same morning you did. He has been in meetings but checked out this morning."

Nicki thought, *Todd at the Switzerland Inn, I must still be out of it.* Nicki's posture plunged. She did not have the energy to walk up the slight incline to the restaurant. Jobi helped her to the table.

The restaurant was beautiful, having a full view of the mountains. Jobi ordered her a special. The coffee slowly revved Nicki's engine. "What could Todd be doing here?"

Jobi said, "He stops by from time to time."

"Really, Nicki almost shouted. How does he get around so much? What is with him?"

"Let's talk about you for a minute," Jobi said with her big smile and comforting voice. "Howard and the boys found Craig alive. He fought off the bear only after being bitten several times on the legs. The bear dragged him almost a quarter of a mile. It is quite a story. I knew you would feel better knowing he was alive. He is in a Hospital in Asheville. God only knows how he fought off that bear. He must be one hard-hitting guy."

Nicki smiled a confident smile and said, "he is."

"I have some things to do today. I will meet you tomorrow for breakfast and spend the morning together. We can walk around the property, meet some guests, and enjoy the shops across the street. I live up the road about a third of a mile. There are 46 full-time residents in Little Switzerland. Susan knows how to get me if you need me. She can get your clothes washed and any health-related products." Jobi stood and said, "Later in the week, we will turn you back into a girl," She ran her hands through Nicki's nasty hair.

Nicki was happy Craig was alive, but she couldn't show it.

She thought *forty-six people were four times the population of Cumberland Island. I guess the munchkins will show up soon. You are not in San Francisco anymore, Nicki. The house did fall on the wicked witch, but there is no yellow brick road, only dirt paths and mountain trails. I need a lion, a scarecrow, and a tin man.* She did crack a small smile at her outrageous thoughts.

Nicki headed back to her room but became distracted by the grounds. The well-cared-for landscaping was enticing. Flowers were neatly in pots, and the scent of roses flowed gently in the mountain breeze. Some outbuildings that had once been hotel rooms were mini-conference centers with small groups moving in and out. The property's backyard ran mildly down to a fifty-foot-wide fire pit. Maximizing the experience were a dozen rocking chairs. Nicki heard you had to fight for a chair after dinner because the crowd could not get enough of the view. The moonlight enveloping the mountains with cool white light was inspiring. The grass was manicured and dark green. The people seemed to be in positive moods, smiling, giving hugs, and walking close to each other. It felt friendly.

Nicki walked up to the shops close to the main building. Crossing the parking lot, she saw a line of twenty-five low-slung Ferraris. *Wow, she was thinking, what's going on here?* As she watched a group of older men and younger ladies enter the cars, they wore leather jackets with Ferrari clubs on the back. She thought they must drive the parkway as fast as they could. The shops were not touristy but elegant and had great value and beautiful items. Each shop had a specialty, including an ice cream shop. Nicki had no cash and was under strict orders never to use her debit cards. One swipe of her card and the government would be on her in a minute. Continuing her stroll, she walked up the peaceful road, and on the left were three A-Frame cabins, and across the street on a slight hill, a red clapboard Church. On Sunday morning, Nicki could visualize all forty-six church members singing the great hymns and praying. Nicki was in a small slice of heaven, with rooms with beds, showers, people, and a restaurant. She went back to bed.

⌒

Ninety-five miles northwest of Atlanta, twelve men converged on a remote meeting lodge in the North Georgia Woods. Bobby and Robert Boaz had been lost twice because of GPS's inability to work in this isolated part of the country. The dirt road was long but beautiful. On the left was a waterwheel mill from an 1800s painting. The forest colors were light green, and the sun filtered through the trees to multiply the bright golden rays. Bobby inched down Col. Hough Rd. However, he was supposed to be on Baer Gap Rd. He was lost and had to turn around twice. Bobby needed help deciphering the roads' names or their direction. He decided to continue the long dirt road. They were ready to give up again when they saw the lodge on the left. While Bobby found the front office, Robert called the other attendees to give accurate directions.

The large wooden building was well-maintained. The lodge was famous for its secure location and restaurant. The rooms were small, with no TV or telephones.

Bobby called the meeting to order after the other attendees arrived late afternoon. The meeting room was in an outer parcel building with two large rooms with food and drinks. The twenty-foot folding glass doors at the front were open to the beautiful fall weather. Bobby and Robert Boaz and five Presidents of the largest United States Corporations were in the room. Taylor Samms, Bernie Maker, and the two leaders of Billy's Boys were also in attendance. Charlie and Beth Tender joined via a video call from Connecticut. They sat around a round table, looking like they had just come to a funeral.

Bobby Boaz opened the meeting with a warning," Four months, gentleman, it does not look good, only four months before the election. Let's go around the room and get a fixed position on our plans."

Bob Boaz showed a video clip of his headquarters in San Francisco, where it looked like everyone was packing for a move. He talked about Tim Boaz's work in building a new plant in South America. He reported in a depressed tone their decision to burn down the plants and headquarters before they left.

The Captains of Industry talked about their progress in moving their business out of the United States. They did an extensive whiteboard drawing of how to move billions of dollars of cash out of the country. Three of the men were vehemently opposed to moving before the election. Their hope in the nation was strong, and they believed the people of the United States would stand up and vote. Dr. Maker discussed the Churches' total collapse and how the deep sense of the end depressed the country's congregations. Taylor Samms discussed the trade situation, focusing on New York and Los Angeles. Hundreds of trading vessels were sitting offshore, awaiting some sign of trust in the United States. No foreign country would trade where there was no transactional protection by law. The United States' credit was no good.

Along with its monetary problems, it had stopped producing its food and depended on importing commodities and staples. The environmentalists and the taxing authorities had put all the big farms out of business. The mining and production rights to ferrous metals used for electronics, defense, and manufacturing had been sold to foreign countries. There were only a few manufacturers of consumer goods owned by individuals. Robert Boaz reported that the government had to lay off people. The state governments were helpless as the Federal Government had stopped letting them collect taxes for themselves. Things had gotten so bad that you either worked for the government or didn't work. The government was teetering, ready to fall. Things were hopeless, and people walked around with their mouths open in horror. The final blow would come in a hundred and twenty days when Prelate Malum would be elected President of the United States. The net effect would be that the country would bow down and worship Francis Vile. The nation's Pastors called her the beast.

The meeting took a downturn as each man discussed the outlook for their business and the government's intent to nationalize them. Several men were deeply concerned about the people who once were full of the American Dream. The government had exported freedom, just like manufacturing. Hope was not a topic of discussion. Enslaved people are what they had become: enslaved people in this great country of plenty, serfs in their land. Elites were prodding the people like workers on cotton plantations. The population growth had come to a standstill. People were dying faster than children could be born. Abortion had become compulsory for all but the chosen. In the name of goodness, children born to people experiencing poverty were swept off to government schools for indoctrination. The men at the table all but wept. A godless government raped their country. The men at the table had acquired wealth from hard work, visionary thinking, and the flood of help from once-great America. Collectively, they owned a seventh of the world's corporate wealth. The government saw them as evil and talked about their business activities as robbing low-income people. The government hated these few men's power and ability to get things done. The founders of these companies were determined not to bow to the government cronies.

But today, things looked unbearable.

After the room shared the bad news, the boys' leaders turned the floor over. Joe Frank showed an overhead of his ten thousand men and women around the country. Todd Miller discussed leadership levels and their success in informing influential groups. Beth and Charlie discussed how Todd's organization had provided an excellent service to their underground movement. There were strongly dedicated cells with skills and expertise in every city and metro area. He describes some of their work secretly moving people around the country.

Joe stood up confidently and said, "We can reach the people and get things done. The people have the heart for the right things."

One of the Corporate leaders said, "We would not have a chance. The government controls all the communication, TV, internet, and newspaper."

Joe said again, "We can touch the people."

"There is no way in our limited time," said another leader.

Joe repeated, "We can influence the people."

"How can twelve men change the world in such a short time?" one said in a deep voice.

"Todd said, "I believe there is a precedent for twelve men changing the world."

Joe said, "Bobby, how did you sell it when you invented your solar equipment?"

Bobby beamed, "No business or bank would give me a second look; I went door to door?"

"How did it work?"

"Joe, it worked but was not easy. I got my message out, which was my message, not some advertising agency. My faith in my product was the key."

"With the men in this room and Todd's organization, we can get the message out. It will be intense, our last chance to cast a vote. We can break it down. Dr. Maker can lead the religious side of the movement; Joe can work with the states to take back their power from the Central government. Taylor can work with trade organizations to secure our trading abilities. The five of you can reach the people in your organizations and geographic areas. The message must be truthful and intent. Todd and his men can move you and your message throughout the country, organizing and multiplying our communication. The journalist will be ready to help. The government removed their freedom of speech, and they are dying to create a new message. It is an information cascade waiting to be ignited.

The men in the room looked at each other with encouraging faces. Joe stood and said, "No guns or swords are needed. The people already possessed the power. The founding fathers prepared our country for this time and set things up so the people could always change Representatives with their votes. The people have been lied to about the power the founding Fathers had given them."

The men sitting at the table looked more expressive; their shoulders were broader, and their chins were squared off. Plan A had been to give up and leave the country. Now, Plan B has taken on a life of its own. The energy called on was the power of the people. "The power of a small change could be enormous," Todd Miller said.

Joe suggested a vote. Dr. Maker kneeled and prayed. His prayer was as powerful as any Psalm, his words reaching the souls of the men in the room. He prayed repentance for our evil deeds and said he was sorry for our self-interest. He teared up for our spitting in God's face with our immortality. Moaning a high moan and bellowing for God's help, as Jesus did, he cried out three times, recognizing God's power as omniscient. He finished in a low, loving voice, "Your will be done, and Lord, we twelve are willing. "After the prayer, the room remained soundless. In the silence, something had penetrated the room. You couldn't see or touch it, but it moved around all the men.

Bobby Boaz asked confidently," Is there any reason for a vote?" All twelve men formed a circle and put their arms around each other.

Todd and Joe spent the rest of the days meeting and creating the plan with the men. The Boys would be the group that moved people, materials, and messages around the country. They were powerful and organized for a group so far underground.

The organization's meetings lasted three days. The mighty men were exhausted, but they were excited. There would be no giving up, giving in, or walking away.

The men gave big, manly hugs at the dawn of the third day. The men who arrived three days ago were defeated. A positive strength became a common brotherhood at the end of those days. The cars pulled up the steep driveway and turned to Bear Gap Road; lite dust kicked up behind each vehicle. Like Lazarus's death, it was evident that the world was about to erupt into chaos.

CHAPTER 15

If you have a place at the table, use it.

Mae Jemison

Nicki slept until seven. Rising slowly, she gazed at the mountains, and to her surprise, she craved to be on the trail, a thought that was hard to believe for a girl terrified of the woods. She took a shower and, with scraggly wet hair, proceeded to the restaurant for breakfast. Enthusiastic groups were talking and moving around in pods of five and ten. It was like high school, and it carried excitement and enthusiasm. Nicki thought *It was great to be around people.*

Nicki looked around the three-room divided restaurant for Jobi Jones but didn't see her. Finding a table near the glass window with a scenic view, she ordered eggs benedict, "Oh yes," she smiled as she drank her orange juice and coffee. After three days of rest, Nicki was alert, robust, and excited to be in civilization. Eating her breakfast as fast as possible, Jobi Jones pulled up a chair and said, "Good morning, Nicki; how are you today?"

"I am physically good but uncertain where and why I am here. But truthfully, I have felt this way for a year."

Jobi said with a smile, "I would like to make a schedule for you."

"What do you mean schedule?"

"This is not only a retreat but an educational facility."

"What is it I need to learn?"

"Well, Nicki, this is not a college. It is an educational facility at a higher level."

"I am confused. I have a law degree. Isn't that high enough?"

"Yes, Nicki, that is particularly good, but there is more. Let's eat, and we will go for a walk. You are going to find this a prodigious place."

After the delicious breakfast, they walked out to take in an overview of the mountains. A blue haze floated over and through the peaks. "Are you in charge of me?" Nicki said to Jobi.

"That is a profound question," Jobi laughed.

"Let's sit in the rocking chairs. Tell me your story, Nicki."

Nicki was not yet sure of Jobi, but she did feel as if Jobi was sure of her. All these people had some connection, and she knew Todd. Really, how could she know Todd?

Nicki started slowly talking about her kidnapping in high school and her relationship with her mom. Then, her slow start took off like water at a broken dam. They rocked, and Jobi nodded. The early morning she turned into the late afternoon. Nicki's story slowed as she talked about her mom's death and unexpected journey. "This expedition has been uncertain at every step, but I keep meeting these eccentric people who have some affection for me. The only thing that saved me was how quickly last year transpired. It is just like now, as I settled with Craig and trusted him to take me to Harpers Ferry, now I am here."

Jobi never said a word. She just smiled.

Nicki said, "On top of all this, I have a file folder of my mom's. It appears to be her notes for an important speech she will make in the fall of this year. I cannot decipher her hen scratching or make sense of it, but I keep at it. I am committed to continuing her work. By the way, do you know what a DUTO is?"

Nicki talked from morning until four-thirty in the afternoon. Jobi said, "I am sure there is somebody here who can help you make sense of your mom's notes. But next on your schedule is some new clothes. After breakfast, we will go to the shops and get you some off-the-trail clothes. It is dinner time for me, and I must return home. I will see you in the morning. Feel free to enjoy the resort and meet some of the people."

"Jobi, what am I doing here, and where do I go from here?"

Jobi smiled, "To dinner."

"Very funny," Nicki relaxed. Jobi was purposeful but measured in her approach to Nicki. Never in a rush or controlling, just insightful.

Nicki returned to the restaurant, the only other place she had been that day. Looking over the menu, she decided on a hamburger, French fries, and a coke, a meal she had dreamed of on the trail. Thinking about her day at Switzerland Inn, Nicki laughed to herself. She had talked all day and poured out her life story and more. Jobi had not said a word. Nicki's day-long purging felt therapeutic. She felt open to the next and the new.

After dinner, Nicki went to her room and sat on the balcony, receiving the full moon's light. The Valley lights interested her as she tried to visualize the lights in things like houses, stores, and roads. It was beautiful. Nicki was always on guard on the trail, watching and waiting for some danger. She liked the fact that she could dream instead of responding. She drifted into a deep sleep, the mountain air her drug of choice.

~

The week of July 4th, Robert Boaz had returned to San Francisco with the love of his life, Tracey, now six years old. His Mom's sister, Aunt Maggie, kept her in Plentywood, Montana, at the Boaz family home. During the week, he included some work but mostly fun for Robert and Tracey. After a morning at the office, Robert and Tracey took off for Muir Woods to walk in the big Red Woods. Tracey became a Junior Ranger as soon as they entered the National Park. The crowds were thick because of the holiday. Just off the crowded main path, Robert and Tracy took a trail that eased up the mountain. Twenty minutes into their hike, Robert heard noises in the leaves to his left rear in the quietness of the climb. He stopped and looked, thinking this trail was probably full of hikers. Fifteen minutes later, Robert heard the rustling again, but much closer. He stopped and looked around. The feeling in his gut told Robert to turn around. He escorted Tracey down the mountain at a faster rate. The noise followed them. Down at the main trail, the path was overflowing with people. Robert picked up Tracey and hurried to the car.

Opening Tracey's back door and leaning in to buckle her seat belt, he felt a violent thud on his back and fire in his upper shoulder. He fell a short distance to his knees. It felt like a baseball bat. Staggered, he pushed up, slammed Tracey's car door, and rolled to the passenger door just in time to miss a two-handed blow that dented the car's roof. The assailant took another swing and caught Robert in the kidney, knocking him down. He brought a final swing to his head while Robert was on the ground, a glancing blow that put him out. The bat-swinging man rolled him into the ditch in front of the cars, throwing the bat in after him. With his elbows on Robert's roof, he called his boss and reported Robert's death. He asked about the girl, and his superior told him to leave her. The assailant sped off in his car. Robert rolled over in the ditch and heaved himself into the sand parking lot.

Blood poured out of his head and mixed with the dirt in his mouth. He made it to Tracey. He quickly exited the parking lot despite a tremendous headache and blurry vision. His goal was to get back to San Francisco. He headed for the Redwood Highway and sped toward the Golden Gate Bridge. On top of the bridge, calmer and with better vision, he decided to head home to Plentywood, Montana, and not to stop at home or the office. Robert called his grandfather and explained the situation. Jon Marie listened carefully and told Robert he would meet him in Plenty Wood. Robert's Grandfather called Todd Miller and had one of the boys follow Robert's car. Robert needed to stay dead. He also needed to pray for peace as he was angry that somebody would want to hurt his daughter. He had come too far for that.

Bobby Boaz landed in San Francisco at 4:00 PM. He rented a mid-sized car and headed toward his corporate office downtown. He expected to catch up with Robert and Tracey just outside the airport. He waited his turn at the four-way stop outside the rental garage, inching into the intersection. Once he had committed to moving through the intersection, he heard screeching tires, and he glanced to see a large Ford pickup barreling in on him. The truck t-boned him. The truck had approached the intersection at a high rate of speed, and the screeching was not of stopping but the acceleration. It was a perfect terrorist attack on the driver's side door. The truck pushed Bobby's mid-sized car sixty feet across the road and spun it up on the sidewalk, where it flipped over. Smoke poured from the totaled vehicle. From a pedestrian point of view, there was no hope for the driver.

The Prelate made sure the news traveled quickly to Francis Vile. Proud of himself, he had kept his promises. Nicki Boaz's family was dead.

⸻

In the peace of the mountain retreat, July passed rapidly. Nicki acquired new skills from the people teaching at the Switzerland Inn. Her friendship with Jobi had become a great blessing. Although Nicki worked for part of her room and board, part of her stay was a scholarship. Her favorite place of sanctuary was the rocking chairs overlooking the mountain range and the valley below. The fifty-foot-long fire pit created a magical stage. She hated that she used the word magic, believing this place was like sitting in God's hand.

Jobi had remade the mountain girl. New hairstyles and clothes made Nicki a lady again, not quite as stiff as a San Francisco lady but a radiant, confident, and influential one. Jobi would mentor Nicki in faith and teach her like Connie. Jobi taught her to look back at her life and see God in the events, no matter how painful. Jobi was the real deal. She spoke from some fundamental understanding or experience.

Jobi finished a short lesson on fear, explaining that you must be afraid before courage can exist. Then Jobi turned her conversation to Todd Miller out of the blue. Todd left this for you a month ago. She handed a little box to Nicki.

"What do you think it is? Everywhere I go, Todd shows up and leaves me a little gift. It is not much, mostly a little trinket."

"What do you do with them?"

"I save them."

"You know, Nicki, a gift is how we build a relationship with somebody we love. It is a way to move to the next level. Todd must love you."

Nicki rolled her eyes, "I saw Todd on TV the other night at some event in Washington, and he had a beautiful, I mean stunning blonde on his shoulder. She was looking at him with desiring eyes. Oh no, he doesn't love me. He always, and I repeat, always leaves me. I hate him for that."

"Nicki, he shows up every place that you go. He saves you most of the time and then leaves a love token. He does love you."

"I wish that were the case, but he has never said he loved me."

"I think he has."

August 1st arrived in the full blast of the end of summer. Nicki had worked in the restaurant, pulled linens, and helped in one of the shops. After dinner, she headed to her rocking chair. Nicki was tired and thought deeply about her out-of-control life over the last year. Nicki chuckled, realizing she focused on herself a lot, even thinking of herself as selfish. Everything was so out of her comfort zone. Getting a grasp of all that transpired from her mom's memorial service to the moment was inconceivable. She felt purpose in her soul but couldn't intelligently define that purpose, and she was tired of thinking about it. She could only exist in the now.

A deep, soothing voice from behind, "Mind if I sit next to you? I am Peter Thornton from New York."

The man was older, wearing a London fog jacket, blue button-down shirt, khaki Dockers, and boat shoes. He talked in a firm but wise manner.

"Sure, be my guest. I am Nicki Boaz."

Peter said, "This is a view beyond compare. You are Carrie Marie's daughter, aren't you?"

"How would you know that?"

"I am a friend of your mother's. I used to read her Bible stories."

"What? My mother is dead."

Peter grinned, "Actually, your mother asked the same questions you do."

"What do you mean."

"Your Mother wanted to know what to do."

"Did you tell her?"

"No"

"I did help her reflect on her current reality and share a few stories with her."

"Did she get it?"

"Your Mother was smart and determined, and yes, she did get it, and even more importantly, she acted on it."

"Mind if I share a story with you?"

Once upon a time, there was a war between two countries. I will call them the good and bad guys for ease of storytelling. A man of God had the power to understand the evil guys' plan, like eavesdropping from a mile away. He would hear about it whenever they planned to attack and inform the good King. The bad guys were tired of getting defeated, and the Bad King called his officers together to ferret out the traitor in his mist. They said, "It is not us, oh King, but God's Prophet. He tells the good King everything.

The evil King was upset and got word that the Prophet was in a city not far away with his assistant. One night, the wicked King secretly sent a massive army with chariots, horses, and troops to seize him. The formidable army covered every inch of the hills overlooking the town. The sight was frightening. Not a ray of sunshine passed between the warriors' shoulders.

The Prophet's assistant woke up first the following day and looked outside the city. To his horror, he saw troops, horses, and chariots.

Terrified, he cried, "Master, what will we do now?

"Don't be afraid!" The Prophet told him calmly, "For there are more on our side than theirs." Then the Prophet prayed, "Oh Lord, open my servant's eyes and let him see!" The Lord opened his assistant eyes. He saw ten thousand angelic war horses and chariots of fire on the hillside surrounding the city and an orange glow filling the horizon.

"Great story but long, Mr. Thornton, a Bible story, I assume? What does that have to do with me?"

"A story for a future time. I am here for a few more days. I wonder if there is anything I might do for you?"

"Like what?"

"I understand that you have some files you got from your mother's office and might need help to put them in order and define her purpose."

"How did you hear that."

"Your Mother and I did the same thing years ago in New York. We found clarity in her work. You can check me out with Jobi or even your dad."

"Maybe I will."

"Let me finish the story. The bad King's army advanced toward the city, and the Prophet prayed, Oh, Lord, make them blind," And the Lord did. The Prophet walked out to meet them and said, "You are going the wrong way. Follow me, and I will show you the way." He led them into the headquarters of the good King.

"Really, Mr. Thornton, that sounds like a fairy tale.'

He continued with an amazingly confident smile, the kind you see on a person when they know the truth, "The prophet prayed and had the Lord open their eyes."

They saw that they were in the stronghold of their enemy. "The good King shouted, "Prophet, should I kill them?"

The Prophet replied, "Of course not. Give them some food and send them home."

The good King made a feast and sent them away, never hearing or seeing them again.

"What do you want me to do with that story, Mr. Thornton? I am not at war, and I don't have an army, and I can pray all day long, and nothing happens. Plus, I would have killed the bad guys." She showed him her switchblade.

Nicki spent time with the sojourners in August, learning in informal groups. As the weeks passed, she transformed into a teacher. Teaching what she had learned on her Island and paradise, she transferred wisdom from her friends Dr. Maker, Taylor Samms, and Connie. Unknown to herself, she absorbed understanding from her friends and valuable information others needed. She was shocked at her knowledge. Her new friend Peter Thornton added a how-to element to her education.

⌐

Todd Miller and Joe Frank transferred Taylor Samms and Dr. Bernie Maker around the country to make disciples of men, businesses, and local governments. The people were anxious for freedom and excited to return to the country's original blueprints. The people were equipped and informed. They understood that, for maybe the last time, they held power, not the National Government. They were ready for action but realized that the government held strong authority over the citizens. It was a headwind for Taylor, Dr. Maker, and the Boys. The people would have to bite the hand that feeds them, an act of faith at the highest level. They ask people to repent and pray. They encourage the population to pass the word that the founding Fathers gave them a way out. The people could replace anyone who didn't represent their needs. Crisscrossing the country, Taylor and Dr. Maker stirred the people's hearts. The Chairmen of the largest companies worked to set the stage for the economy's comeback. They were champions of capitalism at their best, ready to get the wheels turning again. Beth and Charlie worked to move freedom fighters to safety. They used their considerable influence on the Congressional members, sharing the truth of all that had happened before their eyes.

The encouraging word among the helpless and hopeless was growing with potency. Expectations reverberated from the underground.

Todd Miller arrived at the San Francisco hospital within the same hour as his friend Bobby Boaz. Along with several of the boys, they quietly stole Bobby Boaz out of the ICU facility. They returned to Plentywood, Montana, in a private ambulance with an EMT on board.

The sun had difficulty rising above the gray skies, consistently covering the country. Still, there was hope internalizing like a cadence of beating drums. You could see people join in step with the expectation of a new life.

Todd, Dr. Maker, Taylor Samms, Joe Frank, and the boys headed east toward Washington, D.C., with a message and a plan.

～

Late summer found Nicki still unable to discover a speech hidden in her mom's notes. Nicki desperately recruited Peter Thornton's advice on deciphering her mom's notes. He had an uncanny connection with her mother and was a big help in putting things in perspective. Peter helped her pen an outline for the speech her mother might have made. He could interpret many of the scribbles in her mom's notes. But Peter left Nicki with the mystery to solve on her own. Peter implied that her mom's words would have to become her words. Her delivery would have to be the best speech of her life and powerful enough to stop the country in its tracks. Peter was able to decipher the clue to uncover a piece of hidden information that would clarify things and lead back to freedom. *Her mom described the location as being in the Sully on the Hill.* Nicki didn't know what she was looking for: a book, a paper, or a recording. They decided that her mom leaving a blank beside the #1 on the list of five essential people was also a clue. Peter had suggested that the names listed as numbers 2,3,4 and 5 were the names of men who had provided the most influential speeches in our history. Nicki was grateful for the information Peter Thornton had provided her. She was sure that apart from his relationship with her mother, she would never find meaning in her mom's notes.

Nicki sat at the firepit the third week of August, and Peter Thornton slid into the seat beside her. Nicki, It is time for me to leave. I went a long way to spend time with you; it has been meaningful. All I told you is yours to keep and use it as necessary. I know you will succeed in your mission. As a matter of confidence, remember that evil always moves toward power. Do not give up, give in, or walk away. I have had great joy in our conversations.

He stood, rubbed her cheeks, and kissed her head. I will miss you, Nicki. He walked up the stone pathway. He stopped, turned, and spoke back to Nicki. DUTO, do unto others, Nicki beamed. And just so you know, my sweet child, I did not know your mom; I know her. He lifted his arm fist clinched with the victory hand pump.

Nicki looked at him, dropped both arms to her sides, and a deep peace came over her. She had tears in her eyes for a reason she could not define. She felt a part of something beyond her understanding.

At the resort, the number of groups and people arriving had increased. Intelligent, committed people had come to meet, plan, and prepare for better times. Nicki became a sought-after leader. On Tuesday, she joined a group discussing Washington's current leadership, which led to a serious discussion about the election in a little over two months. The Prelate was the topic. No one believed that he was a God-anointed Bishop, but no one could pinpoint his power source and how he rose to influence. Some in the room reported rumors of him having special powers. Others said his eyes turned a light fluorescent green when he got angry. Nicki's Dad had told her about a man who once held the world's power in his hand; unfortunately, his hand was evil. Nicki's mom had a lengthy legal battle between him and his Company. Carrie's Dad was confident that The Prelate was one of his colleagues. The group believed that he was not the power but a servant. Nobody knew anything about Bishop Boyer except he seemed to be the real deal, a servant of God. It seemed apparent that the Prelate would be the next President, and the people's freedom would disappear like Venezuela's rights. The Prelate and his supporters promised to take from the rich and give to the poor. The reality of this populist promise is that they take from the rich, but they give to themselves.

Nicki had a dark feeling about the conversation about the Prelate and laid it out for consideration. "I think there is something more to this election. I believe that there is another force other than two political parties. I feel that evil intends to take control of our nation. It will do it by dressing up as the Prelate's promises. The purpose is simply a battle between good and evil, not political parties but supernatural forces. Powers you can't see or touch but are real enough to mark you. The room was dead silent. Aghast with the thought of magical powers. Nicki looked at the group with a most surprised look, surprised these words and ideas flowed from her mouth. Never had she considered spiritual warfare. They all left the room in silence, wondering what had just happened.

Jobi Jones found Nicki walking the upper road above the Retreat, a winding gravel road with beautiful mountain homes. Jobi lived on a gravel road that looked like a painting. She lived a distance well removed from the retreat. Nicki loved the walk. Just passing the A-frame houses, the road turned from paved to rock and turned ninety degrees to the right. As you turn, you disappear into a canopy of trees that make the lane look like a pixie paradise. Like a fairyland, one old house had a rusty tandem bike attached to the green molded wooden garage. Each home was inviting, homey, and breathtaking. Flowers and lush landscaping made it appear the area was staged for some TV show. "Nicki, hold up; come over to the house for a minute."

"Sure, Jobi; what can I do for you?"

"Come out to the deck and have a seat. "Jobi pulled over a stool and sat. She looked into Nicki's eyes and touched Nicki's hair. She ran her hands slowly down both sides. Jobi was sad. She put a barber cover over Nicki and tightened it around the neck. The boys are transporting an essential person to New York, and they will pick you up in the morning and drop you off in Harpers Ferry. We need to make you look as inconspicuous as possible. It would help if you were a different Nicki than the world knew over a year ago.

Nicki was instantly shocked. She wasn't ready to go. She had not been a member of the outside world in over a year, nor had she been in charge of herself. The people at Switzerland Inn Retreat didn't know her as anything but a guest. Switzerland Inn had no survival pressure, and Nicki quickly became comfortable at her mountain hideaway.

"Jobi said, smiling through light tears," A regular boy's haircut or a regular boy's haircut?"

"Does it have to be that bad?"

"Afraid so."

"Jobi went to work remaking the beautiful girl into a beautiful girl with a boy's haircut."

Jobi took her phone, snapped a picture, and then forwarded it to someone.

"Nicki said, what is this for?"

"For your future."

"I am going to Harpers Ferry. I don't know why. I assume that the Prelate and his men are still after me. But you know my crime was so little and so long ago. I can't believe they would waste that much effort on me."

"Well, Nicki, somebody tried to kill you and Craig just a few months ago. I would suggest that there is more to it than you know."

Jobi sat on the stool facing Nicki and looked at her with a prideful grin. I have watched you grow in your time here. You are quite a teacher, influential, and knowledgeable. You have created a large following of essential people while you were here. You have used what you have learned well.

We have a few more minutes to wait, and I want to review a few things. Make sure you wear your trail clothes on your trip. It is helpful to keep your switchblade in your front pocket.

There was a knock on the door, and Jobi answered; a young man handed her an envelope. Jobi put it on the table next to Nicki's side.

"Nicki here is a debit card and a driver's license. You will need to use them to move around in the city."

"Harpers Ferry?"

"No, Washington."

"Oh."

"So where do you get debit cards and driver's licenses high in the Mountains?"

"Just part of the charm of this Mountain Retreat."

Nicki, I want to give you something else as you go forward. It is a true story from the Bible by an eyewitness. You have heard this story before, but I want to give you a new perspective.

Jesus and his twelve disciples were on the sea. Then suddenly, a terrible storm came up. The waves were breaking into the boat. Jesus was sleeping. The twelve were in a panic and afraid, and they woke Jesus up by screaming and shouting, save us. They expected Jesus to be as panicked as they were. They expected him to give them instructions that would save them, like bailing the boat, facing the wind, or dropping the sail. After all, he was the teacher, and they were the followers.

Jesus did wake up, but he wasn't afraid. He was a little sharp with his friends: "Why are you afraid? I got this. You have so little faith."

Then he stood, spoke at the wind, and disciplined the waves. The sea became calm.

The men sat dumbfounded. They never expected this, never even imagined such a thing could happen. All they could do was sit in awe and say, "Who is this that even the winds and waves obey?"

"Help us, they screamed, was a prayer. The disciples did believe he could help them sail the ship. But Jesus wasn't afraid as they expected, and he didn't save them as planned."

"Be prepared, my sweet one. Your prayer will be answered, just not as expected, and chances are it will be spectacular."

"Why are all the stories people tell me Bible Stories?" Nicki said, tongue in cheek.

With a big grin, Jobi said," Girl, you want high octane or ethanol?"

"Enough with the lessons, pack your bag tonight, and meet under the covered parking at 7:00 AM. I love you, my friend, and I would not trade our time together for anything this side of heaven. I am for you, and I cannot wait to see how it all turns out."

"I am afraid, Jobi. What will happen to me in Washington?"

"Just like our sailor friends. Nicki, it is not what will happen to you. It is what will happen because of you. Your story is not a Nicki story but a God story." With smiles, they hugged a mother-daughter hug.

Jobi said, "One final thought: give God time to work. Don't rush things. While you have been at the retreat, I have seen you practice obedience. It looks good on you."

The following day, at 7:00 AM, Nicki stood under the drive-through entrance. There were five large motorcycles. Two were large and bulky, and two were colorful, fast-looking rocket bikes. The last cycle was aerodynamic. Nobody was around. Nicki sighed and felt acid flow into her stomach. She could hear men talking to her left as they came up the path from the restaurant. They rounded the corner, and four had their helmets off and wore big smiles. The fifth man wore a slick helmet, all blacked out. He appeared attractive, even covered in black leather. They shook her hand and introduced themselves as Billy's Boys. She recognized one of the men as an influential Preacher at one of the large Churches in Atlanta. He must be the man they were transporting in the Billy underground. He gave her a big smile.

One of the colorful rockets screeched out of the parking lot with an enormous whine. The rest took their time. All three other riders mounted, and the fifth man climbed behind the man riding the giant bike. The attractive man rode the most aerodynamic bike, and he motioned for Nicki to come over and get her helmet. She slid the helmet over her regular boys' haircut. The man leaned over and softly tightened her chin strap. In a scratchy tone, like a radio station not entirely on the channel, she heard a voice: check, can you hear me? Press the button on your helmet to reply. Nicki felt around for a button on the helmet's right side and pushed it. Then she heard a squeal and said, "Can you hear me? The driver gave a thumbs up and motioned her to the back. She nestled into the man's back like two puzzle pieces fitting together. He said, "Next stop, Harpers Ferry." The bikes moved off smoothly, all with a loud rumble. The last rocket bike stayed in place.

They leaned into two long curves and advanced to the stunning Blue Ridge Parkway with a punch of power. The sweet morning temperature melted into the light haze. Even with the noise of the bikes, you could feel the silence of the winding road. Nicki enjoyed the experience.

The scratchy, squealy voice reported, "Eight hours to Harpers Ferry on the Parkway."

"Thank you," Nicki replied. She thought eight hours would be a long time to ride this bike, but she was surprisingly comfortable. They moved fast as they leaned into each corner. The ride continued as smoothly as silk past Lineville Falls, Grandfather Mountain, Moses Cone Park, and Bluff Mountain.

Nicki could hear some static talk but could not make it out. Her driver replied to the static. The two other bikes took off wildly, giving the thumbs up as they passed. Nicki's bike kept a constant speed. The driver punched it after a sweeping blind corner. Her driver veered off the paved road and diagonally onto a path at a 45-degree angle. She held tight and leaned forward as the bike pushed hard to climb the hill. The bike stopped at a small clearing, thirty feet high, looking down the road. The driver motioned for Nicki to get off, and then he pushed the bike back into the woods and lay down in the brush so that he could see the road. Nicki joined him, lying in the fresh leaves.

She could hear them coming, the roar of the rocket bike from Switzerland Resort being chased by three red rocket bikes. Nicki thought she saw a gunfire flash, but the bikes' noise was too loud to hear. Nicki's excitement had turned into nervousness. Gunfire was severe; the four cycles flashed by in an instant.

Nicki used her elbows to get up from the prone position, removing her helmet. At the same time, her driver lay still on the ground, communicating with the other bikes. The driver sat up, crossed his legs, and removed his helmet.

Nicki's eyes opened wide with a fierce focus, and her jaw dropped. She grabbed a handful of leaves and dirt and threw them into her driver's face. Nicki sprang to her feet and lunged atop the man with both hands extended out.

PART IV

"Everyman is two men, the man he is
and the man he wants to be."
Unknown

CHAPTER 16

A life spent making mistakes is not only more honorable
but more useful than a life spent doing nothing."
George Bernard Shaw.

Nicki jumped on her driver with all her weight, knocking him over
on his back. Her strong arms pinned him down. His eyes locked
on hers. Nicki's left hand immobilized him, her right hand in the
air, ready to punch him. There was little doubt about who would
win this fight. Nicki swung her raised fist high in the air and then
collapsed with the fullness of her body on top of him, embracing
him in a lover's embrace.

"Todd Miller, I have never been so glad to see you." Laying her
face on his chest with a release.

Brushing the leaves off his face, "Nicki, you have a strange way
of showing your happiness."

"What are you doing here?"

"I came to move a prominent person to their next assignment."

"I assume he is safely on his way?"

Todd said, "No, that person is you. I am to deliver you to
Harpers Ferry. But first, I must fill you in on a few details."

"Your Dad and Brother were attacked by the Prelate's men in
separate ambushes."

"Oh no, are they ok?

"Yes."

"I am glad I did not know. I am unsure what to do if anything happened to my dad."

"They are both ok, a little battered but well and working. Your dad and brother plan to arrive in Washington for the inauguration. They are in seclusion in Plentywood. The Prelate believes they both are dead. Things in Washington are different. They have had several small earthquakes. The damage has been small, but several fissures are still emitting sulfur. It makes the city smell bad and overcast, making people sick. The buildings have turned a grimly grey color. Dr. Maker, Taylor Samms, and Joe encouraged the people to vote for our candidate, Dr. Jim Hobson. They are promoting honest lawmakers to replace the congressional members who are not for the people. We feel good about our progress, but The Prelate has a chokehold on the people."

"We cannot give up. This may be our last time to vote. The country is lawless, and everyone is interested in themselves. The people do as they please in the name of democracy. You know Nicki, I may have misspoken the truth. The people themselves are good. It is the power-hungry leaders that are the problem. They have enslaved the people. The Prelate's group says they are for democracy, but they only seek to have the people serve them. They want to heavily tax people, knowing you get their power if you take their money. The government will not tolerate any opposition. They silence their resistance through incarceration and public humiliation. The people speak only what the government says. The leaders believe their power makes their actions holy and right. You are going to have to be careful. It looks like a socialist revolution in a third-world country."

"Aren't you going with me?"

"No, I have a lot to do."

"What do you mean?"

He sat up, smiled a Todd smile, then reached into his inside jacket pocket and pulled out a teal-colored box. He handed it to Nicki and pointed to her like it was a gift. She opened it, and in a matching soft teal bag was a small cross, the corners rounded and smooth. It was exquisite. He motioned for her to put it on. He put his helmet under his arm and said, "Your favorite, a sixteen-inch chain."

"Nicki teared up and beamed at the same time. She 'thought *This is no trinket; it is exquisite* and *just for me.* It paired perfectly with her translucent Faith rectangle charm.

Todd said," We must wait another fifteen minutes, then move on to Harpers Ferry. I will put you on the train to Washington, and you are to go to this address."

She looked at a scrap of paper, 23 Logan Cir NW.

Todd said, "You can walk from the train station. Go around to the alley and enter through the door on the deck. You are to see Dan Smith."

Nicki was silent. It seemed so cut and dry. "What do I do when I get there?"

Todd said sternly, "Nicki, what is your mission?"

"Finish my mom's work."

"Well, then do it."

Todd helped Nicki with her backpack and helmet, "We have several more hours to go. We will get off the Parkway in a few miles and travel along the country roads."

Nicki remained silent. She was angry he was so short with her. She did not want Todd to leave her again.

"Todd, it is tough going it alone."

"I know, Nicki. It might seem like you are alone, but you are not."

Nicki wanted this to be a loving and kind moment, not a business meeting. With her whole soul, she wanted Todd to save her.

⌒

Bobby Boaz and his son Robert directed Boaz Power from Plentywood, Montana, through Bobby's brother Tim. Along with the other Federalist Five corporate leaders, they continued planning to move their vast assets out of the country.

Measuring their progress, Bobby Boaz, Robert, Beth, Charlie Tender, Joe Frank, and the Federalist Five discussed the election. They poured over the polling data on a restricted satellite call, plotting targeted populations. They believed they could easily defeat the Prelate and his band of evil men. They decided they would continue the grassroots campaigns. Charlie and Beth had made tremendous gains in The Senate and the House, painting a portrait of the Prelate's evil plans. The picture was easy to paint. They only had to play the past trailers. In their persuasive manner, the Benders convinced lawmakers of their higher purpose. Taylor Samms convinced the trade community that they could soon trust the system, sell goods to the United States, and collect their money. The state could feel the pressure from Billy's Boys, like a python around a rabbit. While they could feel the group, they could not see them. They put their clandestine mission into high gear six weeks before the election. Assuming defeat for the Prelate, the group plans to meet for the inauguration in January.

∽

Todd walked Nicki to the train to Washington. Nicki was fumbling around as she bought her ticket. It was her first purchase with her Jobi-made debit card.

Todd hugged Nicki.

Nicki exhaled and laid her head against his chest. The hug felt like a heavy blanket on a cold night. The embrace was warm, secure, peaceful, and perfect.

"Todd, when will I see you again."

"We will all be there for the inauguration."

"Keep the news of your dad and brother being alive a secret. Their life depends on it."

Nicki didn't want Todd to leave. She wanted her old, peaceful life back. She felt every step for the last year had been an uphill effort, every place temporary, and every relationship transitory.

"Todd,"

"Yes, Nicki."

"Thank you for always being here for me. Thank you for the exquisite necklace," Nicki said, but she wondered how he could *leave me again after giving me such a special gift.*

"Nicki, what is wrong with you? You live to hate me," he said with a huge grin and sparkling blue eyes.

Nicki wanted to say more, but they had to move on to new, dangerous, and undetermined tasks. A confession of love would be unwanted."

Nicki boarded her train to Washington at the Harper's Ferry Amtrack platform. She waved to Todd out the window as he headed off on his motorcycle, thinking, *Will I ever see him again?*

Nicki settled in for the hour-and-a-half ride. She was restless because she thought something big would happen at Harpers Ferry. Ranger Craig had almost given his life to get her there on time. She focused on her all-consuming purpose. Todd believed the current administration would lose, and a new, fresh group would bring back honesty and morality. She wanted the weariness of revolution to stop and democracy to return to the land. Nicki said aloud, "For the people and by the people," it was like a word from heaven. She leaned back and thought about her mom's notes, moving the terms around on paper like Scrabble pieces. Nicki had put so much effort into understanding what her mom wanted to say. Peter Thornton had helped decipher the words. As Nicki moved the comments about, they gradually became her words and the beginning of her speech.

The train passed over and by the Potomac, hugging tight to its shore. Nicki fell into a peaceful sleep, and the ride was smooth and fast, not the usual clickety-clack of the train. Before arriving at her destination, she noticed how the countryside had changed. The sky was grey and overcast, but not from any clouds. The landscape was unkempt and, in places, scorched. There was no green beauty, no bright blue skies, only dull and dirty. The river was foul and dead-looking. A half-hour late, the train pulled into Union Station.

Nicki had been to Union Station many times and maneuvered skillfully in and out of the station. Her trail pack was steady on her back. She looked like a hiker. She was shocked to see the dilapidated city. She started her 30-minute walk on Massachusetts Ave NE and 7th NW. It had once been the showplace of the country. There were barricades on several streets with cracks in the road with sulfur smoke sluggishly rising. The town stunk. People were scowling and angry. Drivers were aggressive and sped. Massive transformer-like cell towers covered every inch of the city. It added to the oil rig look and feel of the town. Nicki noticed a white six-inch rectangle painted on a pole, keeping a keen eye out for any trouble. She placed her hand on it and saw an identical painted strip on the other side. She laughed aloud," It looks like a blaze. How irrational is that." Arriving at Logan Circle, she found a small park without plants, flowers, or grass in the circle's center. There were several unkept park benches and a statue of John Logan on a horse. Nicki knew this area was once a charming neighborhood. She walked around the circle until she was on the other side of the park, looking directly at the address. She walked clockwise, standing in front of the house. Then, stealthily around the corner, into the alley and up to the deck.

Looking through a glass-paned door, she saw a dining room table. Nicki knocked with her knuckles. No one answered. She hit hard again with her fist. She paused and hung her head, looking at the address on the paper. Then she turned to walk down the stairs.

At the bottom of the stairs, she heard the door open, and an older man with silver-white hair stuck his head out, "May I help you?"

"Yes, I am Nicki Boaz, looking for Dan Smith. The boys sent me."

"Come in, please," he looked around to ensure nobody was watching.

It was old, dark, and Victorian through the door and into the dining room. Dan pointed to her left and said, "Please come into the parlor."

192

She took her backpack off and sat on the delicate sofa. "I got word to expect you. What may I do to assist you?"

"I am fulfilling my mother's purpose. I am preparing a speech she started. That is all I know. The state is after me. I made them angry by writing a few strong essays for the Journal. They are trying to arrest me. My real problem is accomplishing my mission in six weeks."

"I see," said Dan."

"Let me show you to your room."

Dan took her up two stairs to a large, bright yellow room. The room had windows on two sides, and the larger window overlooked the park."

He said, "I must tell you this room can be noisy at night with all the cars passing around the circle. Here are some brochures about the city and two keys, one for the gate and one for the door. Since the earthquakes, the tourist business has been slow, and you are the only guest currently. We have breakfast at 8:00 AM. I will see you then. Enjoy your night."

Nicki got familiar with the room and her location in Washington. She thought she could get to most places in the city by walking. She pulled out her mom's folder and formed words from her mom's scribble. The work progressed as Nicki could associate her mother's notes with her recent experiences.

⤸

Ethel was storming toward Jacksonville, Florida. The Navy was pulling the destroyers and Aircraft Carriers out to sea. The Navy moved the nuclear ships deep into the North Atlantic at the submarine base in Georgia. Ethel was a late September category-four hurricane. She was not the usual hurricane roaming and wobbling over the South Atlantic. Ethel moved off the African coast like a freight train, moving in a fast, straight line toward the slight curve in the coastline between Florida and Georgia. It was a rare storm. It would be a category five storm with 150 miles per hour winds in two days. The Rangers evacuated Jekyll, St Simons, and Cumberland Isle. At Cumberland, they loaded up the students and the new caretakers of Plum Orchard. Connie and Evelyn had decided to stay, but Evelyn's daughter insisted she leave at the last moment. Connie had the Rangers take her to Plum Orchard and make them check the gasoline level in the generator tank. They didn't want to leave her but couldn't make her go. They tried painting a picture of what 150 MPH winds would do to any structure on the Island. They added that it didn't matter because the fifteen-foot storm tide would cover the Island and flow into the river. It did not phase her. She whispered something about God taking care of her one way or the other. The Rangers battened down the house the best they could and left her a two-way radio. Connie smiled and waved the most generous of smiles.

~

Nicki bounced down the stairs and into the dimly lit dining room early in the morning. The table had the most delicious breakfast foods: eggs, bacon, ham, biscuits, and jam. Dan read the newspaper and said, "Welcome, Nicki Boaz. How did you sleep?"

Good, "Mr. Smith."

"The boys let me know you were coming but gave no other explanation. By the way, that would not be unusual. Your business is your business, and If I may help, I would be happy to assist you. I have lived in Washington for forty years and worked as a writer at National Magazine."

Nicki was curious. Mr. Smith, "I am here to give a speech and uncover some secret information. The material is hidden on the *Hill in the Sully*."

"There are seven hills in Washington. Floral Hills, Forest Hills, Hillcrest, Knox Hill, Hill Brook, Meridian Hill, and Capitol Hill. Meridian Hill offers an exciting place for hidden treasure, and Capitol Hill is famous for its riches. But I have never heard of a *sully*."

"On my trip here, I focused on Capitol Hill, and it would seem logical to me. I must get my mission completed before the election. It is daunting. I didn't anticipate searching the whole city of Washington.

Dan said, "Six weeks isn't enough time to find a hidden treasure in a city like Washington. The number of historic and extraordinary places is enormous." Dan looked into Nicki's eyes, deeply interested in her mission." Are you a writer? Are you a platform speaker? You know Washington is home to pontificators delivering unmemorable verbal diarrhea. How will you give a speech that would change the country?"

Nicki looked intently at Dan as he ran his hand through his thick silver hair. "My mother left me the outline. People along the way have helped me understand her intent. At best, it isn't easy. Truthfully, I think it impossible, but I made a promise."

Dan and Nicki sat at the large, wooded table from breakfast to lunch. Dan told her all he knew about the city. He relayed that Earthquakes shook New York and Los Angeles and were in worse condition than Washington. No trade could move in or out of the ports. Commodities were in short supply, and prices were rising fast. People were guarding their food and fuel. He explained that the government had activated the Army to keep the peace and throw dissenters into jail. They said it was all for the good of the people. Dan continued, they even closed Arlington National Cemetery, letting it go to seed so that the past heroes could not shape their plans." Dan said," I expect the Prelate to temporally shut down Congress in an emergency executive order once elected."

"What has happened, Dan? It looks like a textbook takeover. How can this be? We live in the United States, the land of the free."

Nicki, "It's easy. The people were so focused on their wants that they bought the lie that the government would fulfill their every want at no cost. They reasoned that they deserved it. The government promised everything their hearts desired if they would just let them lead. Every moral law transgressed, the government supported immorality and promoted the transgressors to heroes. The state labeled business as the enemy, and the people gladly helped nationalize them. It all felt good, so patriotic. The leaders knew it would appeal to the young, but the old and wise recognized it as feel-good rhetoric. Even the press fell for the story, but once big government took over, the media could only report what the government allowed."

"My dad and his friends stood against them," Nicki said proudly.

"Yes, they did. Bobby Boaz is one of the real heroes willing to give up all they have to save our way of life. The government has labeled them evil, and school kids spit on their products."

"Is it too late?"

Nicki, "It is never too late for good."

Nicki sat silent, her teeth on her bottom lip. He encouraged her, and she said, "Help me, Dan; I must do my part. I promised my mom."

Dan looked at Nicki through his wise and wrinkled eyes. He highlighted a route with a sigh and recommended Nicki start at Meridian Hill. It had the most significant possibility to have a sully, whatever it was. Dan gave her a bus pass he had supplied to his guest. He reached into a table drawer that held all the books he had written and handed her a cell phone. Use it only in an emergency."

Nicki tried to grin but could not, "Do you have a small gun to go with it?

"Make sure you are back by dark. The soldiers pick on people out at night. Our breakfast chef, Dwane, will bring dinner by the house around 7:00 PM."

Nicki walked across the circle past the statue onto P Street, then to 14th St NW. She turned right on V Street, noticing how the gray day made her feel in bondage. A quick turn on 16th and Nicki stood facing Meridian Hill National Park.

Nicki thought *This was a fantastic place; certainly, the sully would be here in all this history.* She started her search slowly near the Joan of Arc statue, then to the James Buchanan Memorial. She dedicated the afternoon to the cascading fountain, a likely hiding place for a sully. Nicki found nothing other than great American History. There were no Rangers on duty, and as dark approached, she decided that since it was only a mile away, she could come back tomorrow and ask someone who knew.

The twenty-minute walk brought her back to Logan Street at 5:00 PM. Dan was not home as she entered the house. Nicki went to her room to work on her mother's notes. Her file was full of scraps of paper. They had become disorganized and loose. Nicki sat the file aside, drew back the sheers on the window, and looked dejectedly over the circle. She watched the cars swish quickly around Logan Circle. She pondered the big story that carried her to this window and her lack of achieving anything worthwhile.

At 7:00 PM, she met Dan in the dark dining room, "Any luck, Nicki?"

"No, but I learned a lot and am going back tomorrow," Nicki asked Dan about his journalist career in Washington.

"Nicki, in the early days, it was great. There was enormous excitement and growth in the city and development in the country. The town became blighted in the late sixties because of riots. Much of the town remained unrepaired. The city went through ups and downs until the late 90s. The Federal Government changed things, and the town became fresh again. In recent years, the city has reverted to its blighted era with shootings, riots, bombs, and even Marshall law. Still, people love this town and its historic surroundings. It was beautiful to be a part of the city's importance most of the time. I have another home in New Hampshire, and my wife lives there most of the year. She does not like the city's turmoil."

Nicki set out the next day full of intent and determination. After Meridian Hills, she searched Floral Hills, Forest Hills, Hillbrook, Hillcrest, and Knox Hill for three weeks. She was confined to primarily residential neighborhoods, didn't uncover a clue, and became stressed over losing priceless time. Nicki was weary of searching. Her best thinking caused her to believe her opportunity resided in Capital Hill. During dinner with Dan, she learned about Capitol Hill. He explained that it was the city's largest neighborhood. He described all its treasured hiding places, The Capital Building, Supreme Court, Washington Navy Yard, and the Eastern Market. With two weeks left, Nicki was sure this was the place for her treasure. She planned her work wisely and according to facts and her gut feelings. Dedicating one week to the Capital Buildings, she knew she would find the Sully on The Hill.

As she looked forward, her thoughts drifted back to her weeks at the historical sites and how they proved fruitless and frustrating. Night and day, back and forth, it was repetitive and unproductive. She needed to draw a bead on her target, find it, and get it to the people. All her senses were drawing her to the Capitol Building. On Monday, she started her full-focused search. She began by talking to tour guides and guards, asking about the Sully, and taking notes. Nobody had heard of it. Each day she would take a tour, she would ceaselessly question the guides. She would leave the tour and wander independently, asking anyone she saw, even members of Congress. She was opening doors she shouldn't open and becoming a nuisance to the staff. Nicki found her way into the Congressional Tunnels, both private and public. She expected that the Sulley would be in the catacombs. On Wednesday, she felt like someone was following her. In a packed crowd, somebody grabbed her arm. Startled, Nicki quickly looked back and forth with her eyes, then turned her shoulders to get a broader view. She moved quickly through the Capitol Buildings. She didn't want to give up but felt like things were becoming dangerous. During the afternoon, Nicki thought she heard someone call her full name. She found nothing. Nobody has heard of the Sulley. Nicki couldn't focus. Time vanished. Failure was in full view. Her walk had slowed, her shoulders dropped, and her head was always lower than her cap. Nicki, yoked by the responsibility she bore, felt her mission had become impossible. Time, her enemy seemed to be pointing a gun at her head. Once a heroine in her mind, now a failure, in fact.

CHAPTER 17

*You're never a failure until you quit, and
it is always too soon to quit.*
Rick Warren

Exhausted, Nicki gave up on her forward motion. The election was a week away. She had yet to find a Sully. She had finished no speech and had no expectations. She needed more time, smarts, or skills to complete her mission. What about her mom? What about her dad and the Boys? So many people had invested in her, so many depended on her. She wanted to bang her head against the wall. Her stinking thinking grew exponentially. Her fear of being discovered was making her sick. How could she give up? She had come so far and was sure her mom would not mislead her. Nicki knew there would come a time when she would have to find the secret in the Sully or flee.

The next day, she miraculously provided an attitude adjustment. She refocused on her purpose and faith. Her self-talk had lifted her spirits adequately to start again.

But it didn't last long. Nicki looked everywhere on The Hill. It was as if The Sulley was a mistake or a myth. Maybe her mother was wrong. She did not know where else to look. Her attitude revival turned into a light depression.

Nicki twisted her hands together so hard it hurt. She stepped forward to the place she promised herself she would never go.

Nicki walked to the back of the Capital and crossed the street to the Supreme Court. She sat on the steps halfway up. She began weeping.

Looking down where the steps meet, the sidewalk was where her mom died.

She could envision her mother's heroics. Her Mom threw her body over a pregnant woman whom a militant group had wounded. She could see her mother's body go limp as a ricocheting bullet struck her in the back.

Nicki talked to her mother conversationally as if she was standing before her on a lower step. Nicki asked, "why, what, and when. What is all this about Mom, why me, and when will it all be over? What can I do? Please, Mom, I cannot do this by myself."

Closing her eyes, Nicki visualized her mother smiling. It was a silly smile, a smile Nicki had seen only once. On vacation in California, her dad and brother Robert had visited Hurst Castle. They had to drag her mother down the mountain to the car. They thought she had had some breakdowns because of her nutty behavior. After Nicki graduated from law school, Nicki's Mom revealed that she had seen a vision at Hurst Castle. It was a visualization of her purpose. It included pictures of all the people that had added to her life. The dream revealed that the problems her mother had experienced were not punishment but training, and all the people in her life were teachers. Nicki smiled a silly smile back at her mom, and the mental picture was over. Nicki felt comforted by her vision but was unclear about what to do.

Nicki left the Supreme Court steps, placing a hand kiss on the bottom step. Her mind wandered on the forty-five-minute walk back to Dan's. She had not heard from Todd Miller, her dad, or her brother in weeks. She could only believe their hard work would pay off and Dr. Hobson would be elected President.

Nicki discussed her hope with Dan. He looked at her with his mouth turned down as if he might cry. He held his head down as he talked. Nicki, your dad's group, and the Boys do not have a chance.

Do you know how you complained about all those nasty-looking cell towers? Those are the high-speed transit systems for everything in communication, TV, education, commerce, entertainment, mail, telephone, and spying. Several years ago, they invented a high-powered signal. Still, it only had a short range, so it needed many more towers. As water is to life, the signal is to civilization. All voting will be conducted electronically over mobile phones, using state-created software. Everyone praised the creation of voting software and its ease and purity. However, it is the government's guarantee of a win. It will be a victory for the current regime."

"No, Dan, it couldn't be so?"

"Afraid so, Nicki; no matter how they paint the picture, it is a con.

Nicki said in an exasperated voice, "Have I been wasting my time, my life?" Really, Dan, "I quit; this has been too hard for a rip-off. What is the use?"

"I cannot tell you what to do, but you have a plan, and you have been part of a plan for the last few years. Maybe your whole life is a setup for this moment. Your Mom gave her life on the steps a few blocks from here for the country she loved. If I were you, I would keep going, not stop, give up, or give in. Besides, you gave your mom a promise."

Nicki had heard those words a dozen times from a handful of people who had helped her,"

Nicki asked Dan for a file folder, went to her room, and wrote across the front, NICKI'S SPEECH. She copied some lines from her mom's original notes. In a felt tip pen on the front of the cream-colored folder, she wrote:

2. Gettysburg Address, Abraham Lincoln, 1863.
3. I Have a Dream, Dr. Martin Luther King, 1963.
4. Citizenship in a Republic, Teddy Roosevelt, 1910
5. Give me Liberty or Give me Death, Patrick Henry, 1775.

Nicki had studied these men's words, four of the five best speeches ever delivered. Their purpose was to set men free. The number one speech had eluded her, and her mom didn't provide it.

Nicki worked for twelve straight hours on her speech. She put it in her Appalachian Trail backpack, took a two-hour nap, and returned to the Capital to find The Sully. During the day, Nicki's paranoia grew as she moved through the crowds. Her disguise had become her identity. She felt the government goons had finally seen through it. Dan's information had unnerved her. If he was correct and usually was, what did it matter? She couldn't figure out why he ended with a don't give up speech when he was confident it wouldn't make any difference. She did not stay out all day; her descending attitude had worn her out, and she returned to Dan's. Crossing the Mall, a large man bumped into Nicki head-on. She thought she felt a gun in his jacket. She spun off the collision and darted to the side, thinking, what a close call. Nicki's fear snowballed.

Nicki reviewed her speech, which didn't inspire her. Disheartened, she stuffed it in her backpack. Gazing out her window onto Logan Circle, her shoulders slumped, and her white blouse was wrinkled. She looked as though she had been wrestling. She lumbered down the stairs when Dan Smith called her from the dining room. She put on a fake smile, placed her bag in a chair, and hugged Dan. "Thanks, Dan; you are the most informed man in Washington, and your advice was invaluable. But even more, your friendship encouraged me. I am leaving Washington. I give up."

"Nicki, you don't know what tomorrow or the next day will bring. Your work may have laid the groundwork for a brand-new way of life. Where will you go?"

"I do not know. I have not had a real home in two years. Today, I am flying back to Florida. I could end up in Switzerland Inn, Plentywood, or Plum Orchard."

Nicki locked the front door, put the keys to the house through the mail slot, stepped down the five steps, and waited for the number 20 bus.

She purchased a seat on the direct flight to Jacksonville using her fake driver's license and credit card. She passed through the TSA checkpoint, which was only a few steps from her gate.

Gate 32 was down a small flight of stairs and only one hundred feet to the second gate on her left. There were plenty of seats in the waiting area. The blue vinyl seats overlooked the new terminal construction. She would have to depart from downstairs on a bus to a makeshift boarding gate on the tarmac.

She had over an hour for her 11:00 flight. The day was brighter than usual. Clouds moved by slowly, alternating sunlight and shadows. Her view from the seat at the window faced North. The panoramic glass window offered a floor-to-ceiling view of fifteen feet high. The city was near and in full view, just to her right. Several new passengers sat in the area. Sitting on one seat on Nicki's left, a nicely dressed lady in her early sixties asked about the gate and the bus.

Nicki held her head, chin down, and hat covering her face, always the phantom. She could sense the clouds moving overhead and the change in the sun and the shadow.

The lady in the next seat was nervous about flying and kept asking her about the gate. Nicki assured her that everything would work well, and she even walked her down the short flight of stairs to show her the gate and bus signs. The lady was grateful.

Nicki gazed out the window, reliving her failure. Her defeat left millions of lost sheep on their way to the slaughter. Her Mom would be disappointed in her. Her Mom was famous for pushing, prodding, persisting, and praying. Nicki thought, I sure have not prayed much.

The clouds passed over, and the area went from light grey to half-bright. Close to the one o'clock position, a large building in the western distance caught Nicki's attention. It was huge, stuck above everything on the horizon, looking like a rocket assembly building at Cape Canaveral. Nicki thought it could be a reflection of the sun, but it stood up and out even after the next cloud brought shade.

Nicki leaned over and asked her new friend if she was from Washington and knew the name of the building on the horizon. The lady replied no to both questions. Nicki stood up, walked to the gate, and asked the attendant the same question. She stepped around the panel with the flight information and glanced, "That is the Washington National Cathedral."

"Really, it couldn't be. I would have seen it while I was in town."

"Can't see it from ground level even though it is on a hill. The only place to see it in the city is from the top of a high building. It is on a hill, and so is the airport. It is only twenty minutes away, maybe 7 miles."

Nicki sat back down, not taking her eyes off the building. It loomed like a Parthenon over the city. Her despair was like diesel fuel for her body. She was twitching, turning, standing, and sitting. They called her flight, and the lady beside her said, "Let's go."

Nicki looked into her eyes and said, "I must go. You will be okay. We have practiced." She hugged her and ran up the stairs around TSA and out the door to the taxi stand.

"Washington National Cathedral," Nicki shouted. *The Hill, on the hill, she thought, why couldn't I see it? In the Sully on the hill, yes."*

The route took her on Embassy Row, once the belle of the ball in Washington. She arrived at the Church office driveway with a sharp right and another quick right into a residential neighborhood. Nicki reached into her flat card case with her credit cards and ID. She quickly paid, followed the visitors' signs, and hiked up the wide uphill sidewalk to the entrance. The Church opened at 10:00 AM, and Nicki and twenty other tourists milled around the Church's closed doors. Nicki looked straight up and tilted backward, almost falling, admiring the spires that reached for the heavens. Walking to the front of the Church, Nicki couldn't grasp the size of the sixth-largest cathedral in the world, more significant than any building she had ever seen.

At 10:00 AM, Nicki purchased a tour ticket to the innermost parts of the Church. She reached into her credit card case again, pulled out her red debit card, and gasped. Shocked, she panicked, realizing she had used her personal card instead of the new blue card.

Shaken by her mistake, she knew the goons would be here soon, *"How could I be so irresponsible,"* she screamed in her mind.

Running back outside, she bolted down the hill to Woody Rd. There were two young men at the bus stop. She took her red card and said there were five hundred dollars on this card. The pin is 4321, and it is yours if you go to Georgetown and spend it. Take your time and use it over the whole day. I know it sounds bizarre, but it will help us both. She walked quickly back up the hill and into the Church foyer. Implanted on the floor was the great seal of the United States and a state seal from all fifty states.

She cautiously entered the great Sanctuary, which was breathtakingly colossal and so immense you couldn't see clearly to the other end.

She stepped inside the Church, looking for the tour guide. She noticed an impeccably dressed older man with pure white hair, wearing a gray suit and Cathedral name badge. He was impressive in his kindness, looking more like a businessperson than a tour guide. She asked him about the tour. In a deep, penetrating, and beautiful baritone voice, he said, "You can catch them just through the gift shop. Ask for Laura." He smiled an embracing smile as he pointed with a crooked finger.

Nicki was sweating not from exertion but from nerves. Following his instructions, she introduced herself to Laura, the tour guide. She and her husband were long-time members of the Church. They took the elevator to the second floor. Nicki was surprised to find a modern kitchen and eating area. Ladies were preparing a luncheon for a group of high school seniors. They proceeded around the room and entered a business-like hallway leading to a training room with all the latest electronic equipment, sound, and audiovisual booths built into the back wall. Nicki could not believe such modern business conveniences in an old church. They exited the back of the conference room to a hallway more fitting to the upper chambers of a revered church. On either side were unfinished walls, boxes, and excess building materials. The hall led to two metal doors. A vast room divided by sheetrock walls and chain-link fences was through the door. The stacks of Art, pottery, locked cages, and religious artifacts were to the left, on the right offices for the maintenance department managers. Laura talked them through the room to the large glass windows.

Nicki could not hold back, "Where is the Sully Room?"

Laura replied, "I am not familiar with the Sully room."

"Is there a Sully alter, bench, statue, or garden?" Have you ever heard of anything that might be called a Sully"?

"No"

Nicki stopped talking and remained with the tour but became aware of her surroundings. She knew they would be here soon. Nicki leaned out and looked out the seventy-foot-high windows. She was checking for the arrival of the state's goons.

Arriving at the top of the Church, they stepped out on the walkway, listening to the explanation of the difference between gargoyles and grotesques. Seeing several black SUVs arrive, Nicki realized she was trapped.

Laura called the group back into the building and informed them they would be starting their descent through the walkway in front of the twenty-six-foot Creation Rose Window. She warned anyone with a fear of heights to wait behind. They would be walking on a tiny ledge high in the back of the Church directly next to the big round Rose window. The window sat over the main entrance to the Sanctuary.

Laura was an expert on the window. The small group stood high on a narrow ledge while she talked about the 10,000 pieces of glass in the middle and unfolded light to the Rose pedals. It would have been an exciting story any other day, but there was a commotion underneath the group. Nicki saw them, four black-suited goons viewing the Sanctuary. They went in two directions. Two goons went halfway into the Sanctuary, looking left and right.

Nobody but Nicki noticed. Even the guides talked in hushed tones, and so did the government goons. The group's tallest was searching near the Lincoln sculpture on the far-right side. He turned left to walk over to the man in the middle, and they stood staring at the alters straight ahead.

A tour with six women from Virginia walked by, and in a loud voice, the tour guide pointed to the window across the Church. Both men turned to look. The men fixed their gaze on the group walking like ants following their queen along the ledge. Nicki's eyes froze on the men, hoping they would not recognize her from two hundred feet away. She observed their body movements.

The short man lifted his arm to talk to his watch. Both men stood in place but jerked around and looked at the group in exaggerated movement.

Nicki knew.

Hugging the wall, she moved around the group as fast as a tightrope walker could move. Instead of going down the stairs, she turned left, running down the mezzanine that held the flags and electrical work. Solid black wires ran the length of the hall. They looked like spaghetti all over the floor and down some enormous pillars. She moved to the end of the landing and followed it to a dead end over the choir seats, fifty feet up.

She quickly looked around the corner to see if anyone was coming. Leaning over the rail, she thought, *too high*. She crouched in the corner. She heard loud talking. She peered to her right to see two big black wires, the size of a great ship's rope, running across the floor and down. Creating a picture outline in her mind, first, get over the railing, the second turn around, the third squat down, four, slide down. Her body possibly would be exposed, climbing over the railing. A fifty-foot hard drop, she felt like she was jumping from a plane with no parachute.

She threw her left leg over and turned to face the railing, pushing the wires between her feet, then slowly squatted down until her right hand touched the cables. She would have to repel about five feet against the header, then let herself down the remaining 45 feet.

Nicki's hands were sweating as she extended the length of her body against the wires. Her feet wrapped around the wire ropes, her hands losing skin on the roughed-up exterior of the cable as she went hand over hand. She looked up, but there was no sign of the agents. She looked down. No sign of the floor either. She increased her descent by loosening her wrapped feet and letting her hands slide down the ropes. Nicki moved faster than she wanted, but she did not have the power in her hand to tighten her grip. The wires were creeping down, coming loose from whatever held them at the top. In an instant, the ropes slipped, and cables let loose from their anchor. Nicki fell the remaining ten feet awkwardly to the floor. Her legs jammed, then rolled on her back just a few feet beyond the first row of benches in the Great Choir.

The thick wire fell and covered her like a python as she remained on the floor. Her eyes clouded, and she could hear her pursuers. Wanting to stand, she felt the cold floor on her back. Before closing her eyes, she last remembered being thankful that I had feelings in my hands.

Nicki felt hands under her arms, dragging her backward on the silky-smooth marble floor. A few minutes later, she was propped up on the kneeling cushions in St. Johns Chapel. She heard a strong voice.

"Young lady, are you okay?" the smooth baritone asked.

"I am not sure," replied Nicki.

"I saw you climb over the railing to slide down the cables. What were you thinking?"

"There are four men after me, and if they catch me, they will kill me. I am on a mission for our country. I need to escape."

"Do you think you can walk?" said the handsome silver-headed man.

"Yes."

He helped her up, and they walked to the side of the Sanctuary.

He assisted her onto a furniture dolly that had carried a bench into the Chapel. He covered her with a drop cloth neatly folded on the cart. He pushed the cart close to the wall for the five hundred feet of the Naïve. Walking, he focused on the Creation window and seemed to chant or pray the entire distance lightly.

The four men moved around upstairs and downstairs, slightly disturbing the tourists.

He pushed the cart with Nicki into the elevator, and they arrived back on the second floor. It looked like the same route the guide Laura had taken before. They rolled through the training room and down the hall to two steel doors with small windows. Nicki stepped off the cart, and they walked down concrete steps into a high, bright, brick room. Nicki saw a steel spiral staircase to the right and a steel-framed elevator on the left. They stood on an elevated concrete cross built on the room floor. The room was sixty feet wide, and shelves lined with empty beer bottles on two walls. It looked like a construction storage room.

He motioned for Nicki to follow him through a smaller single steel door on the far side of the room. Through the door, it was dark. They were on a six-foot-wide wooden landing hovering over the vaulted ceiling of the great Sanctuary, over a hundred feet high. There were two small construction doors on the side of the platform, and he opened them slightly so they had air and light. He locked the door and asked Nicki to sit.

"How do you feel?"

"Ok, I guess."

"Why are these agents after you?

"I am searching for words to free our country and people."

"You think those words are here."

"Yes, I know they are."

"Tell me what these words are."

"A Bible verse, a secret scripture, I don't know."

His baritone voice raised an octave, "You are aware that no Bible verse or scripture has any power that the state has not destroyed. They never even left one copy for fear of its power if discovered."

"I know it is here, maybe in a crypt or secret place. Perhaps unseen in a carved statue."

"Young lady, 400 angel carvings are just outside the building."

He smiled at her with the warmest smile, an inviting beam, a knowing grin.

Alert and revived in the gentle cross ventilation, Nicki looked at the man's name tag: John Sullivan, Washington National Cathedral.

"What do you do, Mr. Sullivan?"

"I am a retired Pastor. I moved home to Washington and have been volunteering here for several years. I am searching, like you."

She stopped, sat up, reached for his name tag, unclipped it from his jacket, and held it close to her face.

"Who are you?"

"What I am looking for is on the hill, in the Sully. She screamed, "You are Sully, aren't you, Pastor?"

"Yes, they call me Sully."

Jumping up, she yelled, "Will you help me, oh Sully, will you?"

"No"

"What do you mean, no! I have been looking for this for two years, and you say no!"

"I guard mightily for that which you search. It is three thousand words of truth and power. It is a twenty-minute read from the lips of God. Supernatural words offer man the life he has always wanted. The words are kind, simple, and can set men free."

"Nicki, these words have been entrusted to me for sixty years. I had come to believe that they would die with me. Many false seekers have come. There is a key to their release, and you must provide it."

"Like a password?"

"Yes, like a password."

"Isn't on the Hill, in the Sully enough?"

"No"

"I don't have a password. My mother didn't leave me one. Dr. Maker never mentioned one, neither did Peter Thornton."

"Pastor Sullivan, Niki said in her most confident tone, "I am the one. Give it to me, please. We are out of time."

"You never run out of God's time."

"Did you know my mom?"

"Yes"

"Then give me the writings."

"There are no writings."

"What?"

"Please, Pastor Sullivan, just tell me where they are."

Sully stood, walked to the construction door, and saw the street below. "Looks like your henchmen are still here."

"It may be over for me. Those goons have been looking for me for two years, and I foolishly gave away my position today. They will not give up. They are terrified I will get my hands on those words."

Nicki wished she had her mother's papers in front of her; maybe there was a clue, but she was sure there was no password.

She closed her eyes and imagined the handwritten first page, the typed scripture, and the list of the five best speeches. She conjured up pages two, three, and four. Nothing remotely close to a secret word.

Nicki felt sick, hearing men's voices in the other rooms. They could hear the doorknob turn and the door rattle, then a light shining into the darkness through the small window reflecting off the upper side of the Naves ribbed ceiling vaults.

The Pastor and Nicki pressed hard against the wall, barely breathing. The voices drifted away. Nicki looked out the window into the room. She sat back down, "Nobody out there."

Nicki stood up, grabbed the wooden rail, and investigated the darkness holding the giant vaulted ceiling. She shined her hiking flashlight into the vastness of the space.

She bit her lip with her upper teeth. Whispering to herself, "The best speech ever delivered." She yelled, "Sully, what was the number one speech ever given?"

Pastor John Sullivan paused for some time, then smiled, "I have been waiting for this day. Well done, you good and faithful servant."

CHAPTER 18

If you are going to be a Champion, you will have to pay
a greater price than your opponent will ever pay.
Bud Wilkinson

Pastor Sullivan beamed a conqueror's twinkle.

"Sit, Nicki; let's unleash the truth for a better life."

Nicki listened to Pastor Sully's words for the next twenty
minutes, memorized in another time, still as fresh as the day he
committed them to his memory. She recorded the comments on
her phone. At every consonant and vowel, she could feel the power.
Nicki clearly understood the authority of the words. She could see
the purpose of the speech. It was like a canvas of a masterpiece
revealed. Wisdom poured out as he spoke. It was easy to see how
far we had drifted from the benchmark. Her excitement and awe,
mixed with hope, allowed her to understand the country's future.
Her mother said, "Hope requires a power behind it." The knowledge
of this truth heightened her capability to carry out her mission. As
the Pastor closed the speech, she knew why the state had destroyed
the message. It was worded as if from heaven. Nicki thought again,
no, they are from heaven.

"Now what, Pastor?"

"Nicki, I have completed my mission. The rest is in God's hands.
He has chosen you to finish this work."

I will go back downstairs to my post and come to let you out a few minutes before five PM.

"Thank you, Pastor Sully."

Nicki helped him up, and out the door, he went. Nicki locked the door again, looking at her watch. It was 3:10 PM. She sat leaning against the wall, feeling the breeze from the open construction doors.

She sighed and thought, *what do I do with this speech?*

She closed her eyes and slept sweetly as if her mother held her.

Nicki tilted to the left and fell over. Still groggy, she looked at her watch. It was five-thirty. Where was the Pastor? She believed him to be faithful to his word. Something must have happened. She looked out the window of the steel door. She went to the small construction doors and looked down at the parking lot and street.

Should she move out of this safe place or stay? She was sure she could survive overnight, but time was the issue. She needed to type and print her message and take custody of these miraculous and healing words for the people.

She slid down the wall again to a sitting, grasping her phone so hard her hands hurt. She lowered her head and prayed a short, simple prayer, and she did not even mention her name.

Unlocking the door, she moved through the big room, saluting the beer bottles on the wall. She looked through the windows of the double steel doors. Only night lights shined in the halls. She crept out, remaining against the wall in the shadows of the dim light. Two lefts, and she was in the training room. In the hall, she arrived at the elevator. Needing to go down, she knew better than to make any noise. She headed down the spiraling concrete stairs. The door at the bottom opened into the foyer with the seals of the States. Nicki stepped out into the hall, seeing brighter lights in the Sanctuary.

Three hundred feet to the left was a dark-headed man cleaning the floor in a khaki shirt and pants. Silently and methodically, he went back and forth, then forward. He was never looking up or turning to the right or left.

Nicki backed off and tried the front doors. The steel gates and glass doors are locked. She went to her left, the wooden tourist doors also solidly locked. She could hear the clock ticking in her head.

Dare she expose herself and ask the custodian to let her out? Could it be a trap? She positioned herself behind the door and kept watch through the crack.

Back and forth, then forward. Nicki saw a heavy key ring dangling on his right, looking for a weapon on the janitor's waist or back.

It looks ok, Nicki thought. *There is so much at stake, more than just me. I must be right.*

She watched, back and forth and forward. The janitor was now ten feet away from the door.

She went down the outer wall to the nook on the side door. As the janitor moved into sight, she was ready to reveal herself as a locked-in tourist. Nicki heard a low rumble of voices not far behind the janitor.

Who could it be? Too afraid to take a chance, Nicki crept back into the dark as the voices got louder. Five men, one in the middle of the other four. It was Pastor Sullivan in handcuffs. They walked past the janitor heading out the back entrance.

"Nicki took her chance, "Excuse me, sir. I got locked in. Can you let me out this door?"

He said, "No key, boss picks me up at ten at the tourist door,'" he said in a strong Spanish accent."

Nicki shook her head in agreement and quickly hugged the wall to the back of the Church. Somebody must let the agents out. Maybe the door is open. Nicki turned into the foyer with the state seals and saw a Priest unlocking the door for the five men to exit. He exited behind them, and Nicki could hear the clink of the door lock. Looking at her watch, it was seven-thirty, and she had to get out to transcribe her speech. The election was in three days, and she had to prepare a digital and hard copy.

She made her way back inside and through the hall into the foyer. She pressed along the west wall until she came to the desk used for buying tickets. She crouched in the desk area, listening and looking at her watch. Nine fifty-six, and she heard the noise of a bucket banging against the steps. The janitor was walking up from the lower bathrooms. She watched him put his mops, buckets, and supplies next to the door and make another trip down the stairs. The noise changed direction, and the door was unlocked and opened from the outside. An older man in the same brown uniform opened the door and grabbed the bucket. He returned momentarily, calling for the other man, and followed the return voice down the stairs. Nicki bolted through the door. Missing the first step, she flew into the air and landed on the concrete driveway. Dragging herself fifteen feet into the landscaping, she paused to regain composure. She crawled on her hands and knees in the undergrowth, watching the area for any signs of the agents. The janitors came out, loaded the truck, locked the Church door, and slowly coasted down the long driveway. Nicki jumped up and limped behind the driver's side rear of the old van. She followed back until they made a right-hand turn. She crouched over, crossed the street, and walked into the trees behind the bus stop. She waited.

Covered in dirt, Nicki exited the bus at "P" street. She took a scooter east. She called Dan Smith and asked if she could return and use his computer to type Pastor Sullivan's speech. Nicki only used her credit card at the Cathedral, so they should not track her back to Dan's.

Nicki burst into exhilaration as she revealed her findings on *The Sully on the Hill*. She asked for a thumb drive and started on her three-thousand-word transcription. The Pastor was so good he included chapters and verses, *astounding*, she thought.

Nicki typed fast with fresh hope as if the words were in her fingers. She saved her work on the hard drive and the thumb drive. Not able to articulate the richness of the text to Dan, her excitement conveyed the worth.

"Now what?" Dan said.

"I have to get it into the hands of every church and Pastor in the country before the election," Nicki said in a rushed tone. It is called an information cascade.

Only your friend, the Prelate, can accomplish that," Dan looked over his glasses.

"Tomorrow, the Prelate and the President will send his monthly rules and regulations to all the Pastors in the country." Nicki raised her eyebrows," It is a power pose for him.".

Dan grinned, "So you will show up and hand it to him and ask him to send it."

"Pretty much," Nicki said. "I will need your help to make a plan."

"The Prelate and the President are scheduled to transmit their updated guidelines to the Pastors at 3:00 PM. The President will speak for thirty minutes, lying to the people, knowing the freedoms he will take away from them. He is such a schmoozer he takes away from the people, and they love him for it. After the President's schmoozing, the Prelate will speak, handling the tactical part of the new policies and placing the hand of God on them."

Nicki paused.

"The rumor was that as part of the austerity program, the government would reduce the number of Churches by half, eliminate their funds, and close private schools. Consolidating the remaining Churches to reduce the number of pastors and eliminating funds would leave only Churches in the hands of the faithful to the Prelate. It would end church services in most rural locations and funnel school children and Churchgoers into the cattle chute for spiritual butchering."

Dan, looking excited, said, let's change the subject, then leaned into her and said, "As you would say, the Lord has provided doubly. Tomorrow at 9:00 AM, a speaker slot opens at the TEDx Talks at the Ford Theater."

Nicki became anxious. Acid filled her stomach, and she wobbled back and forth. Her intense preparation never primed her to give the speech. It was a scenario that seemed far away, if ever. "I don't know, Dan, if I am ready. Maybe I should wait for a better time."

Dan said, "Nicki, there is no better time. It is time to act. We will do a rehearsal tonight, and I will drive you in the morning and wait outside for a quick getaway. It seems fitting that you would deliver your speech in Ford's Theater."

NICKI'S SPEECH

Nicki waited off-stage in the dark at Ford's Theater at 8:45 AM. The veins in her neck throbbed so hard it hurt. Her stomach was churning, and her hands were shaky. The speech carried such a consequence. Failing terrified her, and she had to make several attempts to memorize her fifteen-minute monologue. She had never spoken for more than five minutes without notes. Her promise to her mother pressed down like a weighted vest, forcing her shoulders to slump and elongating her arms. Something inside told her she was ready and that she had been prepared. She thought, *no thing is, one thing.*

"Here is for you and our country, Mom."

The room was full of the young, prestigious, and influential Washington elite. Six hundred people crammed into the Theater for the coveted Ted Talk.

A quiet hum of low conversations blanketed the room after the first speaker.

Abruptly, the room turned dark, not Theater dark but the end of time dark. The back doors of the Theater flew open with a bang, and a loud clack of army boots and heavy marching panicked the crowd. Back-lit by the lobby lights, rows of Nazi-looking soldiers in tight formation filled the four rows on the orchestra level and the six rows on the balcony. Fearsome and unmerciful looking, the gas-masked men marched into the Theater, never looking to the left or the right. The doors slammed shut just as loudly as when they opened. A light-yellow light shined through a haze, revealing the ferocity of the soldiers appearing to be inhuman. Led by a massive transformer-like commander, they stopped in all aisles. Each alternate soldier turned to the people seated before them, took the hose connected to the gas tank strapped on their backs, and aimed at the people. They tried to escape, screaming and jumping out of their seats, but there was nowhere to go. The smell of sweaty fear filled the room. Many in the audience cried as they knew they would die. The audience reached for their phones, but there was no service. The people were as good as dead. Not instantly dead either. It would be a long, slow, gasping-for-air death, a gas chamber murder.

The Master Soldier moved to the front of the orchestra level and, without a microphone, spoke loud enough to be heard throughout the auditorium. In a computer-like voice, he described the process that would take place over the next few minutes. The brightest men and women of the land are to be chipped in the arm with the state's new tracking device. The choice was to do it or die.

The Master Soldier stopped in mid-sentence as if he had been unplugged. His fellow soldiers froze in position. The crowd needed clarification.

A single round light beam shined on the stage, and a strong female voice penetrated the deep darkness.

"If I speak in the tongues of men and angels but have not love, I am a noisy gong or a clanging cymbal. And if I have prophetic powers, understand all mysteries and knowledge, and if I have all faith, to remove mountains, but have not love, I am nothing. If I give away all I have and give up my body to be burned but have no love, I gain nothing.

When I was a child, I spoke like a child, I thought like a child, I reasoned like a child. When I became an adult, I gave up childish ways. For now, we see in a mirror dimly but then face to face. Now I know in part; then I shall know fully, even as I have been fully known.

Nicki Boaz stepped in the lighted circle in perfect posture, firm to the sense. She asked, "Can you live with the fear?"

A version of the Bible, , that has been largely forgotten, The Message, describes our current situation quite well. In John chapter 3, verse 19, it says, "This is the crisis we're in: God-light streamed into the world, but men and women everywhere ran for the darkness. They went for the darkness because they were not interested in pleasing God. Everyone who practices doing evil, addicted to denial and illusion, hates God-light and won't come near it, fearing a painful exposure. But anyone working and living in truth and reality welcomes Godlight so the work can be seen for its God-work."

The house lights came up, and Nicki stepped closer to the audience, close enough for intimacy.

Nicki's intelligent voice spellbound the audience. They could feel certainty in her words, her body large and confident; the audience leaned in for the comments they ached to hear, how she could save them.

"Good morning, I am Nicki Boaz, and I am here to speak to you about our slavery. Yes, we are enslaved people in a Land of Plenty. We became enslaved because we had no discipline; our wants and desires drove us to trade our birthright for a quick meal. We are enslaved because we call good, evil, and evil good. We were led to this place by glad-handing men intent on being gods themselves."

"Can we not compare ourselves to Eve in the garden? Satan said, "Eve, eat the apple. You want to be like God, don't you?" As Eve took the first bite, she whispered, "Of course I do." Like Eve, expelled from the garden, we have been removed from paradise because we obeyed a government that whispered like the devil. Our forefathers' hard-fought freedom was taken away because we wanted everything that was not ours. We lusted for everything beyond morality and lifted anger to the quality of goodness. We claimed enlightenment beyond God. We worshiped reason. We desired power beyond our ability to handle it."

Nicki raised her arms up and out over the crowd like she was parting the sea, and the fearsome soldiers faded away.

"This morning, thanks to the science of holograms, you

experienced the terror of being the slave of an unworthy master. Demons promised you everything your heart desired, and once you answered yes to them, you became meaningless to the evil that called your name. Their promise always ends up with a collar around your neck. It is not very pleasant. If you don't act now, I can assure you that reality is only months away."

Good men have battled these forces and stood and spoke with words and faith that moved mountains. They could see the Eden Garden and knew its full potential. Men like Lincoln, Roosevelt, Patrick Henry, and Martin Luther King. These men intuitively knew the democratic way and that evil would seek to end the miraculous experiment of our Republic.

Embedded in our battle for freedom are five great speeches that turned the tide for the democratic way.

Patrick Henry said, "Is life so dear, or peace so sweet as to be purchased at the price of slavery? Forbid it, Almighty Lord. I know not what course others may take, but as for me, give me liberty or death."

Teddy Roosevelt said, "In the long run, success or failure will be conditioned upon the way of the average man, the average woman, doing their duty, first in everyday affairs of life, and next in these great occasional cries which call for heroic virtues. The average citizen must be a good citizen if our republic is to succeed. The stream will not permanently rise higher than the main source. The main source of national power and greatness is found in the average citizenship of the nation. Therefore, it behooves us to do our best to see that the average citizen's standard is kept high; the average cannot be kept high unless the standard for the leaders is very much higher."

In 1963, Martin Luther King delivered a famous speech that urged people not to seek freedom through bitterness and hatred. Instead, he believed we should conduct our struggle on the high plane of dignity and discipline. By doing so, we could transform the conflicts in our nation into a beautiful symphony of brotherhood.

King believed that by working together, praying, struggling, and even going to jail together, we could stand up for freedom and eventually achieve it.

Standing over a blood-soaked battlefield, Abraham Lincoln said, "The world will little note or remember what we say here, but it can never forget what they did here. Rather, it is for us, the living, to be dedicated to the unfinished work for which they who fought here have thus far so nobly advanced. It is rather for us here to be devoted to the great task remaining before us- that from these honored dead we take increased devotion to that cause for which they gave the last full measure of devotion – that we here highly resolve that these dead shall not have died in vain -that this nation, under God, shall have a new birth of freedom -and that government of the people, by the people, for the people shall not perish from this earth.

These great men of understanding call out from the grave, pointing their fingers at our country's destination. They spoke the words that brought faith to a wondrous land, the free land. They held a divine vision of Democracy.

Yet these great men held high in esteem are pale compared to the speaker of the most excellent speech ever made. The state ripped this divine address from our books. They dreaded the speech and its supernatural power so much that they destroyed every copy, fearing that even one copy would return to the people. They knew they would be seen as liars and lose their power if the speech ever resurfaced. The state feared it as if it was the very words of God.

Nicki gulped, stepped forward two steps, and sat as her legs dangled over the stage. She said with piercing certainty, "I have read this lost discourse." She paused and gazed softly at the audience, "It is life-changing."

"So, here's what I want you to do, God helping you: Take your everyday, ordinary life—your sleeping, eating, going to work, and walking around life—and place it before God as an offering. Embracing what God does for you is the best thing you can do for him. Don't become so well-adjusted to your culture that you fit into it without even thinking. Instead, fix your attention on God. You'll be changed from the inside out. Readily recognize what he wants from you and quickly respond to it. Unlike the culture around you, always dragging you down to its level of immaturity, God brings the best out of you and develops well-formed maturity in you."

"The word that will set our nation free is on its way. With the help of God, it will be in the hands of every Pastor in days. The word will spread, and we will know how to live again, learn how to love, and be free in our land of plenty."

Nicki raised her voice to a higher level, "Act now, cast your vote, and pray. Do not let anyone fool you; this city does not belong to the state; it belongs to you. Take new courage, hope, and power, and restore the land for our people. It is within your reach. Do unto others as you would have them do to you is your weapon. Fight evil with goodness."

A huge cymbal crashed and reverberated, eardrums breaking loud as the lights went dark.

On stage, something was emerging out of the darkness. It was people. It was a family. Moms, Dads, and children smiling and waving. Some groups were children and grandparents. The families dressed in bright white clothing and the audience could feel the intensity of a promising new future. Through the strength of these positive families, the new beginning of the land gained hope. The audience rose with thundering applause and exited with conviction and resolve to stand up for their children's future. The truth was evident.

CHAPTER 19

When you change the way you see things,
the things you see change.
S. Wright, M. Hager, S. Tyink

Pumped up due to her speech, Nicki wanted to finish her work. Departing Dan's home, she walked across Logan Park to Vermont St. At noon, the Prelate's office and administrative staff were in the building.

A few hundred feet into the park, the White House was on her left. The grounds on Pennsylvania Ave. were large and full of picture-taking tourists. Passing under the trees on her way west, she sat on a bench. Pulling her hat down over her eyes, she reached for a small pad and started sketching the Eisenhower Office Building. She had to enter the building and load her data into the server to send along with the Prelate's new deal instructions to the 300,000 Pastors. She sat staring at the facility, needing a more well-defined view.

She leaned forward to stand, and a firm hand on her left shoulder pushed her back down. A calm voice spoke, Miss Boaz, that was a fantastic speech this morning, surely to be greatly remembered. Nicki looked over her shoulder. It was Bishop Mark Toyer, the Prelates assistant and vice-presidential running mate.

Nicki was speechless and instantly nervous. She looked for

224

armed men with him but did not see anyone. She had never spoken with him. Their eyes had met at one other time. She had never believed he was bad, but she did not know.

Nicki looked around again. The area was full of police, but it was the White House. She checked out the route in front of her. Things looked clear for an exit. Bishop Toyer peacefully walked around the bench and sat down close to Nicki. He smiled, "I am Mark Toyer."

Nicki's legs moved back and forth, ready to take her first running stride.

"Miss Boaz, being in the open like this is perilous for you. They know you are here, and it is only a matter of time before they find you. You have hidden well, but you have let the cat out of the bag, and the Prelate is determined to get the cat by the neck."

"Would you please come with me?"

"No"

"I mean you no harm."

"Where?"

"To privacy, around the corner to a restaurant."

"Why"

"Miss Boaz, we only have a few minutes. If I saw you, so did the agents. Please, let's go. I don't blame you for not trusting me, but you know you are found."

She turned her head to check the area for agents. She did not see anyone, but that did not mean anything. There could be a hundred in disguise. She looked into his eyes, and he was gentle of soul.

He pointed the way with his palm up, and they walked south on 15th Street by the Internal Revenue office and crossed the road into the double doors of the Old Ebbits Grill. Once inside, they turned left and went down the stairs into a dimly lit dining hall. The bishop didn't wait to be seated.

He sat and smiled, "I believe that sitting behind a desk is a dangerous place to view the world, so I am out meeting people and listening. I have heard a lot about you. The agents have been looking for you since they tracked you near the Cathedral, and your speech this morning has set off a fire alarm."

Nicki exhaled, "A thoughtless mistake on my part."

"What are you doing here? Layfette Park is not where you want to be. The Prelate's office is just across the street."

"I know."

"Was that your destination?"

Nicki did not answer.

"What are you going to do to me?" Nicki said, looking down at the table.

"I was a friend of your mother's." The bishop said with a smile. "I was the CEO of a large corporation before I went into the ministry. Your Mother gave many speeches to my organization, and she was a leader for good. She became my friend and helped me find my way into God's service."

Nicki said bluntly, "Are you a good or bad guy?"

"My heart tells me I am a good guy, but my actions and associations with the state portray me as bad. I believe that I can serve God better in my current position. I am also a business friend of your dad. We did a few deals together in our younger days. He is a brilliant leader in his own right. You will have to judge me in the future, but today, I am a high-ranking officer in the state department."

"You didn't help me much, Bishop."

"Mark, please."

"Nicki, there is word out that you possess powerful information that could change our country. You said that boldly in your speech this morning. I am certain that the state has long since destroyed every trace of such material. They were wise enough to know that even one written copy could miraculously resurface. He sighed, Nicki, I have hope that God will return to us, restore us, and remake us in his image."

"Mark, do you think such a document exists?"

"It did exist. But we were such fools that we wanted to become our own gods. We had the words for good living, but now it may be too late. Our country's demise is forthcoming."

"Bishop, I heard it is never too late for God."

"Nicki, the Prelate will find you. You threaten him. He will kill you. He works for an evil lady."

"Will you betray me, Mark?"

There was no response from the bishop.

"Will you betray me?"

"Nicki, I serve God, but I work for the state. I am the only one left. The rest have given up. If the Prelate finds out I encountered you and did not apprehend you, he will kill me. It is a vicious business that the state runs."

"Will you betray me?"

"Not today, Nicki, but I cannot speak about the future."

"Give me your cell phone number," Nicki said forcefully.

"He gave her his card and wrote a number on the back in pen."

"Thank you, Mark. You will not be sorry."

Nicki stood up, pulled her hat down, and walked quickly out of the Restaurant. Bishop Toyer put his face in his hands and wept, feeling like he failed everyone, including God.

Nicki walked fast around the Eisenhower Executive office building to get a layout of the entrances. She walked south to the mall, and by the Washington Monument, she sat with a hat over her face and watched the world pass by. She could not help but remember that all this magnificent once belonged to us, *we the people.*

Nicki concluded that she could not get into the building. She needed a plan B, and she needed it now. The government's message to the Churches was sent this afternoon. Once the Prelate had reduced the number of Churches, he would solidify his position in the power trinity of the country.

She rubbed the little hard-drive in her pocket and gritted her teeth. Nicki had succumbed to writer's block and went blank on a plan B.

Back at Logan Circle, Nicki filled Dan in on all that happened.

He was shocked that Bishop Mark Toyer did not turn her in. Dan couldn't believe Nicki's Mom had influenced the bishop to join God's service. He was worried it was a trick, so he looked out the window to survey the area. Nothing seemed too out of the ordinary.

"Nicki, what did he want from you?"

"Nothing that I could tell. Bishop Toyer knew I was going to the Prelate's office."

"What were his last words to you?"

"He would not turn me in today but couldn't guarantee he wouldn't in the future. Then he gave me his number."

Nicki and Dan could not decide what the event meant other than a high-ranking official in the government knew she was there and did not turn her in, maybe because of his allegiance to her mother.

"Why did he give you his private number?"

"Because I asked, Bishop Mark Toyer is a Godly man. I saw it in his eyes. My Mom would not have helped him if he hadn't. He believes his mission is to be in the government for some reason, but today, he does not understand why.

Dan, I will never get inside to install my file. I need someone inside. The Prelate's message will not go out over Wi-Fi. It will move through a wired pathway. If she could get her message into the hands of the Churches, the masses would move.

"Dan, I only have a few hours. The Churches and the country are finished if we do not get this out. The Prelate and his boss will be God in our country."

"Nicki called the number on the back of the card."

⌒

The Prelate's car pulled into Francis Vile's home. Jumping out, he ran up the stairs and into the foyer. Francis Vile moved quickly and powerfully into the room. "Tomorrow, Prelate, it will be ours. How did your conversation with the pastors go?"

"Like taking candy from a baby. There will be only a handful of Churches left, and they will be under our direct control. The people will follow their pastors. Clicking his fingernails, he smiled with his lips, but his eyes did not agree.

"The desecration of the National Cathedral is scheduled for this afternoon. We can blame it on the opposition. The people's remaining faith will drift away like fog over the ocean. They will not have enough belief to whisper a prayer. I will restore the Cathedral in two weeks, and then it will be your temple. Ms. Vile, you will be the Queen goddess on her throne. The celebration will be grand."

"Think of it, Prelate. In two days, you will be standing on the Capital steps thanking the people and telling them how you will care for them. Then, in the official ceremony, the masses will be subservient to the hands caring for them. But Prelate, I understand Nicki Boaz roams freely in our city. I demand Prelate that she stand before me. Do you understand? She must die before our Armageddon. I will not tolerate any failure, understand?

"Yes, Miss Vile,"

↶

The election went as Dan Smith had projected. No one believed that The Prelate could garner 70% of the vote. Voting on Mobile phones was an invitation for government intervention. Nicki was devastated. She had traveled a long, hard road only to fail at the last minute. She thought God sent her on this journey and then made her fall. The air left her soul, and she slumped into a sad posture like a defeated soldier. Nicki felt terrible for Todd, Joe, The Boys, and the Federalist Five; they had worked hard. None of them had planned to be in Washington for the election, only the Inauguration.

Nicki's file had not been sent to the Preachers with the Prelates' notes. Nicki was furious that Mark Boyer had not helped her. She had poured her heart out and trusted him, and he turned on her. Nicki should have known better than to trust him. She still had the original recording on her phone and a copy on Dan's computer. Nicki Boaz punched the wall in Dan's foyer. She had come so far and through so much. "Why God, why?" shaking her fist.

Nicki held herself responsible. If only she could have devised a way to get the speech out to the people, things would have differed. But then she conceded that the people had nothing to do with the Prelate winning the election.

The state immediately called the troops to round up and capture the opposition. Many went to jail, some died, and some escaped. Nicki, the Federalist Five, Todd, Joe, Dr. Maker, and Taylor Samms were high on the capture list. Nicki felt safe at Dan's bed and breakfast but did not venture out during the day—her failure to change things sent her into a deep depression.

Two weeks after the election had been certified, a small stage and grandstand were placed on the steps of the Capital. The Prelate had planned a short acceptance speech. The west-facing platform was ready for a victory oration. The workman finished the last-minute setups. The Secret Service, Homeland Security, and National Guard took their familiar places, hidden and exposed.

There were few dignitaries on the platform, the Prelate now President-Elect, the House and Senate heads, and a handful of the Representatives and Senators. The audience was staged and paid in full to fill the area before the steps. Special passes ensured that only the rehearsed were in front of the cameras. Freedom to assemble was only for the select.

The rear of the National Mall was filled with tourists and locals. Reporters from all over the world made their way to the front of the mall. The police of all varieties moved in and out on scooters, horses, bikes, feet, and motorcycles. The amount or the attitude of the police was not unusual. Peace was the priority and the norm. The government gave the people what they wanted. Anyone who wanted something other than what the government wanted was not in the assembly.

Nicki Boaz entered the mall at Constitution Ave. and 14th Street.

She watched the crowds gather into groups. Moving toward the Capital and heading east on the wide sidewalk, Nicki stopped and looked back west. The people behind her pushed her to the side. Nicki felt watched; she could not see anyone in the big crowd but knew someone was close. She drifted east with the multitude, her head turning back and forth, keeping her eyes under her hat.

⌐

A tall, well-built Priest in black robes took the elevator to the top floor of the National Gallery of Art, East Building. He proudly talked to the visitors about the Stations of the Cross exhibit. Upon reaching the roof, he asks everyone to leave for his special prayer vigil for the new President. They went quickly, and he moved directly to the large Cross on the open deck. He used a key to unlock the remote access. The Priest carefully removed the sealed packing of the gun. Assembling the rifle and the tripod, he then attached the scope. He was placing his sharpshooter rifle on the top of the two-foot-wide ledge of the deck wall. He lay down and focused his body on stillness. His finger wrapped around the trigger, tensing and ready to fire. The roof partially blocked his target, but he could see the small platform the President-Elect would use through the scope. At 700 yards, it was a sure kill shot for Thomas White. The Prelate had scorned and embarrassed Thomas, and now he would return the favor. His finger was steady and ready as he lay still on the ledge.

Breaking the silence came a whirlwind of commotion. Heavy breathing and shuffling of feet caused Thomas to turn his head. Before he could react, two hands landed on the fake Priest. One hand landed on his shoulder and the other on his hip. Robert Boaz pushed with all his strength and whispered, "Goodbye, Thomas, you sack of garbage," Thomas White plunged off the railing to his death. He fired off a shot before his demise. The bullet hit the wall of the Capitol steps. Robert Boaz smiled, but he did not know if it was the smile of a hero or villain, a national hero or a murderer.

～

The shot panicked the crowd, and people dispersed hastily. In front of the Natural History Museum, Nicki felt closed in by the fast-exiting group. The stampede pushed her into the grass, still walking toward the Capital. After five steps, she had two big young men in black jackets on her left and right. She quickly turned to leave the two men. They moved in cadence with her, their shoulders touching hers. A third young man stepped behind her, and a shorter man stepped before her. The four of them tightened the circle while keeping the pace moving forward.

Nicki was sweating and nauseated. Had she been recognized, and capture was subsequent? She took gasping for air breaths.

Nicki moved her hand to reach into her pocket to feel for her knife, but the left hand of her escort grabbed it gently. "Hands where we can see them, please," he said.

The four men moved her to the side of the mall. They pressed tight like a football huddle, "Miss Boaz, we will take your phone."

"No," she said.

"You can see that you have no choice."

"No way"

"They all four put their hands inside their jackets.

Panicked, hopeless, and confused, Nicki handed over the phone. The moment she passed the phone, the men vanished. *Why didn't they arrest me,* she thought? Who were those guys? They did not seem like regular government goons. On the dead grass of the National Mall, she dropped to her knees, a failure. Even her backup plan failed. A sad violin melody played in her head. It had been a devastating week. The election was lost, and the last trace of truth vanished.

The word quickly spread that terrorists had desecrated the Washington National Cathedral. Horrible acts of contempt, immorality, and devastation willfully committed to dishonor God. Evil was the word used to describe the event. Nicki knew it to be the truth.

Nicki Boaz walked back to Dan's home; entering the dining room, she stepped back and noticed the house had been ransacked. She called softly for Dan, but no answer. She listened for noises, and hearing none, she ran upstairs to Dan's office to find everything in shambles and his laptop gone. Nicki's soul sank out of her body. It was over. Not one copy of the speech remained. She had the future in her hands and blew it. Years of her life went down the drain when she was in inches of saving the country. What would her mother say? She staggered downstairs and observed the park outside, but nobody followed her. She sat in the living room with her teeth over her bottom lip, asking why we could have failed. Everything she planned, she executed perfectly. The law was found and ready to be revealed. Freedom was three thousand words away. I should not have trusted Bishop Boyer; what is wrong with me? Panicked, Nicki believed the police would be there soon to put her in prison or kill her.

Nicki recalled Dan's story about a Prophet and his assistant helping the good guys. Their enemy, the evil King, found where they were hiding. It appeared they would be killed by the thousands of soldiers surrounding the two of them. The Prophet's assistant was panicked. Nicki remembered what had happened. The Prophet asked God to allow his assistant to see the present reality, thousands of formidable angels surrounding the evil King's men. Nicki even remembered the Prophet's words, "See, there is more for us than against us." Nicki recalled Dan's advice, "I would suggest you do the same, pray and look to the horizon. I am sure that there is more for you than against you."

She bowed her head and asked, "Please open my eyes."

CHAPTER 20

*Do not think that what thoughts dwell upon you is of
no matter. Your thoughts are making you.*
Bishop Steere

Exhausted from her superhuman efforts, Nicki sat quietly in the corner of the disarrayed parlor.

Dan showed up several hours later. He had been hiding across the park. Knowing they would be back. He sent Nicki to get her backpack and prepare to leave.

Nicki said, "Where are we going?"

"Corner of D Street and 4th Street SW, close to the Bible Museum. A group of men affiliated with Billy's Boys has a safe home. You will ask for Benji Moore. She is well-connected with the people who come and go. I hate to drop you off, Nicki, but we must hurry. I Love you, kiddo; you're the best.

Up the steps with her bag, Nicki rang the bell. A voice said hello and asked her name. She replied, "Nicki Boaz." The door buzzed open. To meet her on the other side of the door was a tall, dark-haired lady covered in layers of jewelry. Her voice was as pretty as she was.

"I am Benji. Welcome, we have been expecting you. Bring your bag into the kitchen, and we will talk for a minute." Benji poured a glass of water and offered Nicki a plate of ginger snaps.

Benji leaned over and put her elbows flat on the countertop, her jewelry clanging on the quartz. Nicki quickly and loudly started to tell her story, but Benji sweetly interrupted her. "Nicki," she said in a southern drawl, we know all about you and your mom and dad. We are friends of the family. Nicki looked puzzled.

Benji explained a few house rules and then told Nicki, you are on your own. This house was built in 1880 and still heats with radiant water. It creaks and moans like an old house. It has four bedrooms and six bathrooms. Three rooms are occupied, and the fourth is available for you. The meal schedule is posted at the bottom of the stairs. There is an electronic key in your room. Men and women of both political parties live here. We have well-attended Bible studies three times daily, and you are welcome to join in.

You cannot talk about "D" street, as we call it, or any people you see here. The men and women who come here come for help and privacy. They will offer you the same confidential privilege. That is it. You are safe here.

"That's it," Nicki said, still puzzled.

Nicki went to her nicely decorated room to look around, got her room card, and went downstairs to meet others. She sat in on a Bible study that included Senators and gardeners. It had been a while since she had attended a formal Bible Study, but she liked it. A man in an expensive charcoal gray suit befriended Nicki. He was a Senator from Texas. He explained he was staying at "D" Street for rehabilitation. Addiction had taken control of his life, and the demon of alcohol led him down the wrong road. Nicki listened but did not feel comfortable sharing her life with him. She met several other Congressmen. They all seemed friendly but in the same boat as their Texas friends. Nicki stayed in the house and made small talk but listened carefully.

On her second day, she walked around the corner to the Bible Museum. She was impressed with the largeness and newness of the museum and all the Bibles on display. The walk through the Museum reflected her childhood and her mother's great love of the Bible. She felt sad that her mom was gone.

Benji found Nicki sitting in on a Bible study and motioned for her to come on the third day. "Nicki, there is someone here to see you."

"Who is it?"

"I don't know his name, but we know him as trustworthy. Maybe you should meet him in the back of the house."

A man in his mid-thirties in starched khaki pants and a shirt greeted Nicki. "Ms. Boaz, I am Major Biggs from Billy's Boys. He raised his shirt sleeve to show her the two "B's." I am here to inform you of the death of your Father, who was bravely serving our country. Nicki could not understand what he said. She thought he had told her dad had died.

"What," Nicki said, "what are you saying? My dad is alive and well."

"Your Dad, The Federalist Five, Joe Frank, Todd Miller, Dr. Baker, and Taylor Samms worked at their North Georgia retreat. Government agents stormed their meeting. Your Dad went over a cliff in his Jeep as agents pursued him.

Nicki fell to her knees, weeping hot, angry tears. "Maybe he is not dead, "she said.

"We were able to recover his body," he said in a stiff posture. Todd Miller and three Federalist Five are unaccounted for, and Dr. Maker and Taylor Samms are in jail. Joe Frank had a heart attack.

Nicki could not get up. The Major gently pulled her up with both hands. Your life is in imminent danger, and we cannot risk revealing your position. Stay at this safe house until a message comes to you. I am so sorry, Ms. Boaz. I understand your mother and father gave their lives in service to God and their Country.

He saluted Nicki.

She saluted back.

Nicki climbed the stairs back to her room, staggering off the wall as she climbed the stairs like a drunk woman. She laid down. Her pain inflicted every inch of her body. She continued, "Why, God, I did everything you asked." She cried with intermittent wailing. She cried because of her loss and because God had let her down. She cried because she was all alone. Nicki cried because the people she counted on were gone. She couldn't even develop a word to describe her hopelessness or pain.

On the fourth day, she remained in bed, longing that her internal pain would vanish or someone would arrive and rescue her. But nothing changed, and no one came.

On the fifth day, the Texas Senator came to her room to check in on her. His kind voice carried a professional tone of comfort. Nicki sat up as his bright blue eyes greeted her. After some small talk, he read the highlights of the state-owned Newspaper to her. "The Prelate plans to introduce his evil, my words, cabinet at the National Mall. Francis Vile will present her dark Priest at her coronation as the High Priestess. The coronation will be in her new headquarters, the National Cathedral."

"Senator, when will all this happen?"

"Two hours," he said, looking at his watch.

"I am going to throw up. Really, could the leaders be any more disgusting, disrespectful, and profane? Anything else in that trash newspaper?"

He continued, "The sulfur levels remain high. There will probably be a few more small tremors. New York and Los Angeles are on fire because of the quakes. According to the state, everything else is excellent: no food, no work, runaway crime, and trash in the streets. Marshall Law did not make the propaganda post. The new President is quite a hit with his new Congress, which he intends to suspend next month. Raising taxes is on his schedule, but nobody will be here to tax; all the big corporations are moving offshore."

"My Dad would have burned his business to the ground before he handed his business over to the government cronies."

"I am sure. So, Nicki Boaz, what are you going to do?"

"I am going to do what a friend suggested. I will pray and look for an invisible army to help me. But as of yet, I haven't seen any fiery angels or chariots. The Prophet in his story didn't give up even after he was found out and surrounded, so I shall not give up and pray there will be chariots of fire on the hillsides."

The Senator said, "I am familiar with that story—two men against a giant army. I am sure somebody will open your eyes, and your help will arrive. We are for you, Nicki, don't give up or give in."

⁓

Leaving the Capital, the Prelate President rode to the Washington Monument in a convertible. He waved at the staged crowd slowly, making for an inspirational news broadcast. The group made it to the small platform on the east side of the Washington Monument.

As Nicki called them, Francis Vile's demon priest prepared the National Cathedral for her coronation. Nicki had a slight grin in her soul. She remembered that although the French tried to kill God off with the horrific desecration of Notre Dame, God did not die. He came back, and so did the impressive Church. She remembered what Craig told her on the trail: no government has lived as long as the Church. The thoughts propelled her forward.

The ceremonies were both set within an hour, starting at 3:00 PM. The clouds blotted out the sun, everything was dark gray, and several tiny tremors had rattled windows. Nicki had taken a scooter from "D" Street. Gaining entrance into the Cathedral, she positioned herself inside the main doors. She leaned her head against the wall in the Foyer with the state seals. She thought, *what am I going to do? Is it just me? My dad just died. She was shaking her head back and forth. I am going to die, and you know what? That is just fine with me. She took a breath that went deep into her stomach.*

The Prelate President-Elect arrived at the platform at 2:55, followed closely by fifteen men and four women. They sat condescendingly behind the podium. The media filled in the dirt and dead grass area before the stage. Bishop Toyer was absent. He was speaking at the afternoon service at Georgetown Presbyterian Church.

At 3:00 PM, the caravan of twenty cars delivered Francis Vile, the country's new High Priestess, to the Cathedrals' front doors. Two black-collared priests opened her door. Francis Viles stepped out in her astonishing beauty. The crowd was mesmerized by her splendor. In a scarlet dress and a headpiece, she stood erect and proud. The entourage of one hundred people bowed and chanted her name.

Her Priest fell in position before and behind her, and the group moved five steps toward the door.

Nicki bolted out of the door, standing as tall as Vile. The crowd booed loudly. Nicki said, "You are not welcome here, Francis."

Francis Vile replied calmly but arrogantly, "Nicki Boaz, finally! I have looked for you for years, and here you are, good for me."

"You are not entering this, Church."

"The last man that said that to me died on the altar of this Church. The Cathedral is mine. You couldn't stop me with an army of angels."

"I am not alone."

"You weren't alone the night my father was murdered. No, you and your mother killed him. Your Mother has paid, and now you will pay with your life."

Nicki unexpectedly lost confidence. What was she saying? Frank Vile was her dad? Nicki lost her concentration and critical seconds in her defense of the Cathedral.

As Nicki sank into hopelessness, she noticed a light orange glow behind the crowd, like a sunrise. But it was afternoon. Floating above the orange was a golden haze, like smoke.

Nicki rebounded.

"My mother did not kill your dad. There was someone else there. He drove a knife into your dad's heart. My Mother said he was her guardian angel."

"No matter, little Nicki, your time is over. You will die in front of your God and these people. I will rule, and your family will no longer torment me. This world will be mine."

239

The group moved forward. Nicki didn't know what to do. She pushed back, but she was no force against a hundred. They shoved her back to the doors. Francis Vile reached out to open the door when her hand touched the handle. Faster than a street thug, Nicki reached into her pocket, opened her knife, and put the blade through Francis Vile's hand. The crowd stepped back and became silent. Francis Vile backed up five steps and held her hand. It was not bleeding.

"Just like your father Francis, a knife through his heart and no blood," Nicki spit her words.

Vile gained size in her anger. Her cape flew back, and she raised her hands to send lightning into Nicki. At that exact moment, a slight tremor rattled the glass doors of the Cathedral and broke the fitting at the gas meter by the door. The gas hissed as it was sent unseen to the parking lot.

Nicki spun around and kicked the pipe to point toward the group in a ninja-like move. She struck her storm match against her watchband in a fluid motion, seamlessly throwing the storm match and igniting the gas. The stream caught fire and exploded to a blast directly at Francis Vile and her priests. She did not catch fire but was instantly incinerated. Nicki and the crowd stood still as the flames separated them.

At the exact moment at the National Mall, the same tremor caused a fissure that opened a six-foot-wide chasm that ran like a tidal wave down the mall. The wave opened to twenty feet wide under the Prelates platform. It sucked the Prelate and his court down to the pit like a vacuum, sulfur spewed one hundred feet high, and the fissure closed.

At 3:07 PM, it was over. Francis Vile and the Prelate President are both gone. The city was still.

There was such an absence of motivation in the following days. When evil ruled, they knew what to do. The constitution required Congress to advance Bishop Mark Toyer into the Presidency. There was no overriding mood. The confusion of the election and the death of the Prelate and his Master Francis Vile left the people tentative. Would Bishop Mark Toyer be a replica of The Prelate, or would he bring change, and would it be good or bad? Nobody knew the bishop except as the Prelate's assistant. But Nicki thought she knew him.

As she stood motionless in front of the Cathedral, the same four men who had taken her phone forced her into a black SUV, removing her as the gas still burned.

Two weeks later, in front of the Capital, a large audience of free people gathered in the mall. They had come on their own, praying for a new day. Gray skies still prevailed, and the mall was depressing with its dead grass and withered trees. At 11:30 AM, the crowd moved toward the Capital, and there was no sign of the state's strong arm of force. The group stopped at the foot of the Capitol steps, and a peculiar noise rose behind them. It sounded like a snare drum and a trumpet. A soft and distant cadence, seemingly drifting in the light breeze from Arlington National Cemetery. The music was familiar and repetitive. People started singing lowly the words of the Battle Hymn of the Republic. *Mine eyes have seen the glory of the coming of the lord.* In each stanza, the crowd grew bold in the chorus.

Glory! Glory! Hallelujah! Glory! Glory! Hallelujah!
Glory! Glory! Hallelujah! His truth is marching on.

As the crowd sang in national harmonies, a vast, dark, flying object came from the south and turned east over the Lincoln Memorial. It wasn't one object. It was tens of thousands of fast-moving sparrows darting in unison and appearing as one. Several people said they were spooked from their homes in the overgrown National Cemetery. The birds, in unison, darted back and forth up the Mall. The people were fearful and oohs and awes blared as the flock circled the Washington Monument. As the sparrows sped up, they broke into small groups like some force had divided them. They came together, then apart in a frenzy, rolling over like a tidal wave. Through a gap between separated sparrows, the cause of the confusion, two aggressive dive-bombing hawks appeared. They jet-streamed the smaller birds into pods so that they could seize them with their claws. It seemed the sparrows were doomed.

Unexpectedly, the crowd beheld an imposing object sailing effortlessly and powerfully into the sky above the mall. An immense American Eagle with a wingspan of over eight feet exploded through the sparrows. It dove toward the ground, and its supremacy manifested through its powerful call, caw, caw. Its gliding turned into a blast like an airplane off a carrier and, in two swoops, had the hawks in its powerful talons. As the magnificent Eagle passed the Supreme Court, the sun appeared, reflecting on the brilliance of the Eagle's white face and tail. It showed like lights from heaven. The Eagle dropped ten feet off the ground, showing off its capture. Then soared straight up to the top of the Capital and perched boldly, proudly, and gloriously.

Bishop Mark Toyer summoned the Congressional Officials, Judges, Clerks, and Aides. They came and stood before the President-Elect on his inauguration day. Bishop Mark Toyer became the President of the United States in the sun's brightness.

His opening remark was, "I considered the Presidency a step down from my job as a man of the cloth."

His speech continued, "Many of you here today had an ancestor who fought for freedom. This land became coveted by other countries who attempted to claim the bounty of the Lord's gift for their own. Your parents surely told you of the glorious celebrations of victory gracefully given to this country. Many died, sacrificing their lives for ours. Many of you remember the life of freedom we enjoyed in recent years. Our land was a land not worked for, a land of incredible beauty that we did not design, a land of pastures, food, fruit, and grain laid at our feet by our creator.

Today, we have years of hard work to restore the gift of the land. You will be free. You will be free to remain as you are or join us in our journey to serve the Lord. It is your choice. You will be accountable, but I shall lead in the direction of God.

His speech was honest and devoted to the hard work of a coming restoration. His address was full of what could be. After his twenty-minute remarks, he walked before the dais and held up a small electronic device. He bowed his head in silent prayer. Boldness showed in his small frame, and the light in his eyes beamed like fog lamps as he announced a new law to be delivered in seconds to the 300,000 pastors in the country. The crowd roared like lions. Somebody yelled in delight that the Potomac River had suddenly turned Crystal Clear.

A large piece of the Washington Monument had broken off during the quakes. The crowd rolled the piece into one of the fissures in the middle of the mall. The granite stood fifteen feet high and was marked a remembrance of the day.

That day, President Mark Boyer placed his hand on a Bible and took an oath. On the second row of the platform, Taylor Samms, Dr. Maker, Charlie, and Beth Tender were in prominent positions. On the fourth row of the bleachers behind the President stood Robert Boaz and two of the Federalist Five. The great freedom fighters all raised their hands in humble victory. In solidarity, they gazed at the third row and saluted five empty seats marked with maroon velvet cloths as reserved. The country never knew the dedication and faith of these men and women but understood that sacrifice is part of victory.

President Toyer stepped down from the platform and mingled with the audience. In the afternoon of his first day, he issued an executive order to restore Arlington National Cemetery. Insisting freedom should be honored, and the country should respect everyone who paid the price. History, he said, played an essential part in our future. The crews arrived by the end of his first day.

In two weeks, President Toyer made public his seven-year plan to rebuild the Democratic Republic. Churches became free from the bondage of the government, and a movement of gratefulness started throughout the land. The resistance was like that of an exorcism.

The priest, preacher President, radiated with an unusual manner of confidence. When he talked, the people believed. When he planned, things happened. He ensured everyone knew it would be a difficult journey to restoration. He promised that no matter how difficult it would be, their journey would be for the people, by the people, and of the people. His belief encouraged the people, and they started to work. They were free people in a land of plenty.

∽

Jim Rowell piloted Miss Kaylynn north up the river. It was a beautiful day, with blue skies and a light east breeze leaving only a tiny ripple on the water. Cruising past giant uprooted trees pushed high on the shore by Ethel, a floating glass ball bobbed calmly in the water close to what once was a dock. A quiet splash came from behind the boat. A young man plunged powerfully and elegantly off the slow-moving boat. He swam against the current with all his might until he could grab the floating glass ball. He wrapped the yellow rope around his wrist and kicked the dolphin kick parallel to the shore. As the fast water kept him a few feet off the beach, he felt a sharp pain in his side, and a firm tug rolled him up on the sand. Todd Miller, I have been waiting on you, and now I will punch you in the nose. He held her swinging arm and, with a Clark Gabel grin and kissed her lips, embraced her securely, and they rolled back on the sand. Two smiles, big and contagious, filled the Island with freshness and hope.

They headed to Plum Orchard. Nicki took Todd through the woods. The mansion appeared magnificently, and on the front porch, Connie waved. Todd jumped up in an exciting motion and ran to hug her.

The three sat on the porch peacefully, and Todd said to Nicki, "I have a gift for you."

"From you?"

"No, from your friend, the President of the United States." He opened his dry bag and handed her an official document. Nicki opened the large, certified envelope.

The grin on Nicki's face grew enormous even before she finished removing the contents. It was the deed to Plum Orchard.

Nicki slipped it back into the official envelope and leaned on Todd's shoulder. With a satisfying smile, she said, "You know, Todd, there is no such thing as a free lunch."

PART V

THE SPEECH ON THE MOUNTAIN. THE GREATEST SPEECH

PART V

CHAPTER 21

"You're Blessed."
Jesus

When Jesus saw his ministry drawing huge crowds, he climbed a hillside. Those who were apprenticed to him, the committed, climbed with him. Arriving at a quiet place, he sat down and taught his climbing companions. This is what he said:

"You're blessed when you're at the end of your rope. With less of you, there is more of God and his rule.

"You're blessed when you feel you've lost what is most dear to you. Only then can you be embraced by the One most dear to you.

"You're blessed when you're content with just who you are—no more, no less. That's the moment you find yourselves proud owners of everything that can't be bought.

"You're blessed when you've worked up a good appetite for God. He's food and drink in the best meal you'll ever eat.

"You're blessed when you care. At the moment of being 'carefull,' you find yourselves cared for.

"You're blessed when you get your inside world—your mind and heart—put right. Then you can see God in the outside world.

"You're blessed when you can show people how to cooperate instead of compete or fight. That's when you discover who you really are, and your place in God's family.

"You're blessed when your commitment to God provokes persecution. The persecution drives you even deeper into God's kingdom.

"Not only that—count yourselves blessed every time people put you down or throw you out or speak lies about you to discredit me. What it means is that the truth is too close for comfort and they are uncomfortable. You can be glad when that happens—give a cheer, even!—for though they don't like it, I do! And all heaven applauds. And know that you are in good company. My prophets and witnesses have always gotten into this kind of trouble.

Salt and Light

"Let me tell you why you are here. You're here to be salt-seasoning that brings out the God-flavors of this earth. If you lose your saltiness, how will people taste godliness? You've lost your usefulness and will end up in the garbage.

"Here's another way to put it: You're here to be light, bringing out the God-colors in the world. God is not a secret to be kept. We're going public with this, as public as a city on a hill. If I make you light-bearers, you don't think I'm going to hide you under a bucket, do you? I'm putting you on a light stand. Now that I've put you there on a hilltop, on a light stand—shine! Keep open house; be generous with your lives. By opening up to others, you'll prompt people to open up with God, this generous Father in heaven.

Completing God's Law

"Don't suppose for a minute that I have come to demolish the Scriptures—either God's Law or the Prophets. I'm not here to demolish but to complete. I am going to put it all together, pull it all together in a vast panorama. God's Law is more real and lasting than the stars in the sky and the ground at your feet. Long after stars burn out and earth wears out, God's Law will be alive and working.

"Trivialize even the smallest item in God's Law and you will only have trivialized yourself. But take it seriously, show the way for others, and you will find honor in the kingdom. Unless you do far better than the Pharisees in the matters of right living, you won't know the first thing about entering the kingdom.

MURDER

"You're familiar with the command to the ancients, 'Do not murder.' I'm telling you that anyone who is so much as angry with a brother or sister is guilty of murder. Carelessly call a brother 'idiot!' and you just might find yourself hauled into court. Thoughtlessly yell 'stupid!' at a sister and you are on the brink of hellfire. The simple moral fact is that words kill.

"This is how I want you to conduct yourself in these matters. If you enter your place of worship and, about to make an offering, you suddenly remember a grudge a friend has against you, abandon your offering, leave immediately, go to this friend and make things right. Then and only then, come back and work things out with God.

"Or say you're out on the street and an old enemy accosts you. Don't lose a minute. Make the first move; make things right with him. After all, if you leave the first move to him, knowing his track record, you're likely to end up in court, maybe even jail. If that happens, you won't get out without a stiff fine.

ADULTERY AND DIVORCE

"You know the next commandment pretty well, too: 'Don't go to bed with another's spouse.' But don't think you've preserved your virtue simply by staying out of bed. Your heart can be corrupted by lust even quicker than your body. Those leering looks you think nobody notices—they also corrupt.

"Let's not pretend this is easier than it really is. If you want to live a morally pure life, here's what you have to do: You have to blind your right eye the moment you catch it in a lustful leer. You have to choose to live one-eyed or else be dumped on a moral trash pile. And you have to chop off your right hand the moment you notice it raised threateningly. Better a bloody stump than your entire being discarded for good in the dump.

"Remember the Scripture that says, 'Whoever divorces his wife, let him do it legally, giving her divorce papers and her legal rights'? Too many of you are using that as a cover for selfishness and whim, pretending to be righteous just because you are 'legal.' Please, no more pretending. If you divorce your wife, you're responsible for making her an adulteress (unless she has already made herself that by sexual promiscuity). And if you marry such a divorced adulteress, you're automatically an adulterer yourself. You can't use legal cover to mask a moral failure.

Empty Promises

"And don't say anything you don't mean. This counsel is embedded deep in our traditions. You only make things worse when you lay down a smoke screen of pious talk, saying, 'I'll pray for you,' and never doing it, or saying, 'God be with you,' and not meaning it. You don't make your words true by embellishing them with religious lace. In making your speech sound more religious, it becomes less true. Just say 'yes' and 'no.' When you manipulate words to get your own way, you go wrong.

LOVE YOUR ENEMIES

"Here's another old saying that deserves a second look: 'Eye for eye, tooth for tooth.' Is that going to get us anywhere? Here's what I propose: 'Don't hit back at all.' If someone strikes you, stand there and take it. If someone drags you into court and sues for the shirt off your back, giftwrap your best coat and make a present of it. And if someone takes unfair advantage of you, use the occasion to practice the servant life. No more tit-for-tat stuff. Live generously.

"You're familiar with the old written law, 'Love your friend,' and its unwritten companion, 'Hate your enemy.' I'm challenging that. I'm telling you to love your enemies. Let them bring out the best in you, not the worst. When someone gives you a hard time, respond with the energies of prayer, for then you are working out of your true selves, your God-created selves. This is what God does. He gives his best—the sun to warm and the rain to nourish—to everyone, regardless: the good and bad, the nice and nasty. If all you do is love the lovable, do you expect a bonus? Anybody can do that. If you simply say hello to those who greet you, do you expect a medal? Any run-of-the-mill sinner does that.

"In a word, what I'm saying is, Grow up. You're kingdom subjects. Now live like it. Live out your God-created identity. Live generously and graciously toward others, the way God lives toward you."

THE WORLD IS NOT A STAGE

"Be especially careful when you are trying to be good so that you don't make a performance out of it. It might be good theater, but the God who made you won't be applauding.

"When you do something for someone else, don't call attention to yourself. You've seen them in action, I'm sure—'playactors' I call them—treating prayer meeting and street corner alike as a stage, acting compassionate as long as someone is watching, playing to the crowds. They get applause, true, but that's all they get. When you help someone out, don't think about how it looks. Just do it—quietly and unobtrusively. That is the way your God, who conceived you in love, working behind the scenes, helps you out.

PRAY WITH SIMPLICITY

"And when you come before God, don't turn that into a theatrical production either. All these people making a regular show out of their prayers, hoping for stardom! Do you think God sits in a box seat?

"Here's what I want you to do: Find a quiet, secluded place so you won't be tempted to role-play before God. Just be there as simply and honestly as you can manage. The focus will shift from you to God, and you will begin to sense his grace.

"The world is full of so-called prayer warriors who are prayer-ignorant. They're full of formulas and programs and advice, peddling techniques for getting what you want from God. Don't fall for that nonsense. This is your Father you are dealing with, and he knows better than you what you need. With a God like this loving you, you can pray very simply. Like this:

> Our Father in heaven,
> Reveal who you are.
> Set the world right;
> Do what's best—
> as above, so below.
> Keep us alive with three square meals.
> Keep us forgiven with you and forgiving others.
> Keep us safe from ourselves and the Devil.
> You're in charge!

You can do anything you want!
You're ablaze in beauty!
Yes. Yes. Yes.

"In prayer there is a connection between what God does and what you do. You can't get forgiveness from God, for instance, without also forgiving others. If you refuse to do your part, you cut yourself off from God's part.

"When you practice some appetite-denying discipline to better concentrate on God, don't make a production out of it. It might turn you into a small-time celebrity but it won't make you a saint. If you 'go into training' inwardly, act normal outwardly. Shampoo and comb your hair, brush your teeth, wash your face. God doesn't require attention-getting devices. He won't overlook what you are doing; he'll reward you well.

A LIFE OF GOD-WORSHIP

"Don't hoard treasure down here where it gets eaten by moths and corroded by rust or—worse!—stolen by burglars. Stockpile treasure in heaven, where it's safe from moth and rust and burglars. It's obvious, isn't it? The place where your treasure is, is the place you will most want to be, and end up being.

"Your eyes are windows into your body. If you open your eyes wide in wonder and belief, your body fills up with light. If you live squinty-eyed in greed and distrust, your body is a dank cellar. If you pull the blinds on your windows, what a dark life you will have!

"You can't worship two gods at once. Loving one god, you'll end up hating the other. Adoration of one feeds contempt for the other. You can't worship God and Money both.

"If you decide for God, living a life of God-worship, it follows that you don't fuss about what's on the table at mealtimes or whether the clothes in your closet are in fashion. There is far more to your life than the food you put in your stomach, more to your outer appearance than the clothes you hang on your body. Look at the birds, free and unfettered, not tied down to a job description, careless in the care of God. And you count far more to him than birds.

"Has anyone by fussing in front of the mirror ever gotten taller by so much as an inch? All this time and money wasted on fashion—do you think it makes that much difference? Instead of looking at the fashions, walk out into the fields and look at the wildflowers. They never primp or shop, but have you ever seen color and design quite like it? The ten best-dressed men and women in the country look shabby alongside them.

"If God gives such attention to the appearance of wildflowers—most of which are never even seen—don't you think he'll attend to you, take pride in you, do his best for you? What I'm trying to do here is to get you to relax, to not be so preoccupied with getting, so you can respond to God's giving. People who don't know God and the way he works fuss over these things, but you know both God and how he works. Steep your life in God-reality, God-initiative, God-provisions. Don't worry about missing out. You'll find all your everyday human concerns will be met.

"Give your entire attention to what God is doing right now, and don't get worked up about what may or may not happen tomorrow. God will help you deal with whatever hard things come up when the time comes.

A Simple Guide for Behavior

"Don't pick on people, jump on their failures, criticize their faults—unless, of course, you want the same treatment. That critical spirit has a way of boomeranging. It's easy to see a smudge on your neighbor's face and be oblivious to the ugly sneer on your own. Do you have the nerve to say, 'Let me wash your face for you,' when your own face is distorted by contempt? It's this whole traveling road-show mentality all over again, playing a holier-than-thou part instead of just living your part. Wipe that ugly sneer off your own face, and you might be fit to offer a washcloth to your neighbor.

"Don't be flip with the sacred. Banter and silliness give no honor to God. Don't reduce holy mysteries to slogans. In trying to be relevant, you're only being cute and inviting sacrilege.

"Don't bargain with God. Be direct. Ask for what you need. This isn't a cat-and-mouse, hide-and-seek game we're in. If your child asks for bread, do you trick him with sawdust? If he asks for fish, do you scare him with a live snake on his plate? As bad as you are, you wouldn't think of such a thing. You're at least decent to your own children. So don't you think the God who conceived you in love will be even better?

"Here is a simple, rule-of-thumb guide for behavior: Ask yourself what you want people to do for you, then grab the initiative and do it for them. Add up God's Law and Prophets and this is what you get.

BEING AND DOING

"Don't look for shortcuts to God. The market is flooded with surefire, easygoing formulas for a successful life that can be practiced in your spare time. Don't fall for that stuff, even though crowds of people do. The way to life—to God!—is vigorous and requires total attention.

"Be wary of false preachers who smile a lot, dripping with practiced sincerity. Chances are they are out to rip you off some way or other. Don't be impressed with charisma; look for character. Who preachers are is the main thing, not what they say. A genuine leader will never exploit your emotions or your pocketbook. These diseased trees with their bad apples are going to be chopped down and burned.

"Knowing the correct password—saying 'Master, Master,' for instance—isn't going to get you anywhere with me. What is required is serious obedience—doing what my Father wills. I can see it now—at the Final Judgment thousands strutting up to me and saying, 'Master, we preached the Message, we bashed the demons, our God-sponsored projects had everyone talking.' And do you know what I am going to say? 'You missed the boat. All you did was use me to make yourselves important. You don't impress me one bit. You're out of here.'

"These words I speak to you are not incidental additions to your life, homeowner improvements to your standard of living. They are foundational words, words to build a life on. If you work these words into your life, you are like a smart carpenter who built his house on solid rock. Rain poured down, the river flooded, a tornado hit—but nothing moved that house. It was fixed to the rock.

"But if you just use my words in Bible studies and don't work them into your life, you are like a stupid carpenter who built his house on the sandy beach. When a storm rolled in and the waves came up, it collapsed like a house of cards."

When Jesus concluded his address, the crowd burst into applause. They had never heard teaching like this. It was apparent that he was living everything he was saying—quite a contrast to their religion teachers! This was the best teaching they had ever heard.

Matthew 5:3 - Matthew 7:29
The Message, 1993, 1994, 1995, 1996, 2000, 2001, 2002 Eugene H. Peterson by NavPress Publishing

Printed in the United States
by Baker & Taylor Publisher Services